I0596827

Cold Faith

Shaune Lafferty Webb

COLD FAITH

Book 1 of *The Safe Harbour Chronicle*

2nd Edition

The moral rights of Shaune Lafferty Webb to be identified as the author of this work have been asserted.

All rights reserved. No part of this book may be reproduced or transmitted in any form or by any means without written permission of the publisher.

Copyright 2017 Hague Publishing

Hague Publishing
PO Box 451
Bassendean Western Australia 6934
Email: contact@haguepublishing.com
Web: www.haguepublishing.com

ISBN: 978-0-9925437-9-2

Cover Art: Cold Faith by Jade Zivanovic
Typography cover design by The Scarlett Rugers Design Agency

Typeset Garamond 12/14

Acknowledgement

I would like to gratefully acknowledge the following people who have freely offered their support to me over the years: my husband, Gregory, who sacrifices countless hours reading and providing invaluable feedback on my writing; friends, critics and fellow writers Danielle de Valera, Anneque Malchien and James Raven; the talented and 'multi-dimensional' Kenny Travouillon; and devoted reader Pamela Cooper.

I would also like to express my sincere thanks to Andrew Harvey, principal of Hague Publishing, Emily Ralph, copy editor, Jade Zivanovic, cover artist, and Scarlett Rugers, typographer, with particular recognition of their cooperative spirit.

Lastly, my appreciation goes to you, valued reader. I hope you enjoy your journey through the following pages - the first installment of The Safe Harbour Chronicle.

Chapter 1

THE old man yawned, discarded his glasses and leaned back into the chair. The struggle to continue reading was too exhausting. Lately, nothing he read seemed to stick in his head and, within a short time, the words would even start to dance across the page in front of him, prompting the old man to fear that he might actually be losing the ability to reason.

When his attention drifted towards the glasses he'd just tossed aside, he began to reconsider. Perhaps the cause of his recent distraction was as simple as failing eyesight and there was nothing wrong with his reasoning at all. Of course his granddaughter would disagree, arguing that his reasoning had never been sound, disposed as she was to disagree with anything he said or thought. It piqued him to admit that she, not he, appeared to have inherited Edward Braham's intellect. It was a pity though that, more often than not, the stubbornness she'd also inherited managed to overshadow it. If only Edward and Sunny could have met, but Edward was long gone now. Still, it would have made quite a spectacle —watching the two of them go at it. One worth buying a ticket to see.

The old man scratched his head, curious why such an odd expression had come to mind. Was it a phrase he'd read somewhere, sometime? Worth buying a ticket to see.

He yawned again and, yielding to the inevitable, set about his preparations for bed. He smiled as he imagined the look on his granddaughter's face if, to spare himself the trouble of the long walk down the tunnels, he ever made good on his threat to set up a cot in the corner of the library.

The smile faded as he reached out to retrieve his discarded glasses, accepting that another appointment with Ruby was probably unavoidable. All those tests she insisted on conducting seemed so tedious, considering that, in the end, she'd just lean into her cabinet, fumble around for a while and then produce the pair of glasses that suited him best. While he considered time spent in the hospital wasted time, he couldn't deny that Ruby did try. And that was all anyone could ask of his people.

Gently closing the book, he slid it across the table. If he returned the book to its proper location on the shelf his granddaughter would just make off with it. Recently, she'd taken to targeting his favourite books, the ones he and his father had brought into the library all those years ago.

Was it back-thinking to reflect on those years? he wondered. Probably. He was frequently guilty of back-thinking, as his granddaughter was quick to point out.

The chair screeched when he stretched and pushed it back, but no one was disturbed by the noise. He was the only person there. While he stuffed his head with unsettling images of long lost places, everyone else slept. Even during the day the library remained deserted. There was an old, almost forgotten rumour that for a long time after the library was built its door had remained locked. He couldn't imagine why—no one was interested in the place. Still. . .there was that intriguing hole in the door in precisely the right place for a lock to have been set. But pondering old rumours, like pondering old times, was just back-thinking and there were good reasons why back-thinking was discouraged; it wasn't at all productive.

As he moved to extinguish the light, the old man had another of his frequent changes of heart. Tonight he wouldn't go immediately to bed, he decided, but wander top-side to sit by the windows awhile and before fatigue saw him asleep in his chair, imagine that for the first time in living memory the stars had finally come out behind them.

Back-thinking! It wasn't at all productive but there were times, every now and then, when it was quite a satisfying thing to do.

Chapter 2

"YOU'RE ready then?"

Startled, Rab dropped his pack. He thought he'd said all his goodbyes and wasn't expecting anyone to come walking into his space. Swinging around, he found Blaze filling the narrow opening of his crumbling doorway. He could just make out the fire red of her hair in the dull morning light. She had come to claim his space for someone else; it was the only reasonable explanation.

Rab turned back to his task, mildly incensed that the elder hadn't had the courtesy to wait until he was gone.

"Almost."

He hadn't bothered to light his cramped quarters and was locating the last of his belongings by blindsight, that comforting and usually reliable awareness that something or someone was there close by in the darkness. Young enough to have acquired the talent, he was also old enough to appreciate its value; he'd already begun to sense Blaze walking up behind him.

"Here," she said, "I want you to take this."

He twisted around to discover her hand extended towards him with something big and bulky hanging from it.

"It was my father's. Too big for me, but I kept it of course. It'll keep you warm."

As he reached out to take Blaze's gift, Rab's fingers brushed her cold hand.

"It has some tears here and there in the lining," she said, drawing her hand away with obvious reluctance. "And the outside's a bit scuffed and dirty, but otherwise it's quite serviceable."

Rab held up the thick garment, checked its proportions. Quite serviceable? It was, in fact, the finest coat he'd ever laid his eyes or his hands on. Like all males in the village, Rab's hair had been left to grow until it draped snugly about his collar and his beard went untrimmed, both miserable defences against the cold when compared to the thick and warmly padded hood of the coat Blaze had handed him. It would be big for him, too, and probably reach mid-thigh. That was good, he thought, quashing a fleeting impulse to decline the gift. After all, Blaze was only doing the logical thing. Survival aids belonged to those with the greatest chance of survival and a chance of survival was something the elder and her thinning community simply didn't have any longer.

"There's a price."

He should have known; there was always a price.

While he'd been busy admiring the coat, Blaze had returned to the entrance. Though barely middle-aged, she had already developed the distinctive cough and laboured gait of someone who'd breathed too much bad air. Rab watched her—a featureless shape that disappeared for a moment between the projecting rough bricks of his doorway. Since his parents had died, he hadn't bothered to patch and mend his space the way other villagers did. The next owners would be obliged to effect some repairs, especially to the doorway. Too much of the mortar had deteriorated and too many bricks had fallen away. The ruined entrance was an open invitation for the cold winds and filthy snow.

Blaze returned, ushering in the village children ahead of her. In her arms, she struggled to hold something heavy. There were only three children of age in the village and it didn't take much guessing for Rab to know that the something Blaze was struggling to keep in her arms was the village's only infant. Six was too many in his tiny space—although the overcrowding made it marginally warmer.

"The coat for the children," Blaze said bluntly. "We all agreed."

By all, she'd meant the thirty-three adults who made up their community, with the exception of Rab, of course, who hadn't been consulted.

"I can't."

Stepping forward, he held out the coat, hugely disappointed all the same to let it go.

Blaze left it hanging there in his hand. "You must. We all agreed."

"No, we didn't all agree. No one bothered to ask me."

"When you chose to leave, you gave up that privilege, Rab. You know the law."

"Take it back. Whether I have it or not, it won't make much difference."

Even Rab found that claim hard to swallow.

"You'll take the coat and you'll take the children. If you refuse, then you won't be permitted to take any food."

Blaze might as well have slapped him in the face.

He'd been raised in this tight community, knew everything about everyone and they knew everything about him. Would they really let him go like that—with nothing? Of course they would and, if the situation had been reversed, if he was staying behind and someone else was leaving, he'd do the same thing.

"They won't last the journey," he said evenly.

Blaze appeared to shrug, although in the darkness it was difficult for Rab to be certain.

"They won't last here, either," she replied.

Predictably she'd used his own reasoning against him. He wouldn't be leaving if he hadn't finally faced up to the inevitable—none of them were going to last here.

"I don't even know how far I'm going."

Blaze didn't answer, but the shapeless bundle in her arms emitted a feeble cough.

Rab's focus drifted to the dark shapes clustered around Blaze. Perhaps the older boy might come in useful. Fin was almost grown, but a reedy kind of kid with the gaunt face and hollow eye sockets so typical of the latest generation. Regardless, he'd probably fare as well as Rab. The little ones were a different matter. Gift was sturdy enough; he knew that. But she'd only seen—what? Maybe six snow times? Taking the younger and smaller Stitch was simply out of the question and the notion of carrying the infant was too ridiculous to even think about.

"Fin then," he agreed. "He can come. And perhaps Gift."

"No," Blaze replied with authority. "Fin won't go without his brother. All or none."

Rab glanced at the little boy. Stitch was thin, like Fin, but had light blue eyes that only accentuated the normal pallor of his face.

"Then it's none." Rab tossed the coat on the floor at Blaze's feet. "How do you expect me to keep Stitch and the baby alive?" He pointed at the bundle in her arms. "That one can't even walk. I have very little chance of surviving. With those two, I have less. With that one," he gestured towards the bundle again, "we have none at all. Face it, Blaze— she's dead already."

Even though he knew the baby's name, he'd intentionally chosen not to use it. Speaking its name would make the inadequate thing real. This morning was the first time he had spoken to Jep since it had been born and only then because he'd felt obligated to say goodbye to a childhood friend. But despite the token farewell, Rab hadn't forgiven Jep for what he'd done. Rab had warned them—repeatedly—but not even Shy had listened. Of course his terrible prediction had come true and the instant their child had entered the world, Shy's fragile and beautiful light had gone out of it. All the young women died that way now.

The decision to snub his friend had been cowardly, the retaliatory act of a jealous man. Since they'd been small children, Shy had always been his. At least he'd thought so, although apparently she hadn't. Unlike Jep, Rab would never have risked her life that way.

During their awkward encounter this morning, Jep hadn't said a word about the infant or his intentions for it. It had struck Rab as strange at the time and now the reason was obvious. Perhaps Jep had been too proud to ask, but more than likely he'd assumed that forewarned, Rab would have just skipped out—and Jep would have been right.

"You'll take the three then," Blaze said. "Fin, Gift, and Stitch. And you can still go now, just as you planned. They're ready. Their food is already packed."

Rab shook his head, though he knew the gesture was futile. Blaze would never see it his way and, even if she could, it wouldn't make any difference. Take the three, he would. There was no decision to be made. Without food, even beginning the journey wasn't worth the effort—and completing the journey was all that mattered to him anymore.

Stepping forward, he stooped to retrieve the coat.

"I didn't get to vote," one of the children said.

The voice was barely audible but Rab recognised Fin's whine.

"Nor did I," Rab replied.

***

Only Blaze had come out to say goodbye. Rab had expected as much, but the children evidently hadn't. Fin first, then Gift, then Stitch glanced hopefully over their shoulders, each desperate to conceal their weakness from the others. Rab pretended he didn't notice.

After a brief look at each child, Blaze turned to him.

"Which direction will you take?"

Rab hesitated for only a moment. He was leaving; he could break the old taboo with impunity now.

"North."

Blaze nodded. "I thought you would."

Her admission came as a shock.

"And you still want me to take the children." He jerked his head towards the empty lane behind her. "Do they know?"

Blaze didn't reply. She didn't have to.

Rab almost smiled. "You influenced the vote, didn't you?"

Though of course she never spoke of it, Rab had always harboured a suspicion Blaze might just be a believer.

"It was always going to be you," she said instead.

He didn't understand.

"You are the strongest," she explained with a smile that was unreadable. "Always have been. You've never broken a single bone or lain sick on your back for more than a day. You heal well. You breathe well. So you see, it was always going to be you. Whether you stayed here or left us." Her head bowed slightly as she glanced quickly again towards the children. "Perhaps someday you'll forgive me for them."

"Perhaps, Blaze," Rab replied coolly, "but I wouldn't count on it."

He turned and left her then. Whether she stayed a little longer, standing vigil, he didn't know.

Purely by accident, he had chosen a good time and could see almost to the edge of the village today. It would make keeping track of his unmotivated brood just that much easier—for a while at least. Sooner or later, he was bound to lose one of them. The question was: would he bother to go looking for them when it happened?

And it seemed he was going to be confronted with that question earlier than anticipated. Fin was already striding out ahead, despite the heavy burden of the oversized pack that contained the children's meagre provisions. Soon Rab would be obliged to call him back. Their direction was supposed to be north towards the City—or at least towards where the City was rumoured to lie. Fin was veering east.

As Rab made his way towards the ragged edge of the village, the ice crunched beneath the weight of his heavy boots, but the children passed over the frosted ground in uncanny silence. He might easily have been walking alone. When he walked by Jep's space, Rab's attention strayed neither left nor right. His friend had always been a conscientious caretaker, industriously patching the crumbling mortar in his walls with clods of frozen earth and sealing each new hole in his corroding roof with reclaimed scrap that would last for a few rains and then require sealing again. Rab never could muster the enthusiasm to make similar repairs to his own space. Maybe he'd always known this time was coming. Maybe he'd always known he wouldn't stay.

Vaguely he wondered if Blaze had returned the baby yet. The faint sound of mewling nearby settled his curiosity and added the heavy burden of guilt to the load he was already carrying. He'd been right when he'd told Blaze that the baby was already dead—everyone in the village was already dead. It was only getting colder. They were edging close to snow time and one more snow time would finish them for good. He knew it and so did they. But, as usual, the decision had been left to a village vote and the vote had come down overwhelmingly to stay. Rab had been at that meeting, unlike the last that had settled his fate with the children. The only vote in favour of leaving had been his. There'd been little argument and none at all once Rab had announced his decision. No one had even tried to dissuade him, not even Jep. It wasn't hard to understand. With him gone, there would be one less mouth to feed.

Rab's thoughts were wrenched back to the moment when something latched onto his hand. He glanced down to find four diminutive fingers clamped around his and Gift's round black eyes staring up at him. Her other hand was locked tightly around the thick padding that sheathed Stitch's upper arm. She was virtually dragging the little boy along behind her. He had a fine party in tow: one patently defiant, one unquestioningly trusting, and the last just plain bewildered.

He attempted a reassuring smile for the little girl's sake, doubting that it had amounted to much.

When he glanced up and saw their shabby cemetery in the field over the girl's shoulder, Rab had a fleeting inclination to stop. After all, he would never come this way again. Had he been alone, perhaps he might have stood some moments there. Instead he walked on by, past the spot where the bones of his parents and his brother lay sealed beneath the permafrost, past the more recent plot where Shy was resting beneath her own icy blanket. Rab hadn't gone to her funeral; he wouldn't have been welcome. Besides, he couldn't have watched them lower her body into the cold ground. When his brother Bird had died, Rab's mother had sacrificed some of her precious scavenged cloth to swath his thin covering of skin. And when his parents had died, Rab had done the same for each of them in turn. Each time, Blaze had vehemently objected. The dead didn't need clothing; only the living did. But much like Fin was now, there'd been defiance in Rab then. If he'd had any say at all about Shy, he'd have done exactly the same for her. But Shy was Jep's wife, not his. And so she'd been laid naked into the frozen ground and, if the standard ritual had been performed, even her long mane of thick black hair would have been hacked away and close cropped to her head. Nothing went to waste in their village. The dead didn't need clothes and they certainly didn't need such a fine insulator as hair.

Who'd be the last, he wondered, as he strode on past the cemetery. Which of his childhood companions would be deprived of a resting place? Most probably all of them, because when the end came, no one would have the strength or the will to battle the frozen ground simply to appease the dead. The dead were just dead and were owed no debts. He had no doubts the first to go would be Shy's child. Perhaps she at least would have a grave. He hoped so; that was one debt to the dead he did feel he owed. Try as he might, he just couldn't shake the memory of the pathetic little bundle in Blaze's arms.

It occurred to Rab that he'd lost sight of Fin in the gloom ahead. He started to hurry, causing Gift to stumble, which brought Stitch down in a heap behind her. With a quick stoop, Rab swept the young boy into his arms. Having lost his hand, Gift grabbed the tail of Blaze's coat. Suddenly the impracticality of the situation became clear; he couldn't traipse on day after day with two packs on his back, one child in his arms, and another fastened to his clothing. Stopping mid-stride, he lowered Stitch carefully onto his feet and then called loudly into the murky air for Fin.

The last time he'd seen the boy, he'd been wandering off in completely the wrong direction.

"What do you want?"

The indifferent response came from directly in front of Rab. In the gloom, Fin had wound his way back unseen. Scooping up Stitch again, Rab strode off in the direction of the boy's voice, dragging Gift along in his wake, and found Fin standing in the middle of a recently decimated 'shroom field. Fleshy grey debris was scattered everywhere, but here and there some of the thick, knee-high stalks had been left undamaged, their tough, hemispherical caps still intact.

"That was bright," Rab said as he deposited Stitch back onto his feet. "You've just cost the village a meal."

"So?" Fin answered with a shrug. "What's it to you?"

"Look kid, this wasn't my idea either. And it's just too bad you didn't get a vote. Maybe needless destruction was how you settled your scores back there. . ." Rab pointed over his shoulder, ". . .but it ends now. I'm in charge here. No more wandering off. And, in future, you'll do everything I tell you to do."

Stripping the packs from his back, Rab dropped them onto the ground. "The next time I catch you destroying food, you're on your own and I'll be confiscating everything you've got in that pack on your back for the little ones. Understand?"

Fin edged back a step. "You can't."

"You going to stop me?" Rab snapped. He kicked at the two packs lying on the ground in front of him. "Take these two packs and, from now on, you're to look after your sister as well."

Fin glanced towards the packs at Rab's feet. When he looked up again, Rab was gratified to discover that his threats had marginally unsettled the boy.

"Gift isn't my sister," Fin shot back nonetheless.

"She is now." Rab nudged a second invitation towards the packs with the toe of his boot. "Packs."

"Why should I carry your packs as well as my own?" Fin snarled.

Rab shrugged. "Fine. Have it your way. I'll take the packs and you carry Stitch."

The packs weren't light, but they obviously weighed far less than Stitch. Rab waited to discover, without further prompting, which way Fin's decision would fall. Would he do the smart thing: put aside his pride and take the packs? He'd better—for all their sakes.

Wordlessly, Fin stepped forward and made an aggressive lunge for the packs. He'd underestimated the weight and was thrown a little off balance. Rab made no move to help, just waited until the boy figured out for himself how best to distribute the additional packs on his back.

"Right," Rab said as he came down on one knee. "Hop up, Stitch."

Obediently, the young boy climbed onto his back, leaving Rab with the hard task of righting himself again. Grabbing hold of Stitch's legs, he settled the boy into a more comfortable position on his back.

"Aren't you forgetting someone?" he called ahead to Fin, who was striding off awkwardly through the scattered ruin of the 'shrooms.

Rab nodded at Gift. She flashed him an unexpected smile and darted away towards Fin, grabbing his hand when she reached him.

"Head for the river, Fin," Rab said, testing out his own stride. "But don't get too close. Do you hear? We follow it until we reach the City."

"What?" Fin pulled up abruptly and spun around, wearing an expression on his face that could have melted packed ice.

"You're not supposed to talk about things like that," Gift said reproachfully.

"That's a village rule, Gift. You can forget about that now and talk about anything you want."

Gift glanced briefly towards Fin, then broke out into a grin.

"Really?" she asked with a trace of lingering doubt.

"Really," Rab replied.

"Good. It was a dumb rule."

Clearly Fin didn't think so. He was still sporting that ice-melting scowl.

"You're making a big mistake," Fin snarled, then stammered over breaching the old taboo as he added, "If the people in this city you're looking for are so clever, then they'd have saved themselves a long time ago."

The kid had a point, one Rab had fretted over more often than he cared to remember. Perhaps they had saved themselves already. But their rumoured plan was a complex one that would take many, many snow times to complete. Maybe there was still a chance. It was what Rab was counting on anyway. Besides, anything was better than sitting around waiting to die.

"Well," Rab sang out, in lieu of tackling Fin's observation, "just because we've lost one rule doesn't mean there aren't some new ones to replace it. Rule Number One. Everyone stays within sight of everyone else at all times." Stitch wasn't listening. Rab could feel the boy swinging his head around, taking in the view, even though a little elevation couldn't have improved it much. "Rule Number Two. No one eats or drinks anything unless I say so and that includes the supplies we've brought with us. Rule Number Three. If we find water, we don't drink it."

"Do you think we're stupid?" Fin called over his shoulder as he set off once again.

"The little ones, no. It's you I'm not so sure about."

He'd really imposed that rule for the sake of Gift and Stitch, but Fin had invited the jibe. Doubtless he'd already passed through the curiosity phase and come out the other side. The stench of the water alone would keep Rab at bay, but the last generation had been born without a sense of smell, or at least a lessened sensitivity. No scent, no matter how repugnant, ever seemed to deter them.

"Rule Number Four. We follow the river only. We never get too close."

"Rule Number Five," Fin interjected. "Rules One through Four are crap."

"Good for 'shrooms. Crap," Rab said evenly. "But that's all the Rules I have for now." Stitch was beginning to slip low onto his hips. He juggled the dead weight, settling the young boy higher up on his waist. "If I think of more, I'll let you know."

Fin muttered some unintelligible reply that Rab didn't bother to pursue. He tucked Stitch's knees closer into his sides, a guilty device to siphon off a little extra heat; the temperature had started plummeting. Ahead, Fin was beginning to slide on the building ice and Rab was obliged to concentrate on his own footing as well. It wouldn't do to come down with the kid still clamped onto his back.

The fall in temperature was a bad sign. The feeble midday light was failing. They had barely come any distance at all and the point of no return still lay ahead of them. They would pass on through it; at least, that was Rab's intention. He gave no thought at all to turning back. He didn't know the thoughts that were lurking in Fin's head though, but if he had a mind to run off, dragging the other kids along with him, the bitter cold would certainly end their prospects of making it back to the village alive.

✳✳✳

As far as Rab was aware, no one in their village had ever come this far out. Perhaps at some time in their not too distant past, someone had passed this way, but none of the villagers possessed the stamina or the incentive to venture so far afield now. And if they had, it would have amounted to nothing but a fruitless and difficult journey. This was a barren place that offered no food, little shelter and a slow death to the inadequately prepared. Silently, Rab thanked Blaze again for the heavily padded coat. He worried about the children though, but perhaps shouldn't. Obviously Blaze had taken great pains to ensure that the children were protected from the bitter cold, leading Rab to suspect that some degree of sacrifice had been made by the rest of the villagers. He'd admit to previously paying little attention to the children, but even so, little ones running about so warmly dressed wouldn't have escaped his notice. It seemed that many of his fellow villagers would pass the coming nights in misery. The realisation weighed heavily on his mind. They pinned too much hope on him, laid too much responsibility on his shoulders. He feared for the time when it would become too heavy a burden.

"Stop."

Fin stopped and turned at Rab's call.

"It's too cold to go on any further today. We'll rest for the night here. Start out again early tomorrow morning."

"Here?" Fin called back to him. "In the middle of nothing? There's nowhere to shelter."

The boy had a talent for stating the obvious. Rab waved him in.

"I can see that," Rab said the moment Fin stomped up and flung his packs to the ground. "But I doubt there's anything much better immediately ahead. We'll have to make the best of it tonight and hope that we'll find shelter tomorrow."

As Gift sauntered up to join them, Fin flicked a tentative glance at Stitch, who was leaning over Rab's shoulder, attentive to the conversation.

"You're going to kill us. You know that, don't you?" Kicking the packs aside, Fin reached out for his brother. "Give me Stitch. If we're going to die here, at least I'm going to die with family, not you."

Rab passed the boy to his brother. It was relief to get the weight off his back. He looked down to find Gift staring up at him.

"What?" he said.

Her little shoulders lifted slightly. "What should I do?"

Rab smiled to himself and reached out to tousle Gift's dark and matted hair.

"Sit down. Open those packs. And find us some food."

"I can do that," she said with enthusiasm.

Dropping to her knees, she set about opening the packs.

It was something to remember in future; Gift didn't like to stand idle. He eased himself to the ground and watched her work. It took his mind off the cold.

Fin had wandered off with Stitch, but came back once Gift produced their food. The boy was infuriatingly stubborn, but not stubborn to the point of letting his brother starve.

Dried 'shrooms were the only food they carried, given the impracticality of trying to bring a colony of grubs, the village's sole meat source which had been bred to survive on the fleshy fungus. Having developed a taste for the stuff, the colony had once broken out and gorged themselves on the 'shrooms in the storeroom. Everyone in the village had feasted that day and the children had made quite a game of finding the fat, little raiders. Blaze, of course, had been appalled at the wanton behaviour. Since it was becoming necessary to wander farther and farther afield to harvest 'shrooms, the loss exacted on their stock, she'd maintained, was a tragedy and the offending grubs should have been relocated back to the colony, not greedily consumed on the spot. At the time, Rab had wondered if he'd been the only one to notice when Blaze had appropriated a few of the treats for herself. It made him smile again now to think back on it.

"Here," Gift said, handing over his evening meal.

Behind him, Fin and Stitch talked softly, but when Gift passed them their share, the boys wandered off once again. She shook her head.

"They'll freeze out there all by themselves," she said to Rab, then reached out to touch each of the packs in turn. "I'm going to make a nest out of these. It'll be nice and warm inside." She glanced around, suddenly looking concerned. "But what about you, Rab? You're too big. There's nothing here to protect you."

Rab patted the sleeve of Blaze's coat. "I've got this and I bet I'm going to be warmer in this than I've ever been in my own bed back in the village." It was a lie, but Blaze's coat should be just adequate enough. Without it, he wouldn't have felt so certain.

Gift scratched at her head. "Do you think I could make them come in?" she asked, getting to her feet.

The girl was smart; she knew better than to suggest Rab do the pleading.

"You could ask."

She failed, of course, and wandered back to him, looking disappointed.

"All you can do is try," Rab said, excusing them both in the same breath.

He saw her comfortably settled, then folded himself up into a tight ball, appropriating the outer side of Gift's nested packs for protection.

The boys didn't freeze in the night, but both looked grim the next morning when they stumbled over for a little food. Stitch appeared to have fared the worst, forcing Rab to a silent decision. Whether Fin approved or not, Stitch would pass the next night under his supervision.

They set out early and wordlessly. Even Gift remained uncommonly quiet, perhaps perceiving what Rab, too, had noticed gradually building on the close horizon. The weather was turning increasingly against them. And after almost two days carrying all of the packs alone, Fin was starting to show the signs of strain, compelling Rab to stop them ahead of schedule again. Though they really should press on, the light was slipping away too fast, dragging the temperature with it.

Rab looked around, desperate to secure them protection. What he found didn't amount to much as far as shelters went, but it was the best he could manage before the wan light failed them completely. The overhanging ledge offered them a little cover and, if they huddled close together, their combined body warmth should see them through the night.

In the time it took Rab to deposit a dozy Stitch to the ground and stand up again, Fin had offloaded the packs, deserted Gift, and disappeared. Retrieving one of his packs from the heap Fin had left, Rab began to ration out portions of dried 'shrooms. As he shared a meal with the little ones, Rab listened with growing irritation to the sounds the boy continued to make in the darkness. He couldn't make good on his threat to withhold food and doubtless Fin knew it. The kid had to stay fit. It wasn't possible to manage the three packs and the two little ones on his own, so he'd placed Fin's share of the food to one side. It was there when Fin came back, carting the rotten remains of an old tree trunk.

Seeing what the boy had in tow, Rab abandoned his quickly rehearsed censure. A little bit of light and a little bit of warmth were what the night was begging for and if the boy had the wits and the savvy to answer the call, who was he to complain? He'd warm his hands by Fin's fire as eagerly as he would his own. Three more times, Fin wandered off into the darkness to return with another scavenged length of tree trunk. When alive, the tree must have been enormous for so much of it to have survived. Enormous or not, as far as Rab was concerned, it was still a miraculous find.

Gift was a practiced hand at fire starting. Rab watched as she expertly stripped away the useless pieces of bark, discarded them behind her then began digging again into the rotting relic to repeat the whole procedure. When the bark proved too tough for her to strip by hand, she took to jumping on it, enthusiastically smashing the pulp into tinder. Rab didn't attempt to stop her. She seemed to know what she was doing and probably wouldn't hurt herself. Besides, the exertion would go some way to warm up her blood. When enough of the bark was stripped, she bent to the task of coaxing the flames along with gauged and gentle breaths. She knew enough to keep her long hair well out of harm's reach and, when Fin briefly turned his back, even leaned in to readjust the tinder he'd been laying as she'd stripped it. The lids of her black eyes lifted and she caught Rab watching her. Discreetly, she raised a finger, placed it against her lips a moment and then smiled at him over the burgeoning flames.

Rab smiled back out of reflex. He hadn't had much to do with the kids in the village. He knew them of course; it was impossible not to, but long ago, he'd made the conscious decision to keep them at a distance.

Satisfied, Gift struggled up from the cold ground and, skirting the fire, made for the stash of 'shrooms Rab had set aside. She glanced at him, apparently seeking his permission and, when he gave it, strode over to Fin and wordlessly passed him the meal. It saddened Rab to watch her making her way back to him. Neither she nor Stitch should have been sent on this journey; it could only drag out their deaths.

She sidled up close to Rab. "Fin thinks you're crazy," she whispered, stretching her little body up to press her mouth to his ear. "He thinks you don't know what you're doing."

Rab dipped his head to whisper back. "And what do you and Stitch think?"

Gift shrugged. "Stitch is too little to think," she answered. "But I think Fin's wrong." She waved her hand, surprising Rab with the precision of her bearings when she began to speak of their village. "They're all going to die back there," she said. "And I don't want to die." She nodded towards the crouched figure of Fin, eating slowly and sullenly, on the other side of the fire. "Nor does he, but he just won't admit it."

The little one's acuity astonished him. But he wondered if Gift had given any thought to her parents when she'd said that everyone in the village was going to die. It could be that her age had her see them immune somehow. Rab didn't push it.

When she dropped her head and fell silent, Rab understood it to mean that her analysis of their circumstances and her travelling companions was done.

"But I am a little worried," she took up again, surprising him. "I'm not sure you can save all three of us." Lifting her head, she looked directly into his face, the black irises of her eyes reflecting their fire. "If you have to make a choice—"

Rab cut her off. "Don't be silly." He was about to offer her some inane platitude, but then thought better of it. "I don't think it will ever come to a choice," he said instead. "But I won't lie to you. It's not going to be easy." He nodded his head, indicating Stitch, who was lying curled up in a tight ball at his feet and sleeping noisily. "Especially for him."

"Yes, I know. And that's why, if you do have to make a choice who to save, well, you understand, it has to be him."

She'd surprised him again. He'd just assumed she was angling for his favour.

"Why Stitch?" he asked, intrigued. "I'm afraid I don't understand."

"Easy," she replied with a smile. "Fin? He's already given up. And me—well, I'll always remember this journey and what we left back there." Again, she waved her hand with unerring accuracy towards their village. "But Stitch—he's only little. He can start all over again without any memories at all—none that'll mean anything to him anyway."

Rab nodded. He raised a hand to stroke Gift's freezing hair as she snuggled into the comfort of his side. "I promise to remember what you said."

Chapter 3

IN THE bleak morning, Rab slipped out from under the two little bodies. He needed to get his bearings and warm up. Fin had passed the night on the other side of the slowly dying fire, as far away from the trio as possible. There was a touch of defiance in the kid but logic would win out in the end. Fin would either have to join the huddle of their little community at night or die alone in the cold.

After walking a short distance, Rab was shocked to discover that their camp was surrounded by the rotten trunks of a long fallen forest. Fin's nocturnal stumble on the cache of firewood had been no miracle, just an incredible stroke of good fortune. Every now and then as he staggered through the debris, Rab's foot caved through one of the rotten logs. Although he could have woven a path around the ruined logs, like Gift, he took a strange pleasure in smashing the things to bits. Hoping to supplement their store of food with something more appetising than dried 'shrooms, he kept alert for grubs, but found none. The forest had rotted out long ago.

Half way up a steep rise, he glanced back and was just able to make out the dying glow of their campfire and the two dark bundles on either side of it. The kids were still there and still asleep, but he had to be back before Fin woke up. The boy had done nothing yet to gain his confidence and simply couldn't be trusted rationing out the 'shrooms.

Rab slipped, slid, and scrambled his way up the last of the rise. By the time he reached the top, his breath was thickly frosting and he couldn't feel his feet any longer. The river couldn't be seen from his village, so he wasn't surprised to discover that, even from this elevated position, it still wasn't visible. He could see the permanent mist that shrouded the river though, clearer than he'd ever seen it before. In the lowlands, where his village was situated, the mist was a colourless, ephemeral thing that drifted in sometimes to envelope them, making breathing even more difficult than usual and seeing more than a few paces almost impossible. But from above, Rab could make out a blurred sort of edge to the mist and the swirling eddies of dirty brown vapour inside it.

His attention shifted to the sky. The ceiling was holding a little higher than usual this morning. He shrugged. It had done that yesterday too, but the improved visibility hadn't lasted. Even so, Rab was grateful for the small reprieve that allowed him to pinpoint the river and fix their location. They were still heading in the right direction. It was a pity that they couldn't track the river by simply walking its bank, but the foul-smelling mist made that impractical. Besides, even if they could have breathed the air without choking, one or other of them would inevitably become stuck in the putrid ooze underfoot. Bad enough to freeze to death in your sleep, which wasn't an unlikely scenario for them all anyway, but it was preferable to a choking-while-freezing end.

With a quick glimpse over his shoulder, Rab confirmed that the kids were still asleep, and he still had a few more moments. He'd found the river again, established that their direction was sound, and discovered a wealth of tinder in the process. But even if he could have got word of the cache back to his village, it was too distant now for them to exploit; and there simply weren't enough people in the village with the stamina to haul it back there. It was also too bulky and too heavy for him and his little band to carry. The realisation that they'd have to leave it behind was just another in a mounting inventory of frustrations. The likelihood of happening on another reserve was remote, because he suspected that only some peculiar quirk of nature must have preserved this one.

Rab dropped to his haunches to consider his next move. If they kept heading north, making the same progress they'd made yesterday, there was just a slight chance they'd reach a safe haven before freezing to death in their sleep. They had to move faster. Which meant what? That they redistribute the packs and both he and Fin carry one of the children? Impossible! That left only one other option—they'd simply have to travel longer each day.

Movement at the camp site below caught his eye; the single bundle that had been the bodies of Stitch and Gift was dividing. Rab sighed and, rising slowly, began readying himself to resume the responsibility he'd never asked for and would probably never satisfactorily discharge. Maybe Gift, with her naive insight, had it right after all. Maybe the time would come when he'd be forced to choose among them.

Fin was rising when he reached the camp site. Gift was already stoking the fire, an enterprise that made Rab smile. As young as she was, Gift already had the habits of village life ingrained.

"Don't bother with that." He kicked at the icy ground with his boot, dusting Gift's stirring embers, then went to rouse Stitch. "There isn't time." As he lifted the sleeping child, he signalled the little girl with a jerk of his head towards the packs. "Just grab some of the dried 'shrooms from that pack there. Keep some out for Stitch and then reseal the pack—tightly."

Gift nodded her understanding.

Fin was standing motionless by the lonely spot where he'd passed the night.

"That's it?" he said. "Get up and get moving?"

"Sounded like it," Rab replied.

The embers hadn't quite gone out, so Rab scooted another bootful of frozen ground towards the fire. If someone should pass this way again, they could make use of the surrounding tinder and a spark from an abandoned fire could easily finish it off.

"What's the hurry?"

Rab glanced up to find Fin still staring at him, arms akimbo.

"We're moving too slowly," he said, "and snow time is coming. Even if we can't make it to the City by then, we at least need to have found some shelter."

Slowly Fin's arms slipped from his hips. A moment later, he charged off towards Gift and wrenched the pack from her hands.

"Snow time! Dry time! Can't see that it makes much difference."

Stitch still hadn't woken, so Rab settled him against his chest, cupping the boys head against his shoulder. He looked at Gift. She was chewing methodically on something.

"Have you got those 'shrooms for Stitch?"

She flipped open the front of her heavy coat to show him. "And some for Fin and you, too," she said.

Rab shook his head. "Not hungry. Save them."

"You'd better save mine as well," Fin said as, juggling the packs into place, he strode off to the fire. "Apparently we're in too big a hurry at the moment." With a wild swing of his foot, he sent a huge cloud of earth into the coals. "Can't even put out a fire."

But Fin hadn't taken full account of the weight he was carrying and the exaggerated swing sent him off balance, forcing him to execute an ungainly little jig to right himself.

When Rab heard a giggle behind him, he looked back and found Gift struggling to stifle another.

***

When she'd left their camp site, Gift had grabbed a long thin strip of wood to use as a walking stick. Rab wished he'd thought to do the same.

Stitch had woken up some time ago. To keep his muscles primed and his blood flowing, Rab had allowed him to walk for a while, a decision he'd quickly regretted. The boy had taken to running forward to Fin and Gift and then back again to Rab, repeating the performance until Rab's patience was about to snap. Happily Gift knew just when and how to calm him. She had timed the appearance of the dried 'shrooms perfectly and on Stitch's last monotonous circuit, flashed open her coat. As soon as he saw the food, Stitch made a grab for the stash and wandered back to Rab with his prize. A tug on Rab's coat signalled he was ready to ride again. He settled in peacefully and for a long time occupied himself by slowly gnawing on the delayed breakfast.

Around midday, Rab called for Fin to pull up. Neither he nor Fin had eaten and there was still a long day ahead of them. He intended to walk them as long into the night as possible. Visibility wasn't their enemy. They'd been born into a twilight world and none of them had ever seen the sun or, for that matter, the moon or stars either. Sometimes Rab wondered if the sun and moon and stars were really up there at all and if everything his father had told him was just foolish folk tales. Maybe the world had always been this way; it was easier to accept that than it was to accept that the world had up and turned on itself. Easier but not logical. All the evidence spoke against it and all the evidence was telling him that he and everyone who would come after him had been cheated.

"What are we stopping for?" Fin demanded as he backtracked towards the spot where Rab was waiting. "I thought we were in a hurry."

"Gift needs to rest," he said, "and you and I need to eat something."

Fin shrugged and then wriggled out of the packs.

Rab lowered Stitch to the ground. Not surprisingly, the boy was travelling the best of all of them since he'd basically been riding most of the way. Rab's arms were beginning to cramp from the effort of holding Stitch's legs so tightly. He'd become accustomed to the periodic twinges surging up along his spine as he walked, but the latest twinge seemed to have lodged itself into a knot at the back of his neck. No amount of bending, twisting, or contorting of his neck muscles showed any promise of shifting it.

Of her own accord, Gift began judiciously distributing the food, prompting Rab to acknowledge that of the three children, she had the most practical mind and was probably the one he could most readily trust. Bending to take the food from her outstretched hand, he seized the opportunity to assess Fin's condition. The older boy sat huddled in an uncomfortable-looking pose, knees drawn tight up into his chest, head drooping to one side. With a great deal of reluctance, Rab conceded his error; carrying all three packs was too much for the boy. When they set off again, he would have to relieve Fin of at least one of the packs. Maybe every so often, Stitch could walk some more. They'd lose some time, but what was the alternative?

As Gift approached him, Fin's head drifted up from its half-mast position. He took the food from her, but immediately began looking over each shoulder until his attention finally settled on Rab.

A moment later Rab realised what was wrong; Stitch was missing.

Rab jumped to his feet an instant before Fin did. Beside Fin, Gift was twirling around, trying to take in all directions at once.

"He can't have gone far," Rab said. That much was true—but it didn't mean he wasn't lying out there injured.

Again and again, Fin called for his brother, but received no reply.

Rab sprinted off to search for the boy himself, but Gift's steady voice quickly called him back.

"Here he is."

She'd found him a short distance away, grubby-faced and casually stuffing rocks into his pockets. He was still struggling to supplement the hoard even as Rab dragged him back to Fin.

"I told you to watch him," he snapped, shoving Stitch forward. A few of the rocks Stitch had gathered, but hadn't stowed, tumbled from his hands. "I can't do everything."

Fin opened his mouth to speak but said nothing.

Rab didn't need to hear any words; resentment was apparent in the set of Fin's jaw and the piercing stare of his eyes. He resented being cast out of the village; he resented taking orders from Rab, the self-styled yet untried leader; but most of all, he simply resented Rab, the person. Given time and the application of a little reason, the boy might eventually come to accept that Blaze, not Rab, had been responsible for his expulsion and that she had only done it in an attempt to save him. And given time, a little experience, and a lot of luck, Rab might eventually convince Fin that

Blaze's faith in him wasn't misplaced, even if he wasn't all that convinced of it himself just yet. But no amount of time and no number of hardships they overcame under his leadership would mellow Fin's innate disposition. The boy just didn't like him. On the other hand, Gift apparently did, a fact Rab couldn't readily explain.

She tugged on his sleeve, drawing his attention.

"The wind's picking up and I think it's going to snow," she said in that practical manner of hers. "Shouldn't we move on now and find some shelter?"

Whether she had intended it to or not, and Rab had the sneaking suspicion that she had, her observation put a sudden end to the tense moment.

His little charge was right. When he looked up, Rab saw for himself that the perennially gloomy sky had deteriorated into something more menacing. There was a greater heaviness to it now and, in places the headwind had dragged the dirty grey clouds down so low, it seemed like he could just reach up and touch them. Gift might be presaging events a little early, but by night, there was little doubt they'd be walking blind into a bitter wind on ground that would be blanketed in slick, brown snow. They had to get moving and find shelter. Despite the incessant pain in his back, it clearly wasn't the best time to relegate Stitch to the ground. He'd simply have to manage Stitch and one of the packs as well. Perhaps tomorrow, if the weather was better, he'd have that opportunity to sacrifice a little bit of time for a little bit of comfort.

Rab struck off for the packs and grabbed the one he judged to be of intermediate weight. "I left you the heaviest," he explained, anticipating that Fin would misconstrue his action. He had no intention of leaving all three children behind. "I'll manage with Stitch and this pack until we get to shelter."

"Whatever you say," Fin answered with a shrug and, walking over, stooped to gather the remaining packs. "You're in charge after all."

"Why can't I carry one?" Gift asked, scooping up her stick.

The wind was beginning to gust and every now and then a random eddy caught hold of her dark hair, flinging the long strands in all directions. She didn't bother to rein them in. For one brief moment as she stood there, defiant of the wind and their circumstances, she seemed to Rab a natural child of this place. Without a doubt she would give carrying a heavy pack one almighty try.

He smiled and motioned for Stitch to climb onto his back. "Maybe when they're a bit lighter," he told her. "After some of the food and water is gone."

That was another question Fin was certain to pose before long, one for which Rab, unfortunately, would have no answer. After some of the food was gone, what then? So far nothing in their immediate environment had looked promising. After they'd left the 'shroom fields, Rab had kept an eye out, hoping to spot something, anything that, for generations, might have been overlooked by the people of his village. It had been a slim chance at best, but his constant scanning had turned up nothing, even in the rotten forest. The landscape was barren, lain waste by bad air and the rare but poisonous rain. Only the constant husbandry of the villagers had managed to keep the 'shroom crops going back home. There was no denying it—for Rab and his sorry trio, the time was undoubtedly approaching when their bellies would be empty and their muscles would be too weakened to continue.

He almost welcomed the distraction when Stitch's elbows dug painfully into his side.

"We have to move faster," Rab said, catching Fin with a glance when Gift ambled out of earshot. She looked to be managing the terrain with ease, the stick Rab suspected more of a hindrance now than a help. "Especially if Gift is right. I'll carry the pack and Stitch today; tomorrow you take all three packs again. We'll continue that way from now on. One day you'll have all three packs, the next day only two. All right?"

Without warning, Stitch listed to one side and the pack to the other, throwing Rab immediately off balance. After centring Stitch again as best he could, he looked up to find Fin still standing in front of him.

"You're asking me?" the boy said, then turning on his heels, inclined his head into the wind and ploughed out into the plummeting cold.

They walked that way for the rest of the day, Fin constantly struggling despite having been relieved of one pack, and Rab with Stitch and the single pack that seemed to grow heavier with each hard-won step.

The wind, as Gift had predicted, grew worse. Rab kept one eye on the ground in front of him and another peeled for any potential shelter. But the landscape remained monotonously featureless without promise of a protective overhang that might give them some relief for the night, and without it Rab held grave fears for their survival in the open.

Their journey certainly hadn't amounted to much: a few days travel. Still, Rab had known from the outset that death was a potential outcome of his journey. He just hadn't expected it to come about so soon, or that he'd be taking three children with him.

When Gift stopped walking, Rab thought little of it. Gathering her bearings, he guessed. He plodded on past her without comment.

"The wind's changing direction."

Her call brought him to a halt.

"Can't you feel it?" she asked when he turned around.

Well, he couldn't feel it, not like she had, but the bitter smell hit him then and he had no inclination to doubt Gift's judgement. Since leaving the village, they'd walked consistently head-first into the wind, now it was shifting, pushing the distinct stench of the river ahead of it. A sudden broadsiding gust confirmed the wind's new direction. Their need to find shelter had just become more immediate. Battling the wind head-on was bad enough but being erratically broadsided increased the likelihood that one or other of them would lose their footing on the slippery terrain. At least the vile smell in the wind told Rab they were still on course; it was also telling him which direction not to go seeking shelter.

He waved Gift off to the right and then called for Fin. The boy was slow in responding and, at first, Rab feared that his instructions had been lost to the wind. But Fin had heard him. The boy glanced briefly over his shoulder before swinging off in an arc to his left. He was taking advantage of the buffeting wind, letting it control his trajectory and speed, rather than battle completely against it. Occasionally the kid displayed unexpected intelligence. Perhaps they'd never bridge the rift between them, but as long as they journeyed in the same direction, Rab didn't particularly care if they travelled on opposite sides of the road.

Gift was beginning to drift out of sight, something he couldn't allow. Stitch, still clamped to his back, seemed to have picked up on the scent of his panic. He'd taken to squirming about in a vain attempt to fasten his thin arms more firmly about Rab's neck. The wind, now gusting directly at Rab's back, was threatening to topple him over, but he had to run if he wanted to catch up with Gift. To his left, he could see Fin struggling to keep balance.

"Hurry! Hurry!" Gift called. She'd pulled up just ahead of Rab and was now jumping up and down on the spot. "I've found somewhere."

Rab just caught her words despite the wind's best effort to steal them away. Trust Gift!

But when he reached her, Rab was disappointed to discover that 'somewhere' actually amounted to little more than a depression in the earth on the lee side of a low rise. Still it was better than he had managed and, at a calmer moment, Fin was certain to remind him of that. He reached out a hand and ruffled Gift's hair. It was somewhere after all.

After hastily discarding his pack, Rab carefully offloaded Stitch. Fin staggered up on the left, sloughed off his packs and slung them down beside Rab's.

"What's she found?" he asked, raggedly snatching a breath. "And what the hell is she doing?"

Rab turned to find Gift on her hands and knees, madly flinging great handfuls of dirt into the wind. The little one had bettered him again.

"What do you think she's doing?" He dropped over the rise to join Gift. "Digging us in."

When he looked up and saw Fin just standing there, wearing a puzzled expression, Rab bellowed.

"Get down here—both of you. And start digging."

***

They survived the night, courtesy of Gift, but hadn't eaten any food or managed to catch any sleep. Even Stitch had stayed alert all through the night, huddled into the crook of his brother's arm. Shortly after they had hunkered down into Gift's shelter, the snow had come. Its freezing, gritty flakes had buried the packs that Rab had stacked above their heads to combat the battering of the wind and every so often a cascade of dirty powder had tumbled down into their laps.

Against his better judgement, Rab had allowed them the luxury of a slow breakfast. There might not be another opportunity to eat again that day as they had to make up lost time. Suddenly the arbitrary schedule he'd set seemed ironic. After all he was only hurrying them off to a place that probably no longer existed, against a deadline that was probably long past.

But it was Rab's day to walk free of the pack and carry only Stitch, so when they finally set out, his dark mood lifted a little. Fin wasn't pleased about the arrangement, but then Fin never seemed pleased about anything. The day dragged out with little time spared for either conversation or food. Gift trudged beside Rab most of the way and when it became too dark to risk walking farther, they stopped, cold and spent. There was no lucky stumbling onto shelter that night and Fin didn't protest when Rab settled his young brother down with Gift.

In the morning, they rose, ate a little, then moved on until they could go no farther and stopped to eat and rest again. The next day, they began it all anew—this seemingly endless journey that offered little in the way of food or hope. For two days, they walked in and out of a strange grey mist, different to the kind they were used to. At first, when the mist was only thin, Rab wasn't concerned. Since leaving the village, they had walked into a headwind and he could still feel the constant wind on his face, reassuring him of their direction. And their thick outer clothing was more than adequate to protect them from the slight moisture, their boots sturdy enough and watertight. It was only when they came upon the first dense pocket of mist, which swallowed up the wind and the few words spoken among them, that Rab's heart began to hammer. There inside those still and silent voids, Rab wrestled the hardest with his fears and doubts. Was he only imagining those fleeting brushes of wind on his face as they moved blindly through the mist? Had he turned them around? Were they travelling in completely the wrong direction?

The mist left as unexpectedly as it had come, taking with it the awful silence and stillness, and returning the scent of the river. Certain then of their direction, Rab turned his face to the wind and pressed on—one full day gently climbing, another just as gently descending until they came upon a barren plain. Day after dreary day, Rab edged them ever northward across that plain, watching Fin grow increasingly more indifferent, trading the burden of Stitch and the packs, until he lost track of just how long it had been since they had left the village. He thought it was about twelve or thirteen days but couldn't be sure.

Today it was his turn to carry Stitch and one of the packs. Around midday, he broke his rule and allowed Stitch to walk a while by himself again, guiltily rationalising that without some exercise the boy would become too sickly to go on. As evening approached, Stitch was on his back once again. The process of taking each step had become entirely mechanical. When Fin stumbled upon a patch of soft snow, Rab called a halt. Here they could at least dig themselves in again, while farther on they might only encounter more bitterly cold open ground.

They passed a better night and woke to an uncommonly clearer day. Rab hadn't intended to doze off again, only to laze a little longer in the hollow they'd cleared of dirty snow. Gift's anxious voice roused him; she was calling frantically for Stitch.

Damn that boy—if he's gone off collecting rocks again. . .

Rab scrambled out of the shallow pit in search of Gift. A second before he found her, he heard Stitch cry out, but the boy's words were largely unintelligible.

Relief did little to contain Rab's anger—with Fin and himself.

"Where's Stitch calling from? I can't see him."

"I think he's over there," Gift said, pointing towards a nearby hill.

Fin came running towards them from the opposite direction.

When Stitch sang out again, Rab thought he could make out what the boy was saying. But the boy couldn't possibly have said that!

"Did I hear right?" Fin asked. His face was bright red and he was gasping heavily. "Did he say—?"

"Launch pad," Gift replied calmly. "He said launch pad."

Without a thought for their abandoned packs or Gift, Rab bolted off towards the hill with Fin close on his heels. Halfway up, he thought to turn and check on Gift. The little girl was stoically plodding up the slope behind them. Rab rushed ahead but, on cresting the top of the hill, failed to see Stitch. After a few anxious moments, he finally spotted him careening down the other side of the hill. The pumping of the boy's little feet was no match for Rab's rapid long strides and he soon had Stitch swooped up.

Behind him, Rab could hear Fin screaming down at his little brother. He turned to see Fin sliding down the icy slope and Gift's little silhouette on the summit. A plume of ice heralded Fin's arrival.

"If you ever—" Fin began.

"Look! Look!" Stitch cut him off.

From the moment Rab had scooped him up, Stitch hadn't stopped flailing to break free. When he glanced downhill again, Rab finally understood the reason for the boy's excitement. From a distance, what Stitch had discovered appeared as little more than a dense black shape dominating the foreground in a diffuse grey background of sky. Still, it had to be a building just the same; it couldn't be anything else.

But something wasn't right. There shouldn't be a launch pad here—surely they hadn't come far enough yet. And what was a launch pad doing right on the river? To Rab's mind, it didn't seem a likely place to have built one.

"Well?" he said, glancing at Fin. "Any ideas?"

"I'm going down there." Without waiting for Rab's response, Fin took off in a tumbling sort of scuttle down the slope.

"Wait," Rab called after him. "We've left the packs behind."

Fin pulled up immediately.

"You wait here with Stitch and Gift," Rab said.

He released the excited child, who promptly shot off after his older brother. If Fin hadn't captured him mid-stride, Stitch would have kept on going all the way down to the river at his break-neck pace.

"We won't move until you get back," Gift said, aiming a reassuring smile at Rab as she passed, heading for the boys. "Promise."

It was madness to trust three children, but someone had to get the packs.

The moment Rab's back was turned, Fin hollered.

"Make it quick."

Somehow he must have drifted off course coming down the hill because when Rab reached the spot where he'd thought they'd left the packs, he couldn't see them. And there was little to differentiate one spot from another—in the wasted landscape, everything looked the same. Rab began to panic. What if he could never find them? Unthinkable! He drew a deep, calming breath and looked around again, sighing with relief when he spotted the packs. They had been right in front of him all along. He'd been gone too long already but sacrificed a little more time to ensure that the fastenings were secure and that nothing had been left on the ground before starting back to the children.

He arrived on the other side of the hill to find Stitch hopping from one foot to the other, Gift settled cross-legged on the ground, and Fin looking annoyed.

"You took your time," Fin said.

The boy had enough misgivings about his leadership, but he'd have had cause for more if Rab confessed that he'd had trouble finding the packs.

"Just keep your eyes on Stitch," Rab said instead, motioning Fin to start out for the river. "Don't let him run ahead."

Easier said than done, Rab conceded, happy for once to have the responsibility of all the packs while Fin was left with the impossible task of reining in an excited child. Reaching down, he hoisted Gift up from the ground.

Her round, black eyes turned on him and she shrugged.

"What?" he asked as they set off down the slope together.

"Can't be what he thinks it is," she said.

"You think so too, huh? What's your guess then?"

"Don't know, but it's not a launch pad."

Gift was probably right. It wasn't a launch pad, but Rab could make no better guess about what it might be, either. And something else was niggling at him beyond an uncertainty about what Stitch had discovered. They'd learn what it was, or confirm what it wasn't, soon enough. But Stitch obviously saw and remembered more than Gift credited. Fin was old enough to have heard the stories Rab's father told. But where had Stitch, and Gift for that matter, heard them? Seemed his father wasn't the only person in their village with a fondness for breaking taboos.

Downslope, Fin was struggling to keep up with his young brother, while Gift was making a game of walking step for step in Fin's tracks. Rab just hoped no one took a tumble.

"There's a kind of road here," Fin called over his shoulder. "And a gate of some sort."

That made sense if the site had been used as a launch pad. In those last frantic days, some sort of security would have been needed. But it still wasn't enough to convince Rab. In fact, the closer he came, and the more he could see of the building, the less he believed in Stitch's over-enthusiastic assessment. The strange complex was intended for some other purpose, but Rab couldn't even imagine what that might be. Their forebears had been notoriously enterprising. At least, that's what his father had said and Rab had never found cause to doubt his father's word on that.

"Wait right there!" Rab called. "Don't go inside."

Either Fin hadn't heard him or he chose not to listen.

"Do you hear me?" Rab yelled. Despite the painful banging of the packs against his back, he risked a run down the last of the slope.

The river and bad smells went hand in hand, so he'd expected a worsening of the stench the closer he drew to its bank, but the air he was rushing into was the foulest he'd ever encountered. And it was becoming obvious that the complex was something very different to what he'd first thought. Looking down from the top of the hill, his eye had been deceived, leading Rab to interpret the silhouettes of two spindly towers, the mounded profile of the surrounding snow-covered earth and three or four badly collapsed outlier buildings as a single structure. But now he could plainly see that the complex was not one sprawling building, but a collection of many smaller units. A short distance from the complex itself, a tall fence sealed off immediate access.

Rab caught up with Fin and Gift by a pair of high wire gates. Stitch had already wandered off to inspect the neighbouring fence line. He'd be looking for breaches and Rab couldn't afford for him to find one and take it into his head to climb through. Dumping the packs at the base of the gates, he hurried off to intercept Stitch.

"No you don't," he said, grabbing the tail of the boy's coat.

"But we can't get in that way," Stitch complained.

"We're not going in." He spun the boy around and, with a slap to his rear, spurred him back towards the gates.

Fin was shaking at the gates when they returned. "They're stuck."

"Good. We can see enough from here."

"Well, I can't."

Before Rab could stop him, Fin lunged at the gates. But his boots were too big to permit a good foothold. As he tried to scramble higher, he slipped and was left dangling from just one hand.

"Get off!" Rab called. "It's not. . ."

The gates began to teeter. Rab made a grab for Stitch and Gift and dragged them out of the way. He'd had no time to rescue the packs. If the gates toppled outward, the packs and Fin would be pinned beneath them.

There was an ominous screech just before the gates gave way. Fin lost his grip completely and, for an instant, he was free-falling as the massive gates collapsed inward towards the complex. The gates came to rest with a thud that shook the ground. Fin came to rest a second later, spread-eagled on top of them.

Gift was the first to reach Fin and had him half on his feet by the time Rab had managed to scramble over the wire mesh.

"Anything broken?" Grabbing Fin under both arms, Rab hauled him the rest of the way up.

"Don't think so," Fin answered, dazed still and struggling for balance on the unstable mesh.

"Then let's just get off before we put a foot through this stuff."

Rab looked around in search of Stitch. The sight of his free-falling brother seemed to have momentarily pinned the boy to the spot.

"Just stay there," Rab shouted and, with Fin in tow, began clambering over the wobbling surface, anxious to reach solid ground.

Gift went ahead of them, her lighter weight making the going easier.

Once back on sound footing, Rab satisfied himself that Fin was indeed uninjured first before venting his anger.

"What were you thinking? Were you even thinking?"

"Got us in, didn't I?" Bending, Fin reached out to capture Stitch who was excitedly running for him. "I'm fine," he said, straightening. "Let's look inside."

"No." Rab moved off to collect the abandoned packs. "We've wasted enough time. We're moving on. It's obvious this place is deserted. There's nothing and no one here." Grabbing the packs, he turned back to Fin. "Besides, haven't you noticed the smell? There's something really bad here."

Fin only shrugged disinterest. "We're closer to the river. What did you expect?"

"I said no!"

"And I say yes." Fin was already making his way around the collapsed gates, carrying Stitch in his arms. "Come on, Gift."

"He's not going to listen," Gift said, tugging on Rab's sleeve. "Shouldn't we go with him? Just to make sure he doesn't do something stupid?"

Furious, Rab dumped the packs on the ground. "He's already done it." Reaching down, he took Gift's hand. "Don't let go, all right? I don't like this place."

"Told you it wasn't a launch pad," she said, latching onto his hand more firmly.

"No, it isn't," he agreed as he took off with Gift across the icy ground in pursuit of the boys. "But I think I know what it could be."

Just then Fin glanced over his shoulder and, catching sight of Rab following, smiled knowingly.

Sooner or later, Fin's recklessness was going to get them all into trouble. He'd been lucky not to have hurt himself when the gates collapsed. It was a pity he hadn't scratched himself up a bit, maybe knocked out a tooth or two and knocked in some common sense.

"Do you think they're all dead? The people who lived here?" Gift asked.

"No one lived here, Gift," Rab answered. "It's not that sort of place."

Fin was nearing the base of one of the spindly towers. If he took it into his head to climb it, he was certain to fall.

"I know they didn't exactly live here," Gift said, sounding mildly offended, "but if they came here, then they had to live nearby, didn't they?"

Rab glanced down at the little girl. Of course they did. He hadn't even stopped to think about it. Somewhere not too far away, there had to be, or at least have been, a town, somewhere the people who'd built this complex called home. Maybe a small number of the community had survived and, even if they hadn't, perhaps some of their dwellings had. Coming across the curious complex might just have netted them something after all—the prospect of cover for the night. Sheltering anywhere near the towers was out of the question. At any moment, one of the snow-capped towers could tumble. And the foul air wasn't fit to breathe for any length of time.

"Maybe you should lead this party," Rab suggested with a smile.

Gift shook her head. "Fin won't do what I tell him, either."

She pointed ahead. Just as Rab feared, Fin had deposited his brother on the ground and was looking for a foothold on the nearest tower.

"Haven't you had enough?" Rab called to him angrily. "It's rotten."

For once, Fin listened. Perhaps the tumble on the gates had taught him a lesson or two. He was still standing at the base of the brick tower, looking up thoughtfully, when Rab and Gift arrived.

"There has to be a way up," he said.

"Why? And what for?" Releasing Gift's hand, Rab reached out and slipped his fingers into a large gap in the brickwork. With little effort he wrenched out the upper brick. Most of it crumbled to dust in his palm. "Rotten."

Fin shrugged and walked away, intent on circling the tower anyway.

"Well?" Gift said. "What do you think this place is?"

Rab was about to answer when a sudden spasm of coughing intervened. By the time the fit was over, his eyes were watering, his throat burning, and Gift was looking up at him, wide-eyed with concern.

"Is it that bad?" she asked. "I can't really smell it."

"It's that bad," Rab replied. "We can't stay here very long. Even if you can't smell it, it must still be doing you damage. And it isn't just the river. It's something else."

He glanced around to find Fin who, having made his way to one of the snow-covered mounds, was busy clawing his way up. He'd been wrong a moment ago; the kid would never learn.

"Get down off there. The whole thing could collapse."

Rab barely had the words out before he broke down into another spasm of coughing. When it was over, he looked up to see that Fin had made it midway up the mound.

"It's safe enough," Fin called to him across the compound.

"It's not! Use your eyes."

Leading Gift, Rab took off towards the mound. In harm's way beneath it, Stitch stood, glancing up.

"You're climbing on a pile of crumbling bricks. This place was a brick factory. You're likely to bring the whole lot down."

"I was trying to get a better view," Fin grumbled. A cascade of loose, dirty snow accompanied his descent, showering the three on the ground below.

Fin's breathing sounded laboured and Rab didn't doubt for one moment that exertion from the climb wasn't the only cause. Perhaps none of the kids could smell the ghastly stench, but it would be playing havoc with their lungs just the same.

"Can you read?" As he retraced his steps around the mound, Fin stooped to collect a shattered brick from the ground. "There's something written here."

Wrenching the brick from his hand, Rab gave it a brief glance. The brick looked to be finely crafted, making the bricks in his village seem crude in comparison, but the marks on it meant nothing to him. "Of course I can't read," he said, tossing the brick aside.

"Figured." Fin shrugged and pointed towards the partly collapsed building behind him. "I'm going inside. What if there's something we could use? You stay here if you want to, or go back with Gift," he reached for his brother's hand, "but me and Stitch are going in."

"There's nothing there."

Fin walked off anyway, trailing Stitch.

"He won't listen," Gift said with a sober shake of her head.

Surely on his worst day, Rab had never behaved as stupidly as this boy. Fin wasn't just endangering himself, but his brother as well.

He set off after the pair, leaving Gift to follow through the debris field of bricks.

"Don't touch anything," he called to the boys.

If there'd once been a dedicated doorway to the building, it was long gone now. Rab scrambled over a jumble of bricks at the wide and ragged opening. Coming off the pile, he landed in an ice-sheathed layer of sharp-edged wreckage. Once inside, it took a moment for his eyes to adjust. He couldn't see either of the boys anywhere, but a pyramid of surprisingly intact bricks off to his left confirmed his assessment of the place. Over-head, a series of catwalks chaotically cross-hatched the open space beneath a sagging ceiling that had enough jagged holes in it to irregularly spot-light the floor below. All around, dirty flakes of snow drifted through the rank and bitter-tasting air.

Rab sneezed violently and then called out for Fin.

"Up here."

Directly over his head, someone was standing on one of the catwalks. Judging by the size of the silhouette, it was Fin.

"I can see the river," Fin called down, then disappeared completely out of sight.

Furious, Rab ploughed through the scattered debris, searching for some way up. In front of him, set into the side wall of the building, were three deep, dark and heavily-reinforced recesses. Hard up against the wall of the left-most recess, Rab found a set of concrete stairs. The edges of most of the treads had been gnawed away and the surfaces showed the usual pits and pockmarks typical of caustic decay, but they looked secure enough. When Rab gripped the gnarled handrail, his glove came away coated in orange-coloured powder. At the top, he stepped carefully onto the mesh floor of the catwalk.

"Here. Over here."

Wan daylight seeped into the upper floor through an enormous cavity in the back wall of the building and Fin, a hazy-edged shadow, was standing at the far end of the catwalk less than a step away from the gaping hole. Stitch was nowhere in sight.

Rab tapped a foot to the mesh. It seemed intact, but through it, he could see to the floor below. The sensation was disorienting. Worse still the quality of the air had deteriorated even more. It was long past time to get out.

He didn't look down again, but threaded his way along the catwalk, heading for Fin and the yawning hole in the outer wall of the building. One slip and the boy would go plummeting out through the hole and into the river below.

Fin turned at the clanging of his footsteps.

"Take a look at this."

Rab ignored the invitation. "Where's Stitch?"

Fin waved his concern aside. "Over there!"

Looking back, Rab spotted Stitch in the distance, waiting on the other side of the catwalk. Cautiously he took another step and, on reaching Fin, peered down and around him into space. He could almost see the surface of the river now through the permanent brown mist. Glancing down, he took stock of the catwalk again. If the mesh would hold him, he could step a little closer and maybe, just maybe, actually see the water. Rab tested his footing once more, then took a tentative step. Nothing. No creaks. No snaps. Three more slow and cautious steps brought him as close as he was prepared to go. The elevation and a want of solid ground beneath made him feel dizzy. Besides, from where he was, he could finally see the surface. He raised his hand, intending to wipe his eyes, but noticed the orange film still clinging to his glove and changed his mind.

But even though his eyes watered and stung, he could still see well enough to make out the broad streams of whitish sludge that oozed away from the bank below, and to notice how each downstream flow seeped into the one ahead of it. The separate dirty bands of brown and grey snaked around the isolated sheets of ice and eventually coalesced with the river's murky scum to create a swirling, frothing soup in the middle of the river. Upstream the water looked uniformly brown and dirty, but there was no evidence of the foul scum. Downstream lay his village and the current was drawing the ice and stained scum directly towards it.

They had to leave—now—because something bad was seeping from this place and emptying into the river.

Suddenly Rab heard a scream. In the time it took him to snap his head around, Fin shot past him. Heedless of his footing, the boy was making straight for Stitch, who at that moment was dangling beneath the catwalk, one arm hooked around a jagged intact section of mesh, the other flailing about in open air.

An instant later, broken pieces of catwalk crashed onto the factory floor below.

"I can reach him," Fin called.

Rab stood motionless, only vaguely aware of Fin calling to him as he ran for the hole in the catwalk. On the floor below, he could see Gift, her head tilted up, staring at the dangling boy.

There wasn't a thing he could do. He certainly couldn't go after either boy. Fin would be lucky if the remaining mesh took his lesser weight. Each time his foot came down, the catwalk bounced. Rab could feel the sickening vibrations. Fin's feet pounded; the catwalk clanged; and Stitch let out another deafening high-pitched wail. On the ground below, Gift lifted her hands to shield her ears. If Stitch fell now, he'd take Gift out with him when he hit the ground.

Frantic, Rab waved and waved again in an effort to attract her attention.

"Gift," he called. "Move back! Move back!"

Whether she'd heard or even seen him, Rab couldn't tell, but she did come at last to her senses. She backed away, but her focus never wavered from Stitch, dangling precariously above.

With Gift safely out of the way, Rab began to inch along the catwalk. One step—two. The mesh beneath him sagged each time he dared to move. He had to get off the catwalk, reach the floor below and find something to break Stitch's fall.

Fin shouted out a plea for his brother to be quiet and stop struggling. The shout grabbed Rab's attention. Fin was almost at the hole now—on his belly, clawing his way along the mesh. All Rab could hear then was the thumping of his own heart in his chest.

"Look around, Gift," he called as he rushed the remaining distance towards the stairs. Though the mesh bounced, it held. "Find something we can use to catch him—anything!"

Launching himself off the catwalk, Rab began to take the steps two, sometimes three, at a time, his eye on Gift who was running from one place to another across the floor of the ruined factory.

"There's nothing. Nothing!" she cried.

At the foot of the stairs, Rab swung around the railing and propelled himself in the opposite direction. As he joined in the search for something to break Stitch's fall, he kept glancing overhead to check on the safety of the boys. He saw Fin lean over the ragged hole and lower his arm towards Stitch. But his attention was back on the ground the moment Stitch actually fell. He heard the plop though. It happened so fast and with so little apparent significance.

Chapter 4

RAB didn't want to look—either at Gift, who'd gone suddenly quiet somewhere, or the little bundle on the floor. He turned and rushed towards the bundle anyway, sickened at the thought of what he might find. When he dropped down beside the fallen child, he was startled to hear a soft moan. Looking up, he spotted Fin still dangling through the hole in the catwalk.

"He's alive," Rab shouted. "But his leg is broken for sure. I can't tell what else. Get down here. But take it slowly."

His attention returned to Stitch; the boy's breath was barely frosting.

"He's hardly making a sound," Gift cried, skidding to a halt by Rab's side. "What's wrong with him?"

"He's unconscious, Gift," Rab explained. Stripping off the warm coat Blaze had given him, Rab thrust it towards her. "Start tearing strips from the lining. Make them as long as you can."

While Rab inspected Stitch's leg, Gift set to work on his coat. If the coat hadn't been so old, her little hands wouldn't have been able to do it, but as it was, she managed to tear length after length from the lining.

"Save the padding," he said. "I'll pack it inside the bandage."

Gift nodded and began stacking the fluffy wads to one side.

It was a bad break—with what looked to be a sliver of shin bone protruding through the boy's skin. Rab did his best to clean the ugly wound. Gift had seen the full extent of damage to boy's leg and although she worked industriously at stripping Blaze's coat, her hands trembled. Rab struggled to keep his own emotions and the shakiness of his own hands in check; he couldn't afford to alarm her any further.

Out of the corner of his eye, he noticed Fin. The boy had made it off the catwalk in one piece.

"Stay out of my way, Fin," Rab hissed. "Just stay out of my way."

***

Fin walked out in front again beside Gift, all three packs slung across his back. Every so often he glanced back.

Rab had been estimating and counting their walks since they'd left the factory—they could have walked at least nine times backward and forward through their small village by now—and it had been an incredibly demanding nine walks for Rab. The boy remained unconscious and the strapped-up leg made carrying him even more difficult than usual. Rab was gambling everything now on the possibility that Gift was right—that the people who had worked in the factory had to have lived somewhere nearby.

The ruined road tracked a little too close to the river for Rab's liking, but he had no other choice. They simply had to find shelter. If they were lucky, they might also find people and maybe, among them, someone who knew better than he did what to do for the boy's leg and the nasty gash he'd subsequently discovered on the back of the boy's head.

Rab's first impulse had been to return to the village and hope that Blaze could do something to help Stitch. It seemed the only option until he looked again at Gift and remembered the promise she'd had him make, the promise to save Stitch if ever the time came to choose among them. He wasn't about to keep that promise. Over the last few days it had become quite clear to him that she was the only one of them worth saving—not Fin, certainly not himself, and not even Stitch. She had the happy combination of strength, cunning and calm that the rest of them lacked. With the right chance, she could make it and, although he hadn't asked for or wanted it, it had become his responsibility to ensure that she got that chance.

"We're coming to something," Fin called over his shoulder. "But it looks deserted."

The boy's news wasn't unexpected. More than likely they were on their own. Well, they'd started out that way and Rab had always known there was a good chance they'd end that way.

"Is there somewhere to shelter at least?"

Fin stopped abruptly in the middle of the road ahead. Gift, too, spun around. She flung the hood back from her head and beamed Rab an extraordinary smile.

"What is it?" he asked, hurrying as best he could manage to catch up.

"The City."

The settlement the children had spotted looked small, an irregular smudge, lying still and silent maybe two walks down the road.

"Isn't it beautiful?" Gift crowed.

"What's beautiful about it?" Fin asked, looking appalled.

"A roof over our heads tonight," Rab replied. "That's what's beautiful and, if we're lucky, maybe there'll be people, too."

Fin just shook his head.

The boy was probably right. The place did appear to be deserted and in as ruined a state as the road that led to it. Still, it did promise that roof over their heads and, for the moment, Rab would settle for that.

"Better get going," Rab said. He was desperate to lay Stitch down somewhere. "And make sure you stay together."

But Fin didn't move.

Gift lingered, undoubtedly waiting on Rab's censure. When it didn't come, she shrugged and set off ahead of Fin.

"All right," Rab said, once Gift was out of earshot. "What's the problem now?"

"What if there are people," Fin began, kicking up a cloud of brown snow with the toe of his boot, "but maybe not the sort of people you want to find?"

Rab had thought about that possibility, too, and had been hoping that neither Fin nor Gift would. At least Fin had had the good sense not to mention it within Gift's hearing, because if there were people there, and not the sort of people he wanted to find, then Rab had no plan whatsoever to deal with it.

"Well, that would just round out this day, wouldn't it?" he said, aping Gift's shrug.

In their world, everything came out of the darkness as a surprise. The settlement they'd found was no different, but Rab's suspicions about its true size and state were confirmed; Gift had grossly overestimated both. The settlement was probably no more than five, perhaps six, times the size of their own village and, while the road to it had fared poorly, the little town itself had fared worse. Time, neglect, and the poison rain had taken its toll. It was unlikely they'd find anyone, friendly or otherwise, inside.

At the boundary of the town, the road split into a number of narrow lanes. As they trudged down lane after lane, all they came upon was the pock-marked wreckage of the squat dwellings that flanked them and, scattered here and there among the rubble, the jagged remnants of the same type of brick they had already seen at the abandoned factory.

The village was eerily silent and Rab didn't need to worry about Fin and Gift staying close. Gift had latched her hand onto Fin's and showed no inclination to let go. But they had to stop somewhere and soon. The dead weight of Stitch on his back constantly threw Rab off balance, making a stumble likely.

"Find some place, Fin. Anywhere," he said. "I need to put Stitch down."

Fin stopped to turn around. "Everything is in ruins. What do you expect me to find?"

Gift let go of Fin's hand, clambered over a large chunk of rough concrete just to the right of them and then started to amble down a row of collapsed shanties.

"Here's all right," she called in a muffled voice. Her head was stuffed inside an off-kilter doorway. "There's still a roof and it looks safe."

"Don't go inside without me," Rab shouted.

Stitch slipped low on his back when Rab scrambled over the debris towards Gift. Her body filled most of the jagged doorway, but looking over the top of her head, he could see enough to allow that she had honed in on one of the few crudely built shacks that appeared to have most of its roof intact.

He called to Fin, standing sentinel-like in the middle of the lane.

"Come over here and take your brother. I want to look inside first. And hurry up," he said, "before I drop him."

Fin took his time and made no attempt to veil his resentment when he lifted Stitch from Rab's back.

Stifling a sigh of relief, Rab took Gift's hand. It was her find and she had the right of a vote.

The place was even darker than his space back at their village. Of course they could always clear away some of the debris to let in a little more of the insipid outside light, but that would only defeat their purpose. When night fell and the temperature dropped further, they'd be grateful for the additional protection.

With his eyes fully adjusted now, Rab glanced up to assess the ceiling. It was largely intact. Gift had found them an acceptable haven—for the night at least. He looked around, desperate to find something useful lying about on the floor; there was only more debris. The place had been scavenged and probably long ago. There was nothing to burn.

Perhaps they would have been better off trying to walk through the night instead.

Rab glanced back past the opening towards Fin. The boy was having a hard time balancing the packs on his back and Stitch in his arms. Even without the packs, it was doubtful that Fin could share the burden of carrying the little boy and, without rest, Rab couldn't manage to carry him for much longer, either.

The decision whether to go or to stay had already been made for him. "So, what do you say, Gift?" he asked.

***

Rab made Stitch as comfortable as possible, stationed Gift beside him to keep watch, then sent Fin out with instructions to walk in a straight line, first one way, then the other. If he couldn't find anything flammable, then he was to come back immediately.

The boy had been gone a long time.

"Why isn't he waking up, Rab?" Gift asked, snatching Rab's attention away from the empty doorway.

He turned, knelt down again beside Gift, and looked once more at the silent boy.

"I don't know," he answered, running a hand through tangled hair. "Maybe tomorrow," he said with a gentle touch to Gift's shoulder. "You stay here. Look after him. I'm going to see what's keeping Fin."

"He's just sulking again," she replied. "He'll come back when he's ready."

"You're probably right." Rab scrambled up from the floor. His feet ached, his back hurt and his spine was a twisted knot at the nape of his neck. "Back soon."

He hoped.

Throwing on Blaze's coat, he stepped out through the ruined doorway. The coat wasn't keeping him as warm as it had before he'd sacrificed much of its bulky lining to bandage Stitch's leg. Even drawing it tightly about his chest didn't make a lot of difference.

Fin was nowhere in sight and night was closing in. As he clambered over the huge slab of concrete near the entrance to the shack, Rab silently cursed the boy and his arrogance. One member of their party was already injured. If a second were injured, they could forget about moving on. Gift's noble directive would count for nothing. There'd be no saving Stitch—or anyone else. They'd die here, all four of them.

Rab kept to the middle of the lane, thinking there'd be less debris there to trip him up. And though he called Fin's name over and over again, the boy didn't respond. At the junction in the lane, which was as far as he'd told the boy to go, he called again. Still no answer. Turning, he started back the way he'd come, passed the ruined shanty where Stitch and Gift were sheltering, and stopped when he reached the place where the lane met the road they'd taken from the abandoned factory. Unless Fin had wandered well outside the village, he had to have heard Rab's call, but only his own voice echoed back at him.

A scraping sound at his back made Rab spin around. Usually he would have sensed something so close. Not this time. He was just too drained.

"Found this," Fin said, appearing suddenly out of the darkness.

"Why didn't you answer me?" Rab demanded, lashing out angrily.

"Just did."

Fin was hauling something large behind him. "I thought we could break this up," he said.

When the thing he was hauling caught on a pile of broken bricks, he gave it a tug to unsnag it.

Rab made his way over to Fin and what turned out to be a splintered piece of door.

"Wood," Fin said. "Maybe we could get Gift to jump on it."

His proud and cocky attitude shattered the last of Rab's patience.

"Maybe you could jump on it yourself this time," he said. "Or are you trying to break her leg now?"

The moment the words were out, however, Rab regretted them.

Fin let go of the broken door and it clattered to the ground.

"I knew you blamed me," he said, advancing on Rab. There wasn't a trace of cockiness in his voice anymore, only that familiar old resentment and anger. "Nothing I do satisfies you, does it? Maybe me and Stitch should just go back. Maybe that would satisfy you." The boy thrust his face up to Rab's, his mission to match heights a dismal failure. "I know it would satisfy me. We didn't want to come on this suicide journey in the first place. Just where do you think you're going? Have you got any idea? Any at all?"

"Better than you, boy. You should have listened to me and not taken Stitch into that factory. Maybe I don't always know the best thing to do, but I can certainly recognise the worst."

"And I suppose finding that cache of wood was a bad idea, too. You seem to have forgotten that if it weren't for me, we'd all be dead already."

The boy had a point.

"All right, Fin," Rab said. "You made one mistake. Before this journey's over, we'll make a lot more of them. Every one of us."

He made to move around Fin, intending to retrieve the discarded piece of door, but Fin grasped him roughly by the shoulder.

"Leave it," he said. "I'm going back to get Stitch. We'll find somewhere else to rest for the night and start for home first thing in the morning. I'll be fair. We'll divide the food, but, after that, Gift and you can fend for yourselves."

Rab raised both hands, feigning surrender. "Fine," he said. "Take Stitch, if you think you can carry him. But I wouldn't recommend going back to our village."

"What do you mean?" Fin asked, clearly suspicious.

"The river flows towards our village," Rab said. "And I'm beginning to wonder if the river isn't the reason we've all been getting sicker as time goes on."

Fin shrugged in the darkness. "We've always got sick. The air is bad."

"That's true," Rab agreed, "and the water's always been bad. But now the ground is going bad, too. Maybe some poison from that place—that factory—got into the ground. What's in the ground gets into the 'shrooms. And what gets into the 'shrooms. . ."

The boy remained silent for a moment. "The village is a long way from here," he said at last. "Nothing bad could get that far."

"Maybe."

"Well, if you thought that back at the factory, instead of walking further away, why didn't we turn around so we could go back and tell them at least? Don't you care?"

"I thought about turning back—at first. Especially after Stitch broke his leg. But then I realised that they'd already made up their minds."

Fin shook his head.

"Think about it," Rab said. "They voted to send the three of you with me and they wouldn't have done that unless they knew they were dying. Giving them a possible reason why they're dying wouldn't make a bit of difference."

"You're wrong." Fin pushed past him, heading for their shelter and Stitch. "You're wrong about the launch pad and you're wrong about that."

Rab let him go. He hadn't managed to change the mind of any one of the people in his village before, so what made him think he could change

Fin's now? Gathering the length of splintered door, he started to drag it down the lane until Gift's urgent call had him running back to the shack, empty-handed.

Ducking inside, he found Fin on his knees, leaning over his brother, and Gift, a tiny shadow in the far corner of the room.

"What's wrong?" he asked anxiously.

"It's Stitch," Gift whimpered. "I think he's really sick."

***

Stitch's fever only grew worse through the night. Fin had relented, gone back and dragged the splintered door into their shelter, but the fire Gift had made with it didn't seem to have helped. In the firelight, Rab had seen the sweat on the boy's forehead and gave a brief thought to removing the bandage to check if the wound was infected. But there wasn't a thing he could do about it if it was. They had no medicines, nothing to bring the infection or the boy's fever down. All they could do was wait and hope the boy had enough defences of his own to combat the sickness.

He was a strong enough kid and that played in his favour, but it was obvious now that Rab had to rethink his plans. They couldn't go on and they couldn't go back, at least not until the boy's condition either improved or. . .no, he wouldn't consider the alternative.

Rab waited until the children began to doze before leaving. He knew he couldn't stay away too long. If Fin woke and found him gone, he might just try to make it back to the village with Stitch. All Rab could do was rely on Gift to make sure that didn't happen. But even Gift couldn't stand up to Fin indefinitely. He had to find a solution and find it quickly, so he took to the tight alleys and lanes, desperately hoping that somewhere inside one of the ruins down one of the abandoned lanes he would find something, anything to help Stitch. If he were lucky, he might even stumble across a villager who'd stayed behind. But it was dark and his search was tediously slow and unproductive.

He'd just crawled out through the doorway of yet another ruin when he was startled by a female voice, too old to be Gift's, calling to him out of the darkness.

"You, Top-sider! What do you think you're doing?"

His impulse was to rush up and embrace whoever had spoken. There were people here. But he couldn't see who had called to him.

The voice spoke again.

"I said you. Answer!"

"My name's Rab," he replied, uncertain where to direct his response. "And I need help."

"Don't we all?" the voice called back. "What sort of help?"

A figure began approaching him from the opposite side of the lane. Rab couldn't see her face; and bundled up as she was from head to foot, there was little indication of her age. She was pointing something at him, although Rab had no idea what it was.

"I have a sick boy," he said. "We need medicine."

The woman began to back away. "What do you mean 'sick'?"

"He broke his leg and now he's got a fever."

"Oh." The figure paused. "Where are you from?"

"A village south of here."

"You're lying," she said. "There's no one alive in the south."

Rab shrugged. "Well, I had to have come from somewhere and I can assure you that there are still people there." Though not for much longer, he thought.

The woman didn't pursue the argument. "What happened to the boy?" she asked instead, stepping closer.

"He fell—through a suspended walkway."

Until that moment, the finest clothing Rab had ever seen was on his back. But there were no visible patches anywhere on this woman's clothing; no tears, no ancient grime; no misshapen, battered boots; and no vulnerable skin protruding through the fingers of her thick gloves as she stood there, still pointing that strange thing right at him.

"You've been to the river?" she said, sounding amazed. Stepping closer still, she lowered the thing she was pointing. "How stupid can you be?"

***

It didn't take much to realise that Fin was hovering too close for the woman's liking. Gift had opted for the diplomatic approach and gone outside, leaving the woman to tend to Stitch as she saw fit. Rab stood at a distance, waiting for instructions, but it was obvious to him, if not Fin, that the woman preferred to minister to Stitch alone.

"Get this boy out of my light," she barked, looking from where she was crouched over Stitch.

Rab stepped forward and grabbed Fin by the elbow.

"We'll wait outside," he told the woman.

"Thanks for telling me. I'd have worried otherwise."

Gift turned as Rab stepped through the door, pulling Fin.

"Will Stitch be all right?" she asked.

Rab shrugged. "I guess. That woman isn't exactly talkative."

Gift smiled back at him. "Who is she anyway? Does she live here? Are there more people?"

Rab settled on the block of broken concrete beside Gift. "I wish I knew. She just appeared out of nowhere."

"Lucky for us," Gift said.

"I'm not so sure of that," Fin observed from the doorway. "What's that thing she was carrying? She won't let it out of her sight. And why won't she tell us her name or where she comes from?"

Rab turned to answer the boy. "Maybe she's just frightened," he said. "She's helping us, isn't she?"

"And after she's tended to Stitch? Then what?"

"One thing at a time," Rab replied, glancing away. Craning his head only worsened the pain in his neck.

"The boy asks a good question."

Rab's head snapped back round again.

The woman was standing just outside the doorway. The skinny metal stick of a thing she'd laid against the inside wall while she tended to Stitch was slung down at her side now. Beside her, Fin began an open appraisal, of both the metal stick and the woman. It couldn't have netted him much; the woman's hood remained drawn snugly about her face.

Rab got to his feet.

"The boy is Fin," he said and gestured towards Gift, who'd also risen from her perch. "And this is Gift."

"Thrilled," the woman replied curtly. "What's the kid's name?"

"Stitch," Gift told her.

"So, what is the plan for Stitch now? Let me guess. You don't have one."

"Well, I wasn't expecting him to break a leg," Rab answered defensively. "We were going north before this happened."

"North to what?"

Rab edged forward. "Look, we're grateful for your help," he said with demanding restraint. "We really are. But you haven't told us anything about yourself, where you come from, what you're doing here, yet you keep asking me all these questions. Give me one good reason why I should answer."

The woman shrugged. "Simple," she said. "You don't have a clue what you're doing. And now you've made me responsible for that kid. . .Stitch." She jerked her head towards where Stitch lay in the dark and partial shelter behind her. "Someone has to decide what to do. And before I can do that, I need to know whether I can trust you. You are a Top-sider, after all."

"I don't think I like the way you say that," Rab shot back. "Just what exactly is a Top-sider?"

After a brief sidelong study of Fin, the woman's attention returned to Rab. "Someone who lives on the top, of course."

"Meaning you don't?"

The heavy hood she wore made it difficult to be certain, but Rab thought he saw the corners of the woman's lips curve upward.

"Up in the bad air? In the dark?" She swung the metal stick up to her shoulder. "It's true. Top-siders are mad."

Rab eyed the stick. He wasn't at all comfortable with the way she casually wielded that thing around. . .whatever it was.

"Are you intentionally talking in riddles?" he demanded. "Just tell us who you are."

The woman stamped a foot to the ground. "I come from down here," she said. "I'd have thought that was obvious. Well, not exactly down here, I suppose." Raising her hand, she pointed due north. "My city's about a half day's walk that way."

"Your city?" Rab could hardly believe it. Could they really have been that lucky? Was this woman one of the very people he'd come looking for? "An underground city?"

She shrugged. "Now do you want to tell me what your plan was before that kid broke his leg? If not, we'll part company right here, right now."

Rab considered his reply for a long, silent time, deciding that in the long run they had nothing to lose, but everything to gain by explaining. What harm could it do? She'd either help them or she wouldn't.

"I told you. We were going north. We were looking for a way off."

"Off?"

His answer appeared to puzzle her, but if hers was the city he was looking for, she had to have known what he meant.

"You're talking about the launch pad," she said, still sounding unsure.

Rab felt a touch on his hand. He glanced down to find that Gift had stepped up beside him. Judging by the expression that came over her face, like Rab, she hadn't expected the woman to suddenly break out in laughter.

"Top-siders are all mad," the woman said finally. "And vulgar. I should really be offended, I suppose, but it's hard to feel offended by a fool. There is no launch pad. Not here. Not ever. We're all that's left." She pointed to Rab. "A few Top-siders like you," then turned the finger towards herself, "and people like me. Everyone else is dead."

***

"What did you give him?"

Stitch had gone very still. The dead weight was pulling down painfully on Rab's shoulders.

At the woman's direction, Gift and Fin had taken the lead. Gift seemed almost excited, while Fin remained his sceptical, surly self. He'd slung the packs over his back and tramped off without comment.

"Purple mushroom extract," the woman told Rab calmly.

"What?" Rab pulled up and grabbed the woman's sleeve. "You poisoned him?"

Those barely visible lips of hers curved upward again, though it was still difficult to interpret the gesture as something even remotely friendly.

"You really are ignorant, aren't you?" she said. "Purple mushroom extract is not harmful in very small doses. In fact, it has a great number of medicinal applications." She started off after Fin and Gift again, "for one, it can bring down a fever," then glanced back. "What do you use when someone is sick? Incantations and magic?"

Rab struck off in pursuit. "We have medicines," he said, annoyed at how pathetically defensive he'd sounded.

Their medicines usually amounted to water mixed with a little ground up charcoal scavenged from their fires. He wasn't about to admit that. Of course, if his father were to be believed, his people had once had the means and the knowledge to perform miracles with their medicines. But maybe that was just more of his father's loose talk.

And maybe this woman—and everyone else—was right. There were no launch pads and never had been. Why would she lie? And if her people believed it to be nothing but a foolish tale, then perhaps he was wrong. But something nagged at him—if she knew the rumours then who had told her the story?

"I need to make something clear," the woman said, the moment he caught up with her, glancing at him briefly from under the hood of her bulky clothing. "You are not welcome to stay in our city." She nodded towards Gift up ahead. "Especially her. You can remain until the boy is healed or you can leave him with us. It's your choice."

Her pace quickened without warning, leaving Rab behind to struggle on with Stitch. But her brutal honesty had offered him one hope. She seemed confident that Stitch would recover.

As he followed along behind her, Rab studied the woman. She was very familiar with the terrain—that much was clear. Every so often she barked another order to the children ahead, adjusting their course. They had left the main road some distance back and climbed gently for a while, but it was flat going now. The woman claimed her city lay to the north. He had no reason to doubt her, but little reason to trust her, either. For the moment though, it didn't matter. He couldn't go on with Stitch so badly injured.

There was little about the woman that didn't grate on Rab's already tattered nerves, in particular her habit of stopping every so often to glance back before taking off again without comment. What was she doing? Making sure that he was still following? Perhaps she was just checking that everything was still fine with Stitch. Maybe she just didn't like having him at her back. She struck him as the type who had to know everything that was going on everywhere at any given moment.

And what was that curious stick she had slung across her back? Her hand kept wandering towards it, as though she needed to reassure herself that she hadn't lost it. The pack she carried was only small, suggesting she hadn't come far, just as she'd claimed. And it was obvious that she could have walked quite a bit faster than she was doing now. How was he supposed to interpret that little display of consideration?

She stopped to glance back again, but this time raised her hand to point. "We're almost there," she called. "Just a little further on. How's the boy?"

"The same," Rab replied.

At least he hoped so. Stitch hadn't made a sound or a move since the woman had tended to him inside the ruined shanty. For all he knew, the boy could be dead. Maybe that had been her plan all along. To kill them off, one by one. But that didn't make much sense. Then again, it didn't really need to. Besides Rab couldn't see any evidence of a city ahead, just the same empty terrain. Granted she had said they lived underground, but she couldn't have meant entirely. There had to be a way in at least but the flat, featureless plain ahead didn't look very promising at all.

"Fire!" Fin called suddenly.

Rab bolted and as he ran, Stitch's dead weight bumped painfully against his back. When Fin grabbed a hold of his arm, he almost toppled over.

"It's all on fire!" Fin bellowed.

Rab didn't like what he saw or smelled, either. Just like Fin said, the ground ahead of them did appear to be on fire. A low lying blanket of smoke wafted about their feet and the stench of something burning filled the air.

Unconcerned, the woman kept on walking into the smoke. She was actually laughing.

"What is it?" Gift asked, sounding more curious than worried, apparently taking her cue from the woman.

Rab shook his head, realising quickly that he and Fin had got it completely wrong. What they were seeing wasn't a surface fire at all but the build-up of smoke created by the slow pluming of many separate columns out of the ground. The funnels were too numerous to count and, farther away, the gloom and the smoky haze obscured the individual columns completely.

"It's warmer underground," the woman called over her shoulder. "But even we need fire."

Gift's brow crinkled. "What's she saying? That we're standing on top of their city?"

Rab shrugged. He couldn't think what else she could mean. But an entire city built underground? It didn't seem possible.

"It's a trap," Fin said beside him. "The air here is poisoned and she wants us to walk into it."

"I doubt that," Rab replied. Stitch began to stir on his back, allaying at least one of his concerns; the boy was still alive. "She's not likely to walk right into her own trap, is she?"

"I believe her."

Rab turned towards Gift.

"She helped Stitch, didn't she? Shared her medicine? I believe her." Gift knelt and placed the palm of her small hand flat on the ground. "There's a city under here. I can feel it."

Rab spared an inner smile. Perhaps little Gift did feel it. She'd certainly have felt the warmer earth, but that didn't necessarily mean that there was a city under their feet. It could mean anything, including the unthinkable —that Fin was right. But the woman wouldn't walk into her own cloud of poisonous gas. Perhaps she wasn't telling them the entire truth, but she couldn't be lying about the cloud. It was just ordinary smoke, even if it didn't come from the hearth fires of her people.

"I'm not waiting for you," she shouted.

They couldn't delay any longer.

"We're staying with her," Rab said to Fin. "You can come with us or go on alone. But if you go on, it'll be without Stitch and the packs."

"I've already got the packs," Fin reminded him with a smile. "Do you really think you can take them from me?"

Stepping closer, Rab leaned in to tower over the boy. "Do you really think I can't? Or that I wouldn't try? Get going," he said and gave the boy a shove.

***

"Mind your step," the woman advised. "If you fall, I won't go down after you."

Rab stood, with Gift beside him, looking down over the edge of the cliff. The woman had already started down a set of rough-hewn steps that disappeared into the murky depths below them.

Bending, Rab found and hefted a rock, testing its weight, then pitched it out over the edge. A series of dull thuds sounded below.

"Wanna watch where you're throwing things, Top-sider?" the woman barked at him from below.

The cliff was steep, but not bottomless. Still he wouldn't be inclined to clamber down there after anyone, either. And it wasn't going to be easy climbing down the narrow icy steps with the weight of Stitch on his back. He glanced at Gift.

"Do you think you can make it?"

"Of course I can," she answered with a shrug and set off after the woman.

Fin stepped up to take Gift's place.

"What about you?" Rab asked.

"If you can, I can," Fin answered brusquely, and started down after Gift.

For a moment, Rab just watched them both descend. Gift's little feet were taking the narrow steps with ease. Behind her, Fin struggled with his balance, but overall he was managing. The woman was nowhere to be seen. He should have sent Fin down first. If he lost his footing now, he'd take Gift down with him in the fall.

"Come on, it's easier than it looks," Gift called confidently up the cliff face.

Rab hoped she was right. Heights had always been his weakness.

"You hold on tight, Stitch," he said with a glance over his shoulder. "Do you hear me?"

The boy emitted a feeble moan, nothing more.

Tentatively Rab took the first step, staggered briefly, then took the next. Each step demanded discipline and focus. His heart beat madly. His head began to swim. With so much of his attention directed to his footing, he almost blundered into Fin at the bottom of the steps. The woman he soon found perched on a large boulder, waiting for them.

"Took your time," she said, getting to her feet.

They were standing on a large, smooth platform of rock. Beneath them, Rab saw little but gloom. But to the left, he noticed the top of another set of stairs.

"We don't go down there," the woman said, arching her arm. "The city's this way."

It felt good to be on flat ground again.

"What's below us?" Rab asked.

The woman shrugged. "Nothing for you, Top-sider. A few other Top-siders here and there in the valley. Mostly nothing though. It's pretty well played out."

"Played out?" Rab peeked over his shoulder; Stitch hadn't moved.

"Of fuel," the woman told him. "Not much wood there now either." She pointed up the valley. "Some of the people think there's a good supply up that way. I haven't looked. Maybe I will some day."

Rab decided not to mention the broken forest they'd stumbled on early in their journey—not yet anyway. The woman still hadn't earned his trust.

"Is that what you do?" he asked instead. "Find fuel for the city?"

"Sometimes."

"And that's why you were there? In the village?"

The woman stopped walking and turned around. There was little of her face showing, just eyes, nose, and mouth, but it was enough to convince Rab that his question would go unanswered.

When she started off again, Rab glanced behind to assure himself that Fin and Gift were still following. Gift was walking too close to the edge for his liking. The child was too fearless. He waited for her to catch up and then took her hand. A sullen Fin brought up the rear.

Apart from its dusting of ice, which demanded a degree of vigilance, the platform was easily managed. The rock was worn smooth and level, suggesting it might even have been man-made. A short distance away, the cliff face plummeted down again into the valley where the woman said some of his own kind, 'Top-siders', remained. Whenever she used that label, she sneered, clearly disliking Top-siders and keen to have him know it. Rab couldn't imagine what threat the Top-siders could pose to this seemingly impregnable cliff-dwelling. In his village, the daily struggle for survival exhausted both strength and spirit. He doubted that the people in the valley below fared better; they'd have little enthusiasm for trouble making.

The woman soon stopped in front of a large chasm in the rock face, fortified by an elaborately patched network of metal fencing. The bars that supported the mesh had been punched right into the rock around the ragged perimeter of the hole. In places, the metal looked somewhat rusted. There didn't seem to be any way in, until Rab noticed a slightly larger-than-person-sized gate in the middle of the grill.

"You remember what I told you?" The woman glanced at Gift. "About staying?"

"I remember," Rab replied.

A more enthusiastic welcome would have been desirable, but he hadn't set out on this journey only to end it inside a hole in the side of a cliff face. And Rab was beginning to suspect that was all the woman's grand city would amount to. Her talk was simply that—talk! He had no doubt that sheltering inside this inauspicious facade he would find only another band of wretched refugees. The woman must be deluded—or mad. Just his dumb luck. And wasn't Fin going to love being proved right?

Gift tugged at his hand. "What does she mean? Are we going to stay here?"

"Only until Stitch can walk again. These aren't the people we're looking for."

The woman glanced over her shoulder.

"If you don't want to get shot, stay behind me," she said. "Understand?"

"Shot?" Rab asked. "What's shot?"

The woman reached around and patted the strange metal stick she constantly carried. "Guards are stationed at this entrance at all times," she said, drawing something he couldn't see from inside her jacket. "If you try to steal anything, you won't get very far."

She took some pains to conceal exactly what she was doing to the heavy chain that held the gate closed. The chain showed none of the corrosion Rab was used to seeing. Either it was made of some special, unfamiliar material or the city's inhabitants carefully maintained what seemed to be a pitifully inadequate attempt at further security. A good size rock could have smashed the chain with less effort than the woman was obliged to use to release it.

The chain freed, she pulled at the gate and swung it outward, gliding it noiselessly until it finally came to rest flush against the fencing.

"You keep that one under control," she said, pointing at Gift, then stepped through the open gateway.

Gift's hand tightened on Rab's. Her mouth was a thin line, uncharacteristically drawn down at the corners. She'd taken offence at the woman's words and Rab couldn't blame her. Of his three companions, he harboured the least concerns about Gift. For some reason, the woman didn't.

He stepped through into the pitch black cave, disappointed and a little disturbed when normal blindsight failed him. Gift's hand was still latched tightly onto his while, behind him, Fin faintly swore.

"Stop," the woman said.

A rattling sound now, as though she was replacing the chain. There was an inherent sense of finality about that noise that Rab found immediately disconcerting.

"After me," she said with a touch to his arm.

Without his blindsight, Rab was obliged to follow the sound of her footsteps.

"Two more steps and turn sharply to your left."

Rab took the corner too tightly, bruising his left shoulder against a wall of rock.

"Five steps and turn right."

A subtle glow showed ahead of them now and Rab could see well enough to pick out a wall and, to the right, a narrow corridor that seemed to lead back the way they had come. The woman was leading them in circles.

She stopped at the end of the tunnel. Beyond her the way opened out abruptly into a softly illuminated space.

"The guards are just inside." She laid the strange stick she'd been carrying against the smooth wall of the tunnel and began to peel off her outermost layer of clothing. "They'll be expecting me, but not you, so if you don't want to get shot, stay behind me until I explain who you are." Slinging the heavy jacket over one arm, she retrieved the strange stick with the other. "Come on."

Rab felt a tug on his hand and, as he leaned down to Gift, Stitch slipped a little on his back.

"Why does she keep saying that?" Gift whispered into his ear. "I don't like this place anymore. Let's just go. They don't seem to want us here."

When he glanced back, Rab found just what he'd expected, Fin's glower of open contempt.

"We can look after Stitch," Gift said.

Was she trying to convince him, Fin, or herself?

"It's only for a little while," Rab replied, trying to allay their fears, and his. "We need their medicine. Anyway I thought you said you trusted her."

"I did," Gift said with a sigh. "Until now. She's locked us in."

Rab had experienced his own sinking feeling at the sound of the chain being replaced. Even so, if the need arose, he still thought he could smash through it easily enough.

"Well?" Fin snarled. "You're supposed to be in charge, what do you suggest we do?"

"All we can do for now," Rab replied. "Follow her."

The soft rectangular glow they'd been chasing had conditioned him to expect a brighter space, but he hadn't expected to discover such a vast space beyond the narrow tunnel. The place was cavernous—and warm— impossibly, deliciously warm. And, at first glance, it appeared empty, until he looked again.

From the moment he'd started down the tunnel, Rab had just assumed they were heading into a natural cave. He was wrong. The woman was standing in the middle of a huge room, there was no other word for it, that had neatly-laid, square-hewn slabs of smoothed stone for a floor and a huge hearth, glowing red and inviting in the middle of the far wall. Dead centre of the room, wrapped in the arms of an oversized, cloth-covered chair, an old man sat blissfully sleeping.

Rab's attention flicked back to the woman. With her outer clothing removed, he was given his first real look at her. She was younger than he had expected, probably somewhere around his own age, but she had none of the gaunt look of his kind. Her jaw was firm, her cheekbones high and prominent below eyes the colour of muddy water. Her hair, though, was the most startling of her features. Although hacked indiscriminately to varying lengths, it was of a bright yellow colour Rab had never seen before.

He simply couldn't take it all in: the opulence of the room, the apparent age of the old man in the chair, and the odd expression that had descended on the woman's almost pretty face. But he had managed to take in that the promised guards weren't anywhere in sight.

"Grandfather!"

The woman's angry shout startled him.

On the opposite side of the room, the old man began to stir in his chair.

"What did you do with the guards?"

"Sent them away, of course," came the old man's sleep-addled reply.

The woman peeled off another layer of clothing and shed it carelessly to the floor. Along with it came crudely balled up wads of something that fell all about her feet.

"So you're back then." The old man shifted in the chair, stretched once, twice, before angling a glance towards the woman. It was only then Rab noticed that the old man was clean-shaven; not someone who ventured out much onto the surface, he concluded quickly.

"Did you find—" the old man began before the woman cut him off.

"No, I didn't." She pointed to Rab and his companions. "I found them instead," she said and bent to gather the fallen wads. "They claim to have come from the south."

Evidently the old man's bones weren't in the best of shape. His movement was awkward as he twisted around in his chair to study Rab and his party.

"The little boy has a broken leg," the woman told the old man as she continued gathering the scattered wads. "It'll mend."

"Top-siders," the old man observed.

"What else?"

With all of the wads now gathered, she carried them to the far corner of the room and dumped them into a container stationed there.

"But there's no one alive in the south," the old man protested softly.

"Try telling them that. I said they could stay until the boy's leg was healed. No longer. Unless of course," she added with a shrug, "they want to leave the child behind."

The old man struggled to his feet. "I sincerely doubt they'll do that, Sunny." His glance shifted from Rab to the woman. "Don't you?"

The woman just shrugged again and marched back across the room.

Well, Rab thought, at least he'd discovered something about their rescuer —she had a name.

"I'll take the boy to the hospital," she said. "Try to find someone who'll take in the others temporarily."

The old man waved his hand. "No need for that," he replied with a smile that further cracked the skin of his wizened face. "I'll take them."

The offer appeared to surprise his granddaughter. "Even the girl?"

The cracks in the old man's face deepened. "Why not? I took you in."

The woman, Sunny, quickly regained her composure. "Well, you didn't have a lot of choice, did you? You owed me."

Rab watched as the old man's smile slowly withered.

"Give me the boy," Sunny said, turning to Rab.

"I'm not just going to hand Stitch over so you can take him some place where I'll never find him again. We'll all go. Unless you can give me some good reason why we can't."

A snigger sounded on the far side of the room. "Got someone who'll argue with you, eh, Sunny?"

"Keep quiet, Grandfather." Sunny shot him a warning glance. "You just go bring those guards back."

"I'll do nothing of the kind," the old man replied as he drifted towards Rab.

The closer he drew, the better Rab could appreciate the old man's likeness to Sunny. He had the same square set of the jaw and the same prominent cheekbones. But unlike Sunny, the old man's eyes were a weak-looking, watery blue, set shallowly in bloodless, crinkled skin and the remaining tufts of his hair lacked any definable colour.

"Let Sunny take the boy," the old man said. "It's better if you stay out of the hospital anyway. Germs, you know?"

"No, I don't know," Rab barked, uncertain whether an overpowering rush of fear or simple exasperation had sparked his sudden outburst. "What kind of place is this? Who are you people?"

The old man smiled again. "Just that, lad. People." His focus shifted briefly to his granddaughter. "She'll tell you we're the only people. And as for this place—" the smile wavered, "—this is our home."

A shrivelled hand came up to cup Rab's shoulder. "Of course you're not seeing it at its best."

"Grandfather!"

"All right. All right." The old man's smile vanished altogether. "We'll talk more later," he said to Rab. "For now you'd better let my grand-daughter take the boy. I promise he'll come to no harm. She's a pain, I'll admit, but she's no threat to the boy's safety."

Fin shrugged off his packs and stepped forward. "I won't allow it."

"Who's this one then?" the old man asked, peering directly into Fin's face.

They were of a height.

"I'm Stitch's brother and I go where he goes."

"We're wasting time." Sunny shoved Fin aside. "And I've got better things to do. If it'll get us moving, you carry the boy then." She spun on her heels and strode off towards one of two narrow doorways set into the wall between the huge hearth and the left hand corner of the room. "And don't touch the walls on the way down."

What else could he do? Rab turned Stitch over to his brother and watched as Sunny first and then Fin, his arms laden, disappeared through the narrow doorway.

"Thought she'd never leave." The old man breathed a sigh before he began a slow assessment of Rab and, apparently satisfied with what he found, repeated the procedure on Gift. "How old?" he asked, nodding at Rab's little companion.

Rab didn't know exactly. No one slavishly counted years anymore, did they? What was the point? You were born and then you died. What difference did knowing the exact length of the span between make?

"Too young for work," the old man said, accepting Rab's silence, "but probably the perfect age for trade."

Chapter 5

"THERE'S no need to get excited, lad." The old man gasped for breath. "You didn't think I meant we engage in that disgusting practice, did you?" His bony fingers were wrapped around Rab's, as he struggled with little success to uncurl them from his throat. "I was thinking about her safety."

Rab relaxed his grip and the old man drew in a sharp and raspy breath. Gift, who'd been sheltering behind Rab, took a tentative step out from his shadow.

"Don't have to kill me," the old man said. "I'll be gone soon enough anyway." He nodded again at Gift. "There's a market for young girls. Didn't you know?"

A market for girls! Rab had never heard of such a thing and suspected the old man was lying.

"Well, there is," the old man told him, soothing his reddened neck with a trembling hand. "You're a Top-sider. You should know. It's your kind who do the dealing—and the stealing."

"That's a lie." Rab would have made another lunge for the old man's throat right then and there if he hadn't noticed the fear in Gift's eyes. They'd faced some trials together these last few days, but he'd never seen her look quite as alarmed as she did now. Briefly he put a hand to the top of her head, then turned back to confront the old man. "Why would we do something like that?"

The old man shrugged. "A lot of reasons." His thin fingers were still working at the crinkled skin of his throat.

Rab's assault had left an impressive welt and he was beginning to feel a little ashamed of himself. What if the old man was telling the truth? It seemed unlikely. If the old man was to be believed, his concerns were for Gift's safety, a concern Sunny didn't appear to share.

"Breeding mostly," the old man said.

Rab's hand found Gift's.

"We have too many girls." His bony finger poked Rab's chest. "But your kind don't."

That much was true. In his own village, more females than males were born, but like Shy, the young women of his village invariably died in childbirth. Still, if there were such a trade in female children, why had he never heard of it?

"Maybe that's so," Rab said, "but my people don't trade in humans."

The old man shrugged again. "Perhaps you don't." He pointed away to his right. "But they do. The Top-siders out there. We care for our children here, even the girls, but," he raised a crooked finger, "we control how many are born. Baby girls are stronger, so naturally we have more. Another boy in the city is easily accommodated. A girl means work." He ambled away and, returning to the enormous chair, flopped into the lumpy seat. "Work to raise her. Work to educate her. Work to protect her from the raids. Every additional girl we have means one less boy. It's all about balance and keeping a stable population. Understand?"

The old man's talk made a twisted sort of sense, but Rab remained sceptical. "Then why don't you just take their boys?" he asked. "It would solve your problem, wouldn't it?"

The old man's face broke out in a sneer. "Because we're not savages. We're people. Ask Sunny," he said. "Besides, you don't listen very well, do you? I said it was all about balance and a stable population. And there's only so much room." He gestured towards the packs at Rab's feet. "What's in those?"

"Dried 'shrooms," Rab said. "Water."

"Shrooms?" The old man was silent a moment. "Oh, mushrooms," he said finally. "Well, we can always use those. As for the water, I doubt it's fit for humans. Ah—the guards are back."

Rab's attention flicked towards the back of the room. He hadn't even noticed the arrival of the two burly men that were now stationed on either side of the narrow doorway through which Sunny and the boys had disappeared. She'd obviously ordered them back. The woman seemed to wield a certain amount of power in this place.

***

"Didn't I tell you not to touch the walls?"

The old man had but, unable to resist, Rab had touched them anyway. He'd never seen, or even imagined, that there could be anything like this in all the world. The walls of the tunnel were literally glowing, subtly lighting their passage down a slight incline. It was a soft, warm and greenish kind of glow. Each little pinpoint of light was actually quite intense, but the pinpoints emitting that light were so minute that, together, the accumulated effect was a subtle one. And when he'd actually touched the shining wall, Rab's hand had come away damp.

"Is it poison?" he asked, mildly alarmed.

He shouldn't have acted so rashly. Unlike him, Gift had kept her gloves on and her hands to her sides, eyeing the magical lightshow suspiciously as they made their way down the gentle slope.

"Of course it's not poison. I wasn't concerned about you. I was concerned about them." The old man pointed a gnarled finger at the wall. "They're extremely delicate and don't like to be handled. I'd be grateful, and so would they, if you didn't do it again."

"But what are they?"

"Shimmerers. Can't remember the species name," the old man said. "Not my field. Ask Sunny."

It seemed there was a lot he needed to ask Sunny.

"Why are they shining like that?" Gift had finally found her voice.

"Phosphorescence," the old man said, glancing back at her. "Never heard of it? No, I guess you wouldn't," he continued without giving the child the opportunity to reply. "You either, I suppose?" he asked of Rab.

Rab shook his head.

"They're alive, you see. Been growing here since I can remember. And they'll continue to grow here if you keep your hands and those packs off them." He stopped suddenly. "So where exactly is this village you told Sunny you came from?"

"Like I said, way south of here."

Telling Sunny about his village had been a foolish mistake. That damage was done, but he wasn't about to compound the error. Besides he was beginning to have some concerns about the source of a strange buzzing noise coming from the lower end of the tunnel and didn't care if the old man believed him or not.

The old man scratched his head. "But there's no one alive in the south. Even Sunny agrees with that and Sunny doesn't agree with much."

Rab was subjected to another slow and irritating inspection.

"Can't be," the old man declared, starting down the tunnel again. "You must have turned yourself around, lad. Come from the east maybe. You're no ordinary Top-sider. That much is clear. You and those kids are scrawny and dirty, but you don't look feral enough to be one of them."

Rab shrugged his reply. The buzzing sounded louder now.

"Well," the old man said, "wherever you're from, it must be turning bad or you'd still be there. Here we are then. This is our city."

Nothing Sunny might have told Rab about her city could have prepared him. The same phosphorescent glow that lit the tunnel shone out from the walls of a vast space in front of them. And the space itself was bustling with activity. There were more people here than Rab had ever seen in one place before and the amount of noise they made seemed almost deafening. His heart was in his throat, his ears rang, and he simply couldn't believe his eyes.

Gift's grasp on his hand tightened.

"Look," she whispered. "You can't see anyone's breath."

Rab hadn't even noticed, but she was right. He couldn't even see his own and when he thought about it, realised he hadn't since they'd entered the upper tunnel.

Gift's black eyes turned huge with wonder when she glanced up towards the ceiling. Rab followed her gaze and froze. The ceiling sparkled with light.

"Main Street," the old man said with a chuckle that morphed slowly into a sigh. He pointed at the ceiling. "Brightworms. Bigger beasties than shimmerers, but their light is produced by much the same principle. What did you think they were?"

Rab lowered his gaze to find Sunny's grandfather looking at him quizzically. "My father used to talk about stars. I thought—"

"Stars!" The old man slapped Rab's back. "Never seen one for real, myself," he said and brought the hand up to his head. "You think stars look like that?" he asked, scratching the tuffs of his hair for a moment. "Maybe they do at that. Stars!" He chuckled again. "Wouldn't suggest that to Sunny if I were you." He strode off, still softly chuckling. "Come on then," he said with a wave of a hand over his shoulder. "They're closing up for the day."

With Gift in tow, Rab followed the old man down the broad channel he'd called Main Street. Although the ceiling hung low, the cavern was aglow with the soft phosphorescent light of the brightworms and the space was broad and enormous, stretching on and on into the distance. Heavily laden benches of some kind lined both sides of the rock-floored cavern. There were pots, pans, baskets and barrels of all shapes and sizes. Cloth of every possible colour. Foods Rab couldn't identify. Tools he couldn't imagine how to use. Things he couldn't recognise at all.

The old man pointed left. "Food merchants on this side. Goods merchants on the other."

Rab could barely hear him through the din.

"It's not possible," he said under his breath.

The old man just smiled and studied the lines of busy traders for a long moment. "Why, this is nothing. We have maybe thirty traders here. But there used to be thousands of cities with thousands of people doing what we do here. Whole buildings were dedicated to it—whole streets even."

Rab wondered what Gift would make of such careless talk but, when he glanced down, decided she wasn't listening.

For a while, no one seemed to notice two strangers walking among them, despite the occasional knot of humanity Rab was obliged to sidestep. Like the old man, the men went mostly beardless. The women, whose appearance suggested a hardiness Rab had never observed in the women of his village, wore smallish shoes that would have been ruined within a day on the surface and comfortable, well-fitting clothes that were of no particular style, cut, or colour preference. Lingering customers hounded merchants, who themselves were busy stacking and storing their goods into little, four-wheeled, hand-drawn vehicles. Rab had seen the wreckage of similar wagons in his own village, carts that had once been used to transport the 'shroom harvest back from the fields. Long ago, the wood used to construct those carts had become too precious as fuel. But the carts the merchants used appeared to be made of a shiny kind of metal, hammered into thin sheets.

An old woman chose that moment to turn around. She bumped right into Rab. At first, she seemed surprised, then alarmed. With a dip of her head, she hurried off, her purchase tucked close against her chest. Then something behind Rab clattered, causing him to reach out quickly and drag Gift closer. He spun around and found one of the merchants, a smallish, dark-haired woman about Blaze's age, staring right at him. Her mouth was open, as though she was desperate to say something, but the only sound that came out was a gasp.

"Nothing to worry about, Lilly," the old man said kindly, as he bent down awkwardly and gathered a battered pan of some kind from the floor. "Sunny found them." He passed the battered pan to the dark-haired woman.

"We know," the woman said hurriedly and, dropping the pan among the jumble of her wares, darted around the side of her stall. Her actions drew the attention of others who rushed from their stalls to join her. "We saw those two boys, but Sunny didn't mention a Top-side man. . ."

When her focus snapped from Rab to Gift, the little girl huddled closer.

"Or a girl," another woman interjected, making an abortive attempt to push closer to Gift but the gathering crowd had her pinned.

The knot that had already formed in the pit of Rab's stomach tightened, as did his hold on Gift.

The old man shook his head. "She's not one of us, Lilly," he said and, taking a hold of the first woman's hand, drew her forward. "She's a skinny true-breed. . .surface born. See?"

Something vanished in the woman's eyes. . .though her focus remained latched onto Gift, she no longer appeared to see her.

"Too young," she murmured and slowly shook her head.

"They're just passing through," the old man shouted above calls of complaint from the crowd. "They'll be gone before you know it."

As Lilly turned away the mob began to fragment, merchants and their customers slowly drifting back towards the stalls. Rab was surprised at how quickly it actually occurred, these people. . .these tunnel-dwellers. . . clearly respected the old man.

"Nothing to be frightened of," the old man said, bending awkwardly towards Gift. "They thought you were one of our girls." With a gentle touch to Gift's head, he struck off down Main Street once more. "All settled now."

Was it? Rab wondered. Perhaps it had escaped the old man's notice, but Rab was all too aware of the small alliances that had started to form among the dispersed tunnel-dwellers. Drawing a distracted Gift in his wake, Rab hurried after the old man, anxious to put some distance between Gift and the nervous hum and persistent attention of the crowd.

"Where does the food come from, and the cloth?" Rab asked once he caught up with the old man. "Where does everyone live?"

"Why here, of course. Where else?" The old man gestured to his right. "See that alley? There are homes down that alley." His arm swung to the left. "There, too."

A tight clutch of watchful merchants and customers obscured Rab's vision to the right, but to the left, he could clearly make out the entrance to another tunnel running off from Main Street.

"Grocer's Alley," the old man said. "The one on the right we call Chattels Lane."

"Why do you name the tunnels?" Rab asked, struggling to focus on something. . .anything. . .other than those watchful tunnel-dwellers.

"We name everything here, lad." The old man glanced over his shoulder. "That was Market Square."

Rab didn't particularly care what the place was called, he was just glad to be moving on.

Raising his hand to his head, the old man scratched once again among the sparse tufts of his hair. "Look, I can't keep calling you lad. You've got a name haven't you?"

"My name is Rab. The girl is Gift."

"John Braham," the old man said, sounding puzzled. "What sort of name is Rab?" he asked after a moment. "Never heard that one before. More Top-sider nonsense, I suppose."

When Rab declined to answer, the old man, Braham, simply shrugged.

Main Street had come to an abrupt end hard against a glowing wall of rock at the intersection of two tunnels, and the old man pointed to the right. "That's the administrative sector. Hospital, library, council, that sort of thing. Oh, and the threader farm, of course—"

Rab pulled up abruptly and grasped the old man's arm.

"You have animals here?" he exclaimed.

Braham hesitated. "What do you—ah, you mean the threaders. You must have threaders where you come from. Little fellas. . .barely bigger than your thumb nail. They weave webs with their. . .well, thread."

Rab shook his head. "We have grubs."

"Got them, too," Braham replied. "Not the same as threaders. Maybe some time I can show you the farm but the weavers are pretty particular who goes in there. We'll see. Now down there," he said, pointing left as he started off again, "is where the rest of us live, including Sunny and me."

Rab glanced down to check on Gift. Her tightly knit brow and darting eyes spoke the words he couldn't find. It simply wasn't possible that anything they had just seen was real: not the place with its maze of tunnels that bore names; not the garish and edgy merchants and their clients; not the oddly distracted woman who had accosted them; not the cold and unapproachable Sunny, or the effusive but eccentric old man. Surely it was all a dream. Somewhere he was lying on cold ground, nearing death, and dreaming out the last moments of his life.

But what if they were exactly where they seemed to be? What if all of this was real?

***

The old man led them down Braham Street where, again, the walls were alight with shimmerers. This time Rab took special care not to scrape them with his unwieldy packs.

The street, the old man told them with obvious pride, was named after one of his ancestors.

"Talk much about the past in this village you say you come from?" Braham asked.

Rab exchanged a glance with Gift.

"Not a lot," he replied at last.

"Hardly ever, I'd say," Braham observed, "judging by the time it took you to answer. Same here. It's considered impolite. I personally am not offended," he said, affecting a haughty tone. "I do what I like and say what I like nowadays. Guess that's the one advantage of old age. . .that and being a Braham. Sunny and me. . .we're the only ones left, you see and once, before the Pluming that is, Edward Braham was a very important man. A man of foresight and influence. He had money too, of course." The old man waved a hand. "You had to have money in those days. Couldn't do a thing without it. Money built this place. You had to have money. In fact, Edward had so much money that he even funded the early studies."

Sometimes the old man's rambling just made no sense at all.

"Studies?" Rab asked, vaguely listening.

"Feasibility studies, I think they used to call such things. You have to understand that in those days no one was certain that Safe Harbour was even possible."

Rab's head snapped around. Safe Harbour!

"But your granddaughter. . ." he stammered, ". . .Sunny. . ."

"Never mind her," Braham said. "I see she's already given you the benefit of her opinion. Told you that Safe Harbour never really happened. 'Back-thinking' nonsense, she calls it. Don't listen to her, lad. I'm here to tell you that it did happen and that Edward Braham was at the heart if it."

Back-thinking.

Rab had never heard the term, but it was clear what the old man meant by it. And after what Sunny had said, a like offender was the last thing he had expected to stumble on in this place.

"No one trusted his findings, of course," Braham was saying. "Not at the start anyway. But once the Pluming began in earnest—" he raised a finger for emphasis, "then they all stopped laughing." Shrugging, he turned to Rab. "He never intended to go himself though. I'd have gone— sure as hell I'd have gone. But not Edward Braham. Said the future belonged to the young. So he built this place instead. . ." Braham extended both arms, ". . .for himself and the rest of us. I've got the plans," he added, watery eyes twinkling with pride and enthusiasm in the soft, constant glow of the shimmerers. "The original plans. I'll show them to you. Oh—there have been a lot of changes since then. New things have been scavenged, old things recycled, but Edward's vision for the caves is much as you see it now. He blocked off some of the natural tunnels, enlarged others. And there are places we haven't even mapped yet. Of course, I've always considered the house itself the real triumph. You came through it when you first entered the caves." He shrugged. "Doesn't look like much now I suppose. But what it must have looked like once, perched out there at the mouth of the caves like one of those Anasazi cliff dwellings." When he glanced at Rab again, the old man smiled. "Still don't have any idea what I'm talking about, do you lad? Never mind," he said with a kindly pat on Rab's forearm. "I can show you those, too. Pictures anyway."

Rab had no idea what Anasazi cliff dwellings were; he had never heard of an Edward Braham or of any underground city; and whatever the Pluming was, it was apparently something the residents here simply took for granted. So either he was lost within the bedlam of a death dream, where all things, even mad things, were possible, or everything he'd seen and heard since coming off the plateau was real, and that meant someone here, either the woman or her grandfather, was lying. Rab's bets were on the woman.

Should he tell Braham now that he, too, was a believer? Or should he tell him nothing at all? Was it a dream? Was it not? Over and over, Rab's thoughts continued to reel, while oblivious to his internal struggle, the old man just keep leading them deeper into the tunnel.

Braham Street wasn't as broad as Main Street; three, perhaps four peo- ple could walk abreast down the tunnel. The rock floor was similarly worn—either through aeons of natural attrition or the more recent tramping of the city's inhabitants. Perhaps by both. The ceiling was missing the starry scape of brightworms, but in the light from the shimmerers that clung to the walls Rab could see that, just as it had above Main Street, no attempt had been made to smooth it or level out its irregular contours.

Twice their small party passed someone coming from the opposite direction. Both times, the tunnel-dweller pulled up abruptly, anxious eyes turned on the old man who simply waved them on. And the fact that they did go on their way, although guardedly to be sure, meant the old man had to be some sort of elder as he'd more or less implied, especially if his claims about Top-siders stealing children were true.

It was as good a time as any to prod the old man about them again.

"Seems to me," Rab began, "that if your children are being stolen, there are enough of you here to go and get them back."

The old man stopped walking and proceeded to study Rab's face for what seemed like a very long time. "Could just be you're telling the truth about that village of yours after all, young fellow," he said at last. "You don't seem to know much about ordinary Top-siders. They're nomads mostly. Rarely in the same place twice. Follow the wild mushrooms and ground grubs. . .this way. . .that way." He waved a hand aimlessly in the air.

Rab had never heard of, or come across, such people.

"Hard to find someone when there's nowhere in particular to start looking. Wander around top-side long enough, you'll see," the old man told him in what sounded ominously like a warning, then started off once more.

As they continued down the tunnel, the smell of smoke and chatter of voices began to fill the air. Somewhere behind the regularly spaced niches on either side of Braham Street, life in this underground city was playing out, but the odd glimpse Rab managed to snatch didn't reveal much: the glow from the fires he smelled, the shadow of an occupant dancing across the far wall, in one niche, some sort of table in the middle of the private grotto and a thick cloth covering part of the rock floor. It wasn't possible of course: a trick of the light, a chimera; at worst, an element of the dream he was having as he lay freezing to death somewhere under an ailing sky.

"Where do you get your fuel?" Rab asked, just the same.

"Used to get a lot out of the seep," Braham answered freely. "Old man like me can't scramble down into the valley anymore, but we've got young ones to do that. They say it's starting to dry up though. Hardly worth the effort of hauling the barrels down the cliff and back up again for the oil they're collecting off the ground these days."

The people in Rab's village had once harvested oil, skimmed it off the surface of the river until it became too dangerous to go down there. He'd never heard of oil seeping out of the ground before though. It was something about the valley Sunny had neglected to tell him, doubtlessly on purpose. Or perhaps the old man's claim was just another element of his dream.

Gift showed no interest in their talk. She just continued to follow along behind, hand resting in his. He'd become accustomed to her candour, perhaps even relied on it. Now she had nothing to say and her silence only served to unsettle him further. And he had no idea where Fin and Stitch were—other than down the opposite tunnel, if Braham could be believed. In a hospital. Ridiculous! 'Purple mushroom extract'—that's all they had! And the boy need not have been taken away to treat him with that. If Stitch was being subjected to some barbaric ritual, Rab only had himself to blame. He couldn't do much about anything else, but he could do something about that!

He stopped walking. "I want to see Stitch," he said.

Braham stopped and looked at him, puzzled.

"I've only got your word that he's being looked after," Rab told him. "I need to see for myself."

"What's the matter?"

Rab spun around, surprised to find Sunny bearing down on them, that strange metal stick slung over one shoulder as always.

"I told you he'd be taken care of," Sunny said. "I took him to the hospital, just like I said I would. His brother is with him."

She smiled as she drew up to Rab, then planted that stick of hers. A hollow-sounding ring echoed off the walls when the base of it struck the floor. "What did you think I'd do? Eat him?"

"Eat him! That's a good one, Sunny!" Braham hooted, landing a hard slap on Rab's back. For an old man, John Braham still boasted considerable strength.

Smiling, Sunny pushed past her grandfather, who, still laughing, started after her.

Gift's grip on Rab's hand tightened. But what could they do but follow?

Sunny disappeared through one of those niche-like openings, but the old man stopped just outside.

"Home," he said with a flourish Rab took to be an invitation to enter.

Inside, Gift let go of Rab's hand and dashed across the room, making for a fire that was burning brightly in the farthest corner. Rab almost envied her. The day had held too much for them both to fully absorb, so Gift had honed in on the one thing she found familiar; the fire. Rab didn't have that luxury. An unwilling leader he might be, but a leader he was, and with that came the responsibility to sift and weigh and analyse everything, including Sunny and the old man. Regrettably he didn't seem up for the job.

For the moment at least, Gift seemed content enough just to watch the embers dance, so while she did, Rab set about making a bed for her out of their packs. She didn't appear to notice. The old man displayed no interest, either. He was busy rummaging about at the back of the room while Sunny stood watching him from the middle of the room, the strange metal stick leaning characteristically against the side of her leg. Finally she snorted, grasped the stick and turned, disappearing through a recess in the far wall. As he settled Gift onto the makeshift bed of packs, Rab listened to Sunny moving and banging things around somewhere behind the wall.

The moment alone afforded Rab an opportunity to assess the old man's space. There were no glowing walls here; the only light came from the massive and well-stoked fire and it showed Rab a large space filled with clutter. Just to one side of the fire was a low table. Rab couldn't make out what it was made of, but it looked stained, as though drifting ash and soot from the fire had been creeping beneath its surface for a very long time. Whether the space itself had been a natural or man-made cavity, he couldn't tell, but it was obvious that some additional measures had been taken to at least enlarge it.

Unlike the ceiling above Market Square, the rock overhead had been smoothed by someone's meticulous hand; the walls seemed to have undergone some adjustment as well since the back wall abutted unnaturally square against each of the side walls. Rab counted five recesses in total; three in the back wall, including the one into which Sunny had disappeared, another in the left wall, and one midway along the right wall. The old man had generously sized quarters, which he appeared to share with only one other person, Sunny. Such an enormous amount of room for just two people was an indulgence unimaginable in his village.

A jumble of bowls and pots, again of unfamiliar make, lay strewn on top of the low table. Earlier, he had seen similar pieces being stowed by the merchants in Market Square. Where had such fine things come from?

Strangely, the old man's space was devoid of a single chair. Considering the extravagant, though admittedly tattered relic Rab had seen at the mouth of the cave, he'd have thought the old man's space would be similarly equipped. Instead bulky and misshapen clumps, which Rab took to be some sort of seating, were scattered here and there around the room.

His study was abruptly interrupted by Sunny's return, her arms laden with things she'd brought from the back room. She made straight for the fire. Had she found Gift still in her way, Rab had no doubt that she'd simply have kicked the girl aside. A moment later, the old man sauntered back, his arms no less burdened than Sunny's, to catch Rab openly appraising his granddaughter.

He shrugged. "I like to do my own cooking," he said and kicked one of the bulky, misshapen clumps towards the middle of the room and Rab, "but she won't allow it." Just about everything in his overladen arms tumbled immediately to the floor as a consequence of his clumsy drop into the seat. "Thinks I'll set fire to the carpet or something." Leaning forward, he slapped the palm of his hand in the middle of the mess he'd just created. "Sit down. I've brought these to show you."

Rab glanced towards the fire. Sunny had her back turned to him and her hands were busily working at something on the low table. She'd been listening though; the slow shake of her head betrayed her.

No one had invited him to take one of the cushiony clumps for himself, so Rab just dropped to the floor, which, when he reached out to reposition himself and relieve a bit of the tension from his aching calf muscles, felt surprisingly soft and warm under his hand.

The old man leaned forward and gently patted the floor covering.

"Never come across one of these before, I'll bet. Carpet," he said proudly. "Of course, it has seen its best days." He shrugged. "But then so have we."

"What is it made of?" Rab asked, stroking the supple fibres.

"Wool mostly, I think. From sheep," the old man told him. "They'd shear them, you see—"

"Grandfather!"

The cool censure came from the direction of the hearth.

"Sunny doesn't like to hear me talk about the past," the old man said. "Of course, I've never seen a sheep myself," he hastened to add, his old crimpled face suddenly beaming. "Wouldn't that be something?"

"You say that about everything past, Grandfather." Sunny swung around. The face Rab had thought almost pretty before looked hardened and ugly now. "You're always filling the children's head with your back-thinking nonsense. All the sheep are dead. All the cows. All the pigs. Everything! There's just us now. It's not like you don't know better than to talk about such things." Without waiting for a response she turned back to her task at the fire.

Her harsh words failed to upset the old man.

"She's wrong," he said to Rab. "Even she knows she's wrong."

This time Sunny didn't bother to turn around. "If you're talking about that pitiful thing you keep feeding, it won't last another season. We should have just eaten it long ago."

Rab had never heard of sheep, or pigs, or cows and couldn't even im-agine what the 'pitiful thing' Sunny had mentioned might be. This place—these people—were impossible. They simply could not exist.

The old man didn't respond. Instead he spread out a jumble of things, rolls of some kind, onto the floor.

More wonders.

Hesitantly, Rab reached out to touch the closest roll. He couldn't be certain, but it seemed to be made of the same stuff as those wads Sunny had stuffed inside her clothing. Like everything else he'd encountered here, that didn't make a lot of sense.

From the folds of his clothes, Braham drew out a strange looking ob-ject that he proceeded to perch on the bridge of his nose.

"Glasses," he explained, noticing Rab's puzzled stare. "Can't read a word without them anymore."

Leaning forward, the old man attempted to flatten the rolls.

"He won't understand them," Sunny said from the hearth.

The old man ignored her, preoccupied with a struggle to stop the stub-born edges of the rolls from springing back. Finally he was forced to place the flat of his hand on the top corner of the stack and a bent knee on the lower.

Sunny was right. Rab couldn't make anything much out of the neat lines and mysterious script. When he glanced up, the old man's face collapsed into a frown.

"What is it? Oh, of course," he said. "The paper. You've never seen that before, either. The library here is full of it. People used to depend on paper," he added with a glance towards the hearth that went unanswered, "for purposes other than burning."

"You used that word 'library' once before," Rab said, leaning forward.

"That's where we keep the books. . ."

"Books?" Rab interrupted.

The old man glanced past Rab towards Sunny, but evidently she'd given up listening. His lips quivered as he let out a puff of air.

"My father talked about books," Rab added.

Braham hesitated. "Well, these aren't books. They're plans." He stabbed at the paper. "That's the original house at the mouth of the cave. These are the doors." His finger glided over the sheet. "These, the windows. There, the tunnel leading to Main Street. Everything down to the smallest detail is recorded here."

Even if he couldn't fully understand the scribbles and scrawls on the paper in front of him, or appreciate the old man's enthusiasm, Rab could make out the long curving line that represented the tunnel they'd walked down to reach Main Street as well as another curving line the old man hadn't mentioned. It had to be the one he had seen on the left-hand side of the enormous hearth. He leaned forward to study the paper more closely, thinking that it wouldn't hurt to learn everything he could about this place.

"Get that stuff off the floor before I burn it! It's time to eat."

Rab jumped. Sunny was looking down at them. She had a large bowl in her hands and the familiar look of disdain on her face. Little wonder her grandfather was so eager to show him these 'plans'. His education had had nothing at all to do with it. The old man was simply enjoying an uncommonly civil audience.

"Here." Sunny thrust the bowl into Rab's hands, then returned to the table and retrieved two more bowls. One she passed to her grandfather, who accepted it eagerly. Kicking the rolls of paper aside, she dropped nimbly onto the floor still holding the second.

Cautiously Rab sampled the contents of the bowl. There was an undertaste of 'shroom to it, but the remaining flavours and textures were entirely foreign. Despite the old man's declaration that he preferred to fend for himself, he appeared to appreciate his granddaughter's cooking well enough. He was sitting bolt upright, legs crossed awkwardly in front of him. Beside him, Sunny also appeared equally engrossed in her dinner.

Rab glanced towards Gift asleep among the packs, wondering if he should wake her to share his bowl of food. The little girl had barely eaten anything all day, but she'd finally found a moment of peace in this strange world and Rab simply couldn't find it in his heart to steal that from her. Besides he doubted that he'd have much success coaxing her to try the odd concoction Sunny's fireside labour had produced.

As he ate his attention glided back to the old man and then on to his granddaughter. There were so many questions he should ask, but he doubted the old man was capable of answering or the young woman, willing. Sunny was tolerating his and Gift's presence, nothing more.

Her meal completed, Sunny rose gracefully to her feet.

"The girl can sleep there." She pointed towards the far corner of the room, opposite the fire. "Or leave her where she is. I don't care. Just make sure my grandfather doesn't trip over her. I don't need more broken bones to deal with."

She reached down for Rab's empty bowl.

"What about Fin?" he asked.

"I told you." She grabbed the bowl impatiently. "He's staying with his brother."

"I want to see him," Rab said, getting to his feet. Allowing them to be separated had been a stupid mistake.

"The hospital is closed," Sunny said sharply as she turned away. "You can see him in the morning. Ask Grandfather to take you. I've got better things to do."

Rab glanced briefly at the old man. He wasn't even listening, intent instead on scooping up the last of his meal from his bowl.

"How do I know he's safe there?" Rab demanded, turning again to Sunny.

She was standing, back turned, in front of the table. As she swung around, Rab's bowl fell from her hands, landing noisily on the table top. "I guess you don't. Just like I don't know if we're safe here with you." Without looking, she reached out to retrieve the strange metal stick she'd set against the back wall and laid it across the crook of her arm. "But I wouldn't think about making any trouble if I were you. I'm a good shot and I never hesitate."

Whatever that stick did, Sunny seemed confident of its effectiveness as a deterrent. She kept it with her, balancing it and the bowls she'd retrieved from the table as she started towards the recess in the back wall. "Look at it this way, Top-sider, those boys are a lot safer now than they ever were with you."

"Don't worry about her," the old man said. "That thing has no bullets and it's busted. She just likes to carry it around." He smiled proudly. "She wasn't lying about being a good shot though." One warped hand found the small of his back and, rising stiffly, he began to make his way a little crookedly towards the dark opening where Sunny had vanished.

"But what is it?" Rab called after him.

The old man stopped and turned around. "It's a gun, of course. For killing things." His head cocked slightly to one side. "Well, like I said, it's nothing to worry about. Sunny's gun doesn't work and there aren't any more. Nothing to shoot at now, anyway. Except Top-siders," he added with a little chuckle before he, too, disappeared behind the back wall.

Alone now, Rab considered his options. If the old man were telling him the truth, then Sunny's fondness for lugging around such a killing tool, functional or not, didn't persuade him to trust her or her people any better. But the old man struck Rab as a little crazy and it was beginning to look as though his granddaughter might be even crazier. More worrying still, it seemed to him that Sunny had let his little band enter the tunnels a little too easily. Something was very, very wrong. There'd be no one in this place who could help them. It was up to him. Always had been, he supposed. He knew he could find his way out of the tunnel city, but he had no idea where Fin and Stitch had been taken. And even if he did, he couldn't possibly care for the boy. Though Rab was loath to admit it—he had no options.

His concentration was broken by a strange sound like that of water running behind the back wall. The extraordinary noise stopped and almost immediately, Sunny sauntered back into the room, the old man trailing behind her. She was still carrying that killing stick—that gun.

"You sleep over there, too," she said and, using the tip of the gun, pointed towards the same far corner of the room where she'd indicated Gift should sleep. "You can use some of the cushions." She swung the gun towards the left. "That's Grandfather's room, so remember to keep that girl out of his way."

Instead of wandering off towards another of the recesses as he had expected, Sunny strode right past him. On reaching the opening to the old man's space, she glanced back at her grandfather. "You need me, you know where I am," then disappeared into the tunnel outside.

She didn't even live there! And there was all this space, just for one old man.

"Here."

A large cushion landed at Rab's feet.

"Take as many as you need."

Rab did as Sunny suggested and used three of the big and billowy things to fashion himself a bed. Grabbing another two, he repositioned Gift well clear of the old man's sleeping quarters. The little girl didn't even stir when he moved her.

As soon as his head hit the comfort of the cushion, Rab didn't care anymore if it was all a dream. He didn't care if Sunny came back into the room and 'shot' him with that gun of hers, either. It was a far better place to die than any other, lying there cradled in the soft embrace of the old man's cushions with a fire burning warmly nearby. After one brief moment of panic over the fate of his two missing charges Rab, too, slipped into an insensible sleep.

When he woke, it was from a swift and sudden stab into his chest.

Chapter 6

RAB'S eyes sprang open to find Sunny standing over him, the tip of the gun pressed hard against his heart. If the old man hadn't told him the weapon was useless, he'd have been more alarmed by such an unorthodox wake up call. Instead, he found himself vacillating between indignation at her cavalier methods and compassion for a woman whose sense of security was so clearly hinged on an ineffectual artefact. He'd barely seen it out of her hands and, even then, she kept it within easy reach.

"Get up," Sunny snapped. "If you want breakfast." The gun swung towards Gift, lying undisturbed and barely visible inside the folds of the bed Rab had made for her. "Her, too. Grandfather's already eating."

Across the room the old man smiled back at him, while beside Rab Gift began to stir. Sunny headed back to the low table by the fire as Rab disentangled himself from the cushions. It was a struggle; he seemed to have aged many snow times since he'd left home.

Though unusually quiet this morning, the old man was very obviously alert, his attention being hungrily shared between his bowl and Rab's exchange with his granddaughter.

By the time Rab had himself raised into a sitting position, Sunny was back. With outstretched hands, she indifferently offered him two bowls. He took the closest, anticipating a meal similar to the one he'd been given last night. Variety wasn't something the people of his village expected. Instead the bowl contained a squarely cut slice of some other oddity.

"What is it?" He poked hesitantly at the softly textured slice.

"If you don't want it, don't eat it."

Sunny turned her back on him, leaving barely enough time for him to grab the second bowl for Gift.

"Just put it back on the table," she said. "We don't waste food here."

It was a bold claim as far as Rab was concerned. His kind, 'Top-siders', weren't wasteful, but judging by what he'd observed so far the same couldn't be said for these tunnel-dwellers.

He scooted across the floor and nudged Gift's shoulder with the second bowl, startling her from her observation of Sunny.

Rab was pleased to see that the night's sleep had done her some good. There was no trace of fatigue in the big, round eyes she turned up to him —just disappointment.

"Why is she so mean?"

"Maybe she's just scared," Rab whispered back.

Gift took the bowl from his hands and snuggled in close. "Of us?"

The notion seemed equally absurd to him; he shrugged a puzzled reply. Sunny did appear to be scared of them and something about his rag-tag little band of refugees obviously troubled her. But they posed no apparent threat to her city—two small children, a youth little more than a child himself and a sole adult. They were woefully outnumbered, obviously unarmed, and patently uninformed. Perhaps he and Gift were merely misreading a simple, if admittedly extreme, case of un-friendliness. Though prone to rambling, the grandfather seemed affable enough. But another glance at Gift changed Rab's mind. They couldn't both have misinterpreted Sunny's behaviour. Gift was the most astute of his companions and Rab wasn't about to dismiss her judgements lightly.

"That's Sunny's own recipe."

The old man gestured enthusiastically towards Rab's bowl. His mouth was crammed with food.

"You should at least try it," he said, then jerked his head at Gift. "The girl looks like she could do with a good feed."

Obviously the old man wasn't completely distracted. If they were to leave this place, then Gift had to be fit and healthy. And Rab did intend to leave—soon—with or without Fin and Stitch.

He tapped the bowl lying limply in Gift's hands. "He's right. You need to eat."

Gift eyed the bowl, clearly suspecting the same thing he had for one brief moment last night. Sunny wouldn't be averse to poisoning them. But whatever she had in mind for them, it wasn't poisoning.

"It's all right," he told her, and taking the wedge of strange food out of his bowl took a cautious bite. Not surprisingly, it tasted of 'shroom.

The old man nodded his approval while, from her position by the fire, Sunny made something of a clatter, deliberately Rab suspected, by dropping her empty bowl on the table.

When the old man finally rose to carry his own empty bowl to the back of the room, Gift tapped Rab on the shoulder and whispered.

"She's not going to let us go, is she, Rab?"

***

There were only a few people out and about on Braham Street. Perhaps it was still early. Sunny struck him as the type who'd roust an old man from his bed at a time better suited to her convenience than his comfort. Before they'd left for the hospital, she'd disappeared again into the recess by the side of the hearth. For all Rab knew, she was still there.

At home in his village, Rab had developed a talent for estimating time, despite the perpetual gloom. He couldn't explain how he did it. Like blindsight, it was something he had intuitively mastered but lost inside this underground city. Its loss revealed what benchmark he'd been using for time all along. And the answer was disappointing. He didn't possess some mystical internal gauge that kept ticking off each moment of his life; something about the dying sky had still been telling him when it was morning, midday and evening. It hadn't been anything special at all; just an innate ability, common to all, overlooked by most. But here he could gather nothing about the time of day based on the constant and regular glow of the delicate shimmerers that lined the walls of the tunnels.

At the intersection of Braham and Main streets, Rab began to hear the distant buzz and clang of activity down in Market Square. But to his relief, the old man bypassed the turn-off to Main Street and wordlessly started down the tunnel that, so Braham had claimed, would take them to the hospital. Rab almost found himself missing the anticipated monologue.

People came and went more frequently in this tunnel and each time they passed someone, Gift's grasp on his hand tightened. He was starting to lose all sensation in his fingers. News of their arrival must have spread during the night. The eyes of each person they passed scanned Rab from unshorn head to shabby boots, but their study of Gift was especially intense. Her mounting uneasiness at such unbridled interest fed Rab's own fears. These tunnel-dwellers were only tolerating their presence courtesy of the old man and his granddaughter.

It was unlikely that Stitch would be in any condition to leave or Fin of a mind to abandon his brother and that kept Rab circling back to the unthinkable. He worried how Gift would take to leaving both boys behind. It was probably the most difficult choice anyone could be asked to make—and she was still so very young. Would self-preservation override loyalty? If she baulked, she'd be setting his course as well. He simply couldn't leave without her.

"The council chambers," Braham said.

Rab glanced to his right. There was nothing to see but an old and heavily panelled door recessed into the glowing stone wall. He had rarely seen doors and then only when his fellow villagers had been lucky enough to stumble on some wreckage. . .the way Fin had stumbled on that cache of tinder. But this door wasn't just any ordinary relic. A door that size could have warmed his fellow villagers for an entire day. The more he saw of this underground city, the more convinced Rab became that despite their show of order and sophistication, these tunnel-dwellers were an arrogant, extravagant breed with little understanding of the world above and no tolerance for those who struggled to survive in it.

Rab counted three more of the richly panelled doors before they came to a cross tunnel.

"The hospital is this way," Braham said, pointing right. "Not far now."

They soon came to another wooden door barring their way.

"Here we are then," the old man said, giving the door a mighty push. "We keep the hospital as isolated as we can. Germs, you understand. The boy is the only patient at the moment. Otherwise you wouldn't be allowed in." He took off ahead of Rab. "Can't afford to infect the rest of the city."

Braham was rambling again. No doubt germs were just another invention of his overactive imagination.

"There he is. Just like Sunny told you."

Spying Stitch and Fin, Gift suddenly released Rab's hand and flew across the tiled floor.

There were provisions for forty perhaps fifty people on the most wasteful sort of bedding—wooden framed cots with padding as thick as Rab's thigh. Stitch was at the far end of the spacious room. Fin was slumped in a chair at his side. On the opposite side of the room, a round-faced, fizzy-haired woman was seated behind a large desk in front of a huge open hearth. She was looking down, absorbed with something laid open on the desk in front of her. Rab couldn't be certain but his guess was a book. There were more books, too, stacked neatly on the two sets of tiered shelving that occupied the space on either side of the fire.

The woman's head jerked up from her study.

"We've just come to see the boy, Ruby," the old man told her. "He belongs to this Top-sider."

There was a loud clatter at the far end of the room. Fin was on his feet and the chair he'd been sitting on, lying toppled on the floor. From the look of him, he'd passed a sleepless night.

"He's my brother, old man," Fin barked. "If he belongs to anyone, it's me and I don't belong to him."

Braham shrugged. "Have it your way," he said as he wandered away from Rab, heading for the round-faced woman. "Makes no difference to me."

Finding Stitch awake and alert seemed to have lifted Gift's spirits. Having adjusted his bed coverings, she began to fuss with the boy's hair, though Stitch did his best to fend her off.

He was still grappling with Gift when Rab came up to his bed. Fin was righting his chair.

"Stitch looks fine, doesn't he?" Gift said confidently, then set about plumping the boy's pillows. "Everything's going to be all right now."

While Stitch didn't look fine exactly, he certainly did look better. His face was no longer chalky white and his leg had been expertly re-bandaged with some sort of fine white cloth. There were supports of some type on either side of his leg, but the bandaging prevented Rab from discovering very much about them.

"How did they do it?" he asked, glancing at Fin.

The boy shrugged and pointed towards the woman behind the desk. "Ask her," he answered. "She did it."

"Purple mushroom extract, sulfur, and a pair of splints," the old man called out. He was sitting on the edge of the woman's desk and swinging his legs. "Mushroom extract for the pain. Sulfur for the infection. Splints so the bone knits straight. Simple."

Gift stopped rearranging the bedding. "What's 'splints'?" she asked Rab.

"Don't know and please don't ask. We don't have the time for an explanation."

She smiled and returned to her task.

"Satisfied?" the old man asked. "Ruby here didn't eat him after all. Top-siders!" he snorted, sharing a laugh with the frizzy-haired woman behind the desk.

Tunnel-dweller sarcasm was beginning to grate on Rab's nerves. He was ignorant about a lot of things in the world; that much was true. But despite Sunny's show of bravado, he doubted that even she'd last long out in the open without her fancy potions or the support of her tunnel-dwelling comrades. On the outside, he'd stack Gift up against any tunnel-dweller.

"Books?" Rab asked, pointing towards the row of shelves he'd noticed.

The old man stopped swinging his legs and glanced at the woman behind the desk.

"Yes, they're books," he told Rab.

"Then this is the library as well?"

The old man pushed off from the desk and walked over to Stitch's bed. "Where did you say you were going?" he asked so quietly it would have been impossible for the woman at the desk to have heard him.

"North," Rab replied.

"Just you and these three children?"

Out of the corner of his eye, Rab noticed Fin stiffen. Not even he called Fin a child.

"Come with me," the old man said.

Rab glanced at Gift who just gave him an answering shrug.

***

Rab's eyes had finally adapted to the constant glow of the tunnel city and he could finally see clearly enough to make out the details he'd been missing before.

"The library's down that tunnel."

Rab had been counting every door they passed and the number of paces between and when he glanced back to check on Gift, trailing obediently behind him, and saw her mouth constantly moving, he realised she'd been counting steps, too.

Even blindfolded, he could return to the hospital without missing a step. Being able to find the hospital again unaided was one thing, but Rab had a nagging suspicion that while he could make his way back to the mouth of the cave easily, getting out of this place wouldn't be as simple.

Sunny had made it plain that they weren't wanted here, so logically she should be happy to see them leave. But Rab's mind was uneasy. He just couldn't see her letting them go at a time of their own choosing. Despite appearances, something was amiss here and whatever it was, it went beyond bringing an injured child into their midst and tapping a supply of limited medicines. It went beyond bringing in an unwanted girl as well. Sunny needn't have done it. She could have sent them on their way. No one had to know that she'd come across anyone out there. She could simply have lied and, in his estimation, Sunny wasn't the type to have any qualms about lying.

"I'm guessing you can't read," the old man said, without giving Rab the opportunity to answer. "But there are plenty of pictures to look at. The little girl should like that."

The tunnel ended abruptly at another extravagantly carved door that had an oddly shaped and ragged hole about half way up its right-hand side. The old man gave the door a shove and it opened inward with a weary creak, venting cool air. Rab wasn't prepared for the comparative darkness or the sudden chill.

"Can't have a fire in here, the whole place could go up," the old man muttered. "And the shimmerers don't like it in here. Too cold. Just let me get some lights going." He ambled away, his voice drifting off into darkness.

Rab heard a brief clatter.

"Wish Sunny would stop moving things around. Ah! Here's one."

A feeble yellow light began to glimmer. A second later, another popped up.

"A few more should do it."

Another yellow light materialised and one of them began to glide Rab's way.

"Come on in."

The old man was swinging some kind of elaborate contraption to and fro in his hand.

"If you sit at that table over there, I'll bring the rest of the lamps."

As Rab stepped through the doorway, something caught in his hair, the old man being too short to have disrupted the gossamer veil. Inspecting the delicate threads he was startled when a tiny black creature crawled out onto his hand and instinctively he flicked the thing away. The thought struck him then that he may just have dispatched a roving threader. Neither Braham nor Gift seemed to have noticed anything, so Rab kept silent.

He found the edge of the table by colliding into it with his hip. His stumble set something rocking and, when he reached out to steady whatever he'd bumped, discovered the cold, hard rung of a chair.

The old man's leading light drifted off again and suddenly his movements weren't piloted by one glowing ball of light anymore but by two and then three. The trio of lights bobbed towards Rab, accompanied by the sound of a shuffle as the old man covered the floor.

"That's better," Braham said, plopping the three lights down on the table.

Rab could see the top of the table clearly now—and the chair he'd nearly overturned. There were four other chairs beside the one he'd bumped, spaced regularly around the wooden table. All looked battered and scarred. A long time ago, someone must have brought them through the tunnels and here they had stayed, just like the incised doors, defying the fate of most wood in their fuel-impoverished world.

"Sit." The old man began to position the lamps at equal distances down the length of the table. "What first?" he muttered to himself and walked off again.

Rab pulled out the nearest chair, seated himself, then tugged on Gift's sleeve.

When, with a little jump, she seated herself, Rab noticed that her feet didn't touch the ground. It was only a small thing, but it was enough to remind him just how young she really was.

Her fingers began to weave little circles on the scored table top in front of her.

"Damn that woman!" Braham's curse echoed off the walls.

Rab sought out the drifting circle of light that would pinpoint the old man's position and found it some distance away, hovering at a considerable height overhead. It seemed he'd greatly underestimated the size of the room. The light drifted sideways before it began to descend. The old man had to be climbing down some unseen ladder.

"She's been plundering my books again."

The light stopped descending and started to drift waist-level towards the table where Rab and Gift sat waiting. Such a pity that shimmerers found the library so inhospitable. Rab would like to have seen this place in its entirety.

As he drew near, the glow from the sphere of light reflecting off those odd looking 'glasses' he'd donned made the old man's face look sinister.

Gift leaned in closer to Rab.

"Thought the little one might like to see this," he said, positioning the light in front of Rab.

Beside the lamp, he tenderly placed something else: a squarish-shaped book that was covered in some sort of greenish material.

Braham flipped the book open. "Take a look," he prompted.

Rab looked down at a profusion of colour. Out of the corner of his eye, he could see Gift still staring up at the old man.

"Birds," Braham explained, as he rounded the table to take an empty chair. "The whole world used to be full of them. Turn the page," he suggested.

When Rab just sat there, the old man reached across the tabletop, took the extraordinarily thin strip of paper between thumb and forefinger and turned it himself. "Keep going," he urged.

As Rab turned each new page, another new and crazy splatter of colour and shape was revealed. Of all the things the old man could have chosen to show them, it had been birds. Rab felt like laughing. Perhaps he had, because Gift's attention suddenly snapped to the book.

"What's the matter?" The old man eyed him suspiciously.

"My brother," Rab said. "His name was Bird."

"Ah." The old man smiled. "Top-siders and their strange names. Well, there were over 10,000 species of birds in the world once, young man. This book. . ." He reached in again and tapped the page, ". . .has pictures of about two hundred of them."

Rab flipped more pages. Every so often, Gift stilled his hand and leaned in a little closer.

"So many," Rab said to himself. "All gone."

"Maybe. Maybe not. Who's to say? Just because we never see them, doesn't mean there aren't birds somewhere in the world still. But you're probably right." Braham slid another book across the table. "Mountains of the world," he said and spun the book around. With little effort, he found what he was looking for. "The Himalayas," he said with another tap on the open book. "Tallest in the world." The third book he shied towards Gift. "Fish." With just as little effort, he located the page he was seeking. "Whale shark. Biggest fish in the world." Rising to his feet, he gathered one of the lamps. "Take your time," he said and started to wander away. "There's more wonders still to see and hundreds and hundreds of books to see them in—unless Sunny's burned them all."

Rab's head shot up. "Burned the books?"

Before he'd sat down at this table, 'book' was just a word, but now Rab was beginning to understand the old man's passion for his books, appreciate how each page preserved a shadow of things that had come before, things that were gone forever and could never return. No sane person could possibly take it in their head to destroy even one of those fragile shadows.

The light bobbed away again, but the old man's voice reached him loud and clear.

"For fuel. Kindling's running low in the storeroom. Foragers aren't finding much lately. Got no animal dung anymore, either," Braham said calmly. "And like I said, the seep is starting to dry up. So Sunny burns the books. Wads it up sometimes, too, so she and the other foragers can stuff it under their clothes to protect themselves top-side."

Of course!

Rab should have guessed that already. What was it Sunny had said? The valley was 'played out'. There was little left. In time the tables and chairs and even the ornate doors would be consigned to the fires. And once those relics, too, were all gone, the tunnel-dwellers would find themselves confronting the same situation Rab's people had been facing for a very long time now. One they'd be completely ill-equipped to deal with. If the illustrious Edward Braham had cached a substantial reserve of fuel in that 'storeroom', it must be all but gone now. If it wasn't, Sunny wouldn't have resorted to burning the old man's books. These tunnel-dwellers had fared a little better than his people for a little longer— nothing more. It made Rab wonder what else they might have neglected to consider. What else he had been slow to notice.

He should tell them about the fallen forest, because for the moment at least they had the means and the manpower to exploit it. If they managed the supply carefully, they could extend the life of their city for perhaps an entire season. A season was a long time for Rab's people and, although it likely wasn't judged so by these tunnel-dwellers quite yet, they'd soon come to gain the same perspective. But still, he just couldn't bring himself to tell the old man.

He swivelled around in his chair to locate the bobbing light.

"I don't suppose there's a picture of a rabbit in any of your books?"

The light stopped bobbing.

"A rabbit?" came the old man's reply. "Of course I've got pictures of rabbits. But there are many types of rabbit. Which one?"

"Does it matter?"

"It does to the rabbit, lad." The old man chuckled and the light began to bob again.

Beside Rab, Gift slowly flipped more pages. Every so often she traced a finger along the outline of another fish. While he waited for the old man's return, Rab watched as the shadows of an obsolete world gently nudged Gift's misgivings aside. He'd become so absorbed with the transition, he didn't hear the old man approach and jumped in his seat when another book dropped by his elbow.

"Rabbits," John Braham said before returning to his seat. "Domestic and wild." His head cocked slightly askew. "Is there a reason you're so interested in rabbits?"

"It's my name," Rab said.

Gift's attention shifted abruptly from her book.

"My brother was Bird and I am Rabbit." He shrugged. "Although I doubt my parents had ever seen either."

"I'm sure of it," the old man replied. He stopped talking for a moment and the lines marring his forehead deepened. "Your father seems to have been something of a back-thinker," he said at last. "Talking to you about books and stars and such. Naming his children that way. Here." He flipped the book open. "Flemish Giant. Biggest rabbit breed in the world."

The old man seemed to have a preoccupation with size. So far he hadn't shown them the smallest or the shortest of anything. With no means of comparison, the latest picture meant little, beyond leaving Rab disappointed. Birds appeared to be rather proud and colourful creatures that demanded and captured the eye. Even the fluid lines of Gift's fish suggested a certain amount of power and control. But the rabbit looked to be a rather mundane creature—round, dull, and, from appearances, probably sluggish. Its triangular head and oversized ears suggested that perhaps it was also a little stupid.

Gift's small finger came down on top of the page. "You're named after that?"

Rab smiled and glanced up from the page. "What about stars?" he said. "I mean. . .if they ever existed, then surely. . ."

The old man cut him off. "Been wondering when you'd get around to that." With a sudden whoosh, he sent another book across the table. "Sunny burned most of those books, but there were one or two she missed."

Rab almost didn't want to know. Maybe it was better to keep the fantasy. If it hadn't been for Gift, he might have left the book unopened.

"I want to see," she demanded.

Cautiously Rab opened it and beside him, heard Gift gasp.

"They're just like you said, Rab, only prettier."

Yes, he had been right—but only in a small and very limited kind of way. Instead of the smattering of stars he'd expected, the picture showed hundreds, thousands of tiny pin points of light scattered on a cloud, almost the colour of blood, which looked to be turning madly in nothingness.

The old man reached across the table. "The caption there. . .that writing, see? It says that's a picture of Eta Carinae. Sorry," he added with a shrug. "Can't tell you where that is exactly." He turned a few more pages. "This is the sun, though." His finger stabbed at another picture beneath the astonishing, yellow ball he'd called the sun. "That's the moon. . . Mars. . .the night sky in the Arctic. . ."

Rab's head was beginning to spin—as madly as beautiful Eta Carinae.

"And that's the same sky in summer. The sun never sets there in summer, so the sky glows that weird colour at night time."

"Never sets?"

Rab had never seen it rise. He banged the book closed, causing Gift to jump.

"Now what's wrong?" The old man sounded just as surprised.

"The colour of the sky," Rab said. "That yellow sort of stain. I don't like it." He pushed the book away. "The world looks like that everywhere now."

***

Something strange was going on in the tunnels.

Rab had sensed it ever since they'd left the library. So had Gift. But the old man continued down the tunnel as though nothing was amiss. When another of the tunnel-dwellers came running towards them, Rab finally confronted old Braham.

"Is there something I should know about? That's the third person who's run past us."

"City's a busy place," the old man replied.

They were heading towards the intersection with Main Street, drawing closer to Market Square.

"Are we going back to your space?" Rab asked, growing increasingly uneasy.

"Not yet."

When they came to the intersection, the old man turned left. In the distance, Rab could see the tables set up, just as they had been yesterday, and a crush of people gathered in the Square. But the merchants weren't stationed at their stalls and the clients weren't ambling from place to place, picking over the wares. Instead they'd clustered together in a knot in the centre of the Square.

When Braham took a sharp turn into Chattels Lane before they reached the Square, Gift pulled on Rab's hand.

"Something is happening," she whispered. "Why is he just ignoring it like that?"

Rab shook his head. "I don't know, but it can't be anything important or he wouldn't be ignoring it."

"Maybe," Gift replied, but kept glancing towards the Square just the same.

"Sunny won't let me keep Kix in the house. She says he smells." The old man snorted. "Doesn't smell. Been known to snore though," he added, sounding proud.

Beside Rab, Gift's mouth was soundlessly working again, counting steps. Chattels Lane looked much like Braham Street. It was a little narrower perhaps and the floor seemed a little more irregular, and while Braham Street had meandered, it was straight going down Chattels Lane. But the same greenish phosphorescent glow of the shimmerers lit their way and, just as in Braham Street, niches were hacked into the rock walls with cloth hangings draped at each entrance to shield the inhabitants from the wandering gaze of passersby. There were no elaborately carved doors in Chattels Lane.

Every so often they passed what looked to be bays in the sides of the walls, where secondary tunnels appeared to have been attempted but, for whatever reason, aborted and others that had either been blocked off or, judging by the large boulders choking the entrances, suffered collapse. The administrative tunnel had been quiet and almost deserted. But in Chattels Lane, Rab was constantly nudged sideways by distracted tunnel-dwellers who were all rushing in the same direction—towards Market Square. Still the old man seemed oblivious to the disturbance.

"Kix has a stall at the end of the lane," he told them. "The children here take turns at feeding him." He smiled. "He'll be too fat to move soon. They're not allowed to ride him, of course. Kix doesn't like that."

"Ride him?" Rab asked. "Kix isn't a person?"

The old man erupted into a fit of laughter.

"He thinks he is. Kix is a horse. And Kix is going to get me out of here some day. Despite what Sunny thinks." Abruptly he stopped walking. "You're looking for it, aren't you, lad? You and those children. That's why you're going north. You're looking for the launch pad!"

Chapter 7

"MUST be," the old man said, resuming his trek down the tunnel. "Not even a Top-sider would come out so far into the open otherwise." He shrugged, glancing at Rab. "You've brought the children, haven't you? The only ones left in your village. Doesn't matter if you don't answer. I can figure things out." His feeble hand came to rest on Rab's shoulder. "You and me, lad, we can get out. We can even take the little ones," he said with a fleeting look at Gift. "Kix is too difficult for me to handle alone, but you and that bigger boy can do it. If we talk nice to him, Kix will let the little ones ride him every now and then. He can manage that. They don't weigh much and the further we go, the lighter his packs will become. He'll let them ride sometimes if we ask him nice enough. I know he will."

Rab stopped walking and grabbed a hold of the old man's elbow. "It's past time you answered a few questions, old man," he said, his voice almost shaking with anger. He'd just about had it with Braham and his endless little excursions. "Your granddaughter insists that there are no launch pads and that she only brought us here because of Stitch. It's obvious she'd have preferred to leave us out there, but she didn't. Why? We're hardly a threat to your city and if, for some obscure reason, we are, then why did she take the risk of bringing us in? And there's something very odd going on around here this morning, but you keep pretending that nothing is happening. Why is everyone congregating around the market like that?" Suddenly Rab regretted his rough handling of the old man and loosened his grip. "And while you're answering questions, perhaps you could explain what a horse is."

For what seemed like a very long time, the old man stood staring at Rab. He didn't appear to have understood a word.

"Sunny's telling you the truth," he said at last, "as she sees it. There are no launch pads and never were, as far as she's concerned. You're an oddity, Rab. Just like me. Why do you think I showed you those books if it wasn't to prove we're alike?" He waved his hand. "Oh, Top-siders might believe that the notion was toyed with, but don't try to tell me they believe that even one ship was ever built. They don't. And nor does Sunny any more. Hardly anyone else here believes it either and of those that do, most wouldn't dream of talking about it. I only get away with it because I'm a Braham. If the ships were built, the others think, then why were we left behind? So for them, it could never have happened. They just don't appreciate the time involved to accomplish such an enormous task." He poked a finger into Rab's chest and then turned it on himself. "But you and I do. As to why Sunny brought you here, well, I can't answer for Sunny, lad. No one answers for Sunny but Sunny." He fell silent a moment. "What was the rest you asked me? Oh yes, that gathering in Market Square's got you thinking something is wrong." He shrugged again. "Perhaps it is, but if something has happened, how do you expect me to know what it is? I've been with you all morning. Besides, whether something is up or not, it's irrelevant to us. We're getting out of here. You and me." He raised a finger in the air. "A horse, on the other hand, is easily explained." Lowering his hand, he beckoned for them to follow, a look of mischievous delight crinkling the lines of his face. "You'll see soon enough. We're almost there. Funny," he said, "I'd always assumed patience was one of the Top-siders' few virtues. But it looks like I've been wrong. Valuable information," he muttered to himself as he continued down the tunnel.

Rab had to credit the old man with his insight and logic. In his village, Rab had indeed been an oddity. There was little doubt that only Sunny answered for Sunny. And Braham hadn't strayed out of their sight even once this morning. As far as the horse was concerned, it was obvious all he could do was follow.

A gentle nudge from his hand sent a shocked Gift off after the old man.

The tunnel came to an abrupt end and Braham pointed towards a dark niche in the wall.

"Here's Kix," he said, then disappeared inside the space.

"What do you think it is?" Gift whispered.

Rab shrugged, but froze when he looked through the opening. He hadn't been expecting anything quite so big—or so worn-looking. If the old man had any thoughts of the beast carrying even Gift's trivial weight, he was deluding himself. By the looks of it, the animal could barely carry its own. For once he found himself agreeing with Sunny; they should just have eaten the thing!

He watched from the tunnel as the old man began to tenderly minister to his beloved horse. The thing responded to his touch. Legs that had moments ago seemed like oddly contorted sticks became marginally straighter. Its pathetically sagging spine seemed to stiffen a little. A quiver ran through its flanks and its projecting, elongated head bumped once, twice against the old man's shoulder. Kix was incredibly dirty, but from head to hind beneath the grime and filth, the skin of the beast appeared to be sheathed in coarse hair that, while predominantly white, was randomly splattered with black. Despite the unfamiliarity of its shape and what, in a healthy specimen of its kind, would have been an intimidating size, the feature that intrigued Rab the most was the beast's round, black eyes. It seemed to be communicating with the old man through those eyes. They tracked Braham as he moved about the enclosure and softened when he approached. Even when its attention flicked towards Rab or Gift, there was nothing menacing within them. Perhaps Kix was just too old, too worn to care. Perhaps it simply wasn't scared of people. But it was plain to see that a beast in its prime would be capable of inflicting significant injury to the unwary. Rab kept his distance.

Gift didn't display the same qualms. She'd skirted around him and scuttled out of reach before Rab realised it.

Her quick movement triggered another ripple through the animal's flanks and when she raised her hand, it dropped its head to investigate.

"It likes me," she cried, beaming a broad smile.

An uglier, less responsive beast would have been eaten long ago, so it seemed Sunny might have some weakness after all—the children of the tunnel city. And her grandfather had been just cagey enough to exploit it.

"Here." Braham rummaged in his pockets. "Give him this and he'll like you even better."

The old man dropped something Rab couldn't see into the palm of Gift's hand. Immediately the beast snorted loudly, visibly startling her. When it dropped its head again and began nibbling at the treat she held, Gift started to laugh.

Braham's face burst into a smile, the sight of the little girl and the bedraggled old beast communing clearly giving him joy. But as suddenly as it had come, the smile died.

"Kix is the last of his kind," he said. "There was a time when horses used to roam all around on the surface. Free. But that was before the

Pluming. Poor Kix doesn't remember much about freedom. Do you, boy? Me, either." He patted the horse's flank, then looked over at Rab. "There were still a few horses living top-side when I was a lad. Not many. Only a few tough stragglers. I saw Kix born, you know," he said. His focus shifted back to the horse and his hands took up those long, gentle strokes again. "When he was old enough to leave his mother, I brought him down here, figuring the next hard snow would finish any horse left in the open. First chance I got I went back up. And they were gone," he said with a slow shake of his head. "Every last one of them."

Silently, Rab sighed. Sure. . .he felt a pang of sympathy for the old man. He even felt sorry for the horse. But if he'd only suspected it before, he was almost certain now—John Braham was completely mad.

"Tell me you're not serious about taking this thing?" he said.

"Why?" The old man continued his rhythmic stroking of the horse's flanks. "We'll need to carry food, clothes. Kix can do that for us."

"We'd be better off stealing a wagon from one of the merchants," Rab suggested dryly.

"No. No. No." The old man shook his head again. "A wagon couldn't stand up to the surface; the wheels would fall off or the axle would break. Kix came from the surface. And he can carry that boy, too—Stitch, if you've a mind to take him. Besides," he came around the side of the horse to give the beast two hefty whacks on its ropy neck, "I won't leave him behind."

"Then Sunny will be coming, too." Just the thought of the woman's company on a long journey was almost more than he could stomach.

The old man looked surprised. His hand stopped short of favouring the animal with a third, healthy whack.

"What makes you think that? Sunny doesn't want to go anywhere and I'm not inclined to try and change her mind."

"It's unlikely she'll let you go off with just me and that horse of yours."

"Did I say anything about telling her?" Braham replied with a smile.

"But. . ." Rab began, then shrugged.

What did it matter to him? He had no intention of dragging the old man along anyway. If Braham was content to desert his granddaughter—so what? In the old man's place, he'd happily have done the same. Best to leave old John Braham to his fantasies and concentrate on finding another way out of the tunnel city. Those guards at the cave entrance just weren't going to let them walk out, and Sunny's motives still eluded him. Either the old man was just as ignorant or he was trying to play Rab for a fool.

When the horse suddenly began to flail its enormous head, Rab jumped forward and pulled Gift out of the way.

"There! There! Kix, my old friend," the old man crooned. "Too much excitement." He nuzzled the horse's neck. "Rest now. We've got a long trip ahead of us."

With a final long stroke down the horse's nose, the old man stepped away. Kix's wary black eyes followed every move he made, becoming solemn and sad, as though a light had been extinguished within them. It seemed to Rab that, for a fleeting instant, he'd seen intelligence behind those eyes and a flash of comprehension. He hoped he was wrong. Better for the beast to be insensible and dim-witted than possess the capacity for thought or have even a shred of understanding that the world around it was dying.

"Come on," Braham called.

While he'd been distracted by the horse, the old man had slipped past Rab into the tunnel.

"We've got a lot of preparations to make."

They walked back to Market Square in silence. Rab couldn't stop thinking about the horse and the old man appeared equally preoccupied.

They arrived back in the square to find the number of tunnel-dwellers appeared to have doubled during their absence. There was an exaggerated restlessness to the crowd now. Everyone was moving around so much, the only person Rab could keep track of was Sunny, who was standing towards one side of the shifting crowd in a small huddle with five others. As usual she appeared to be giving orders.

The old man must have seen her, too, but if he had any idea what the commotion was about, he didn't share it.

"Well?" Rab said, stopping to confront the old man again. "Are you going to tell me that's nothing?"

"Wouldn't know," Braham replied with foreseeable disinterest. "Whatever it is, Sunny seems to have it under control. Some Top-sider trouble most likely. Happens now and then." Leaving Rab and Gift behind, he struck off directly towards Braham Street.

"What do you think he means?" Gift asked.

"I have no idea," Rab replied. "I haven't been able to figure out much about anything since we got here. But it's time I began." He bent to his knees, bringing himself eye to eye with Gift. "You stay here. Don't move—no matter what."

"What about him?" Gift raised her hand, one little finger pointing towards the old man slowing disappearing down Main Street. "He's expecting us to follow. When he realises we haven't, he'll come back for us."

As usual Gift showed good sense. Rab got to his feet and turned to assess the mood of the shuffling crowd. Everyone appeared agitated; a few almost frantic. And sure enough, Braham had finally noticed that they were missing. He was scanning the crowd now, trying to spot them.

Pushing Gift ahead of him, Rab skirted the fringe of the crowd and sought out a deserted spot between two of the market stalls on the opposite side of Main Street. From there, he could see what was happening without drawing attention to Gift and himself.

Sunny hadn't moved. She was still standing with the same group of five others, the ever-present gun lying on the ground by her feet. Two in the group were men, much older and much taller than Sunny. Their hair was long and unkempt, beards woolly, and the bland and dirtied clothes they wore further set them apart from the rest of the tunnel-dwellers. The others were children, the two youngest around Gift's age, the oldest about Fin's. All three were female, clinging onto each other in a close huddle, scared and filthy.

Sunny was engaged in an animated conversation with the two men, but Rab couldn't make out a word of it. Every now and then she cast a glance into the crowd, seemingly to assess their mood.

And she had cause to.

The atmosphere was charged.

Gift tugged on Rab's hand. "What's going on?" Her voice barely surfaced above that of the crowd. "Who are those people?"

Rab shook his head. Whatever the matter, the three children appeared to be at the heart of it.

Out in the Square proper, the crowd momentarily surged forward, an abortive swell that soon rediscovered its equilibrium.

"Show us the children!"

The shout had come from the left. Rab looked that way and spotted a big, heavy-set man on the move, pushing his way through the crowd and closer to Sunny.

"Yes," came a cry from the back of the crowd. "Why can't we look at them now?"

Abruptly Sunny broke off her argument with the long-haired men to turn and face a crowd that was clearly on the edge of erupting.

"You know the procedure, Cropper Caine." She'd singled out the big tunnel-dweller. "They have to be cleaned up first and then examined."

The big man had made it to the front of the crowd. "Wasn't that way with those girls last Harvest Time. You let them in right away."

Even at a distance, Rab could see the big man's face flush.

"Quick returns," Sunny said dismissively. "Hadn't been gone for more than a season. But this girl here. . ." She reached out and roughly grasped the elbow of the oldest girl, ". . .she's been gone a long time. Do you want to risk infection?"

The young girl, already clearly terrified, began to shake. Rab felt bad for the kid. It was plain that she didn't understand what was happening to her.

"Didn't worry you yesterday when you brought those four Top-siders in!"

"That's right," Sunny countered. "I brought them in and the only thing wrong with them was that young one's broken leg."

The big man grunted and there was the odd shout of accord within the crowd.

"Once everything is taken care of, you can all have a good look at the girls. You," Sunny pointed into the crowd. "Get these children down to the hospital. The rest of you get back to your own business."

"And what about those two?" someone roared.

"What about them?" Sunny snapped back. "They're my business!"

"We've paid enough!" The big man again. "And we don't even know if the girls are ours."

"Well, at least one of them is." Sunny took a step forward. "The oldest looks like she could be the Benson girl."

Somewhere inside the crowd, a woman gasped.

"And when they're cleaned up and examined," Sunny said, glancing briefly behind her as though checking on the children's welfare, "we'll work out who the other two are."

Her gesture was all show.

"You can trust me. You know you can." She flung out her arms the way someone would to shoo off an annoying child. "So you all just go now and let me do my job."

There were a few half-hearted protests until the tunnel-dweller Sunny had ordered to take charge of the children stepped forward and began to lead them away. When the knot of people started to slowly unravel, a sizeable number following after the girls, Rab grabbed Gift's hand and began to hurry her away from the stall where they had sheltered. If found there, they were certain to be accused of theft.

He didn't get far.

"Enjoy that, did you?" Sunny called.

Instinctively, Rab knew she meant him.

He stopped and, trailing Gift, made his way back through the thin smear of lingering tunnel-dwellers towards Sunny.

"I might have," Rab replied, "if I'd known exactly what I was looking at."

He could feel the cold eyes of the remaining tunnel-dwellers on the back of his head and the shorter of the two men standing with Sunny was studying him with a little too much interest.

"Bit slow on the uptake, aren't you?" Sunny said.

"Captured a Top-sider for yourself, I see," the short man sniggered, prompting Sunny to spin around. "Should have nabbed one a little less scrawny."

"Oh, you're a very funny man," she replied indifferently, then turned to the taller man. "You'll get the regular pay and no more. Three returns. Three bounties. You can get it from the council same as usual. You know where to go."

For a moment it seemed that the men were about to argue. Instead the taller of the pair shrugged, nudged his fellow, and began to walk away.

There was no denying Sunny's daring. On his best day, Rab would never have contemplated taking those two on. They didn't seem to be armed in any way, but something about their demeanour told him that they didn't need to be.

"And don't think you can talk anyone there into paying more," Sunny called after them. "You try anything, I'll hear about it."

The two men just kept walking.

Sunny turned back to Rab. She seemed to be smiling, but somehow he doubted the smile was intended for him.

"Morons," she said. "In the settlement up the valley, they could have made twice what we pay."

"They're captives?" Rab asked.

"Returned captives." Sunny bent and retrieved the gun from the floor.

"I wouldn't have thought you valued girls highly enough here to pay to get them back."

She shrugged. "They're still our girls. We're not all barbarians like you, Top-sider."

"That big man was working his way up to it."

"Ben Caine?" Sunny said with a flip of her hand. "Just proves what I said. Lost his girl to Top-siders a long time ago. Never got her back. Never got over it. Shut up when I told him to though, didn't he?"

Rab declined to point out that it was only under threat.

"And those two men?" he asked instead.

"Bounty hunters. Although, if you ask my grandfather, he'll tell you that isn't quite true. According to him," she slung the gun over her shoulder in her customary manner, "bounty hunters track fugitives. Fugitives. Captives. It's all the same to me. Bounty hunters hunt for bounty. End of discussion."

"Are they Top-siders?"

"Top-siders don't return the children they've stolen," Sunny reminded him.

"Then they're from here?"

"Used to be. I guess you could say they live between now."

Suddenly Rab understood.

"You! You're one of them! That's what you were doing in that village."

Sunny fixed him with a stare. "Do I see disapproval?" Her face twisted into a bitter sneer. "Better than grubbing in the dirt for mushrooms, Top-sider. Besides, Lilly Benson will never know it's not her kid. Everyone wins. Lilly. The girl—and after twelve years living with the Top-siders, she's not likely to reveal who she really is—even if she does remember."

Rab was rapidly gaining an entirely new perspective on Sunny. He shouldn't have been surprised, but he was.

"And what happens if the real Benson girl turns up?"

"She won't."

"That's why you brought us here. You were going to pass Gift off as a returned captive."

He should have thought first before blurting out what was in his mind. Fortunately for him, Gift didn't appear to be listening. Her attention was still fixed on those children who were now gradually disappearing from sight.

Sunny began to laugh. "Her? Oh, I'll admit the thought occurred to me. At first I suspected that she was a captive, until I took a good look at her. But there's more than one generation of Top-sider in her genes. She's wild-eyed—inherently undisciplined. Even the most desperate mother here couldn't fail to see that. No." She turned and began to head out of the Square. "No one would believe she's a person."

***

Over and over again, Rab ran Sunny's words through his mind. It had seemed such a strange thing to say but, on reflection, he realised that John Braham had described Top-siders exactly the same way, calling tunnel-dwellers the people.

Were Top-siders not even considered people here?

If it weren't for Fin and Stitch, he'd likely have taken Gift and tried to leave immediately. But if Top-siders weren't regarded as people in this demented place, then he and Gift had it all wrong anyway. Sunny wouldn't be the least interested in stopping them.

The merchants in the Square had returned to their stalls, the remaining clients to their browsing. Sunny had disappeared down the tunnel that led to the administrative sector, library, and hospital and the old man had never returned. Rab and Gift were on their own.

What harm could it do to go up to the surface and at least see if it was possible to get out. It wasn't as if he was intending to leave right this moment. He wasn't wearing Blaze's coat and Gift was even less adequately dressed for the outside.

"What is it?" Gift asked with a smile. "You're thinking about something. You always get this tiny crease between your eyes when you do."

Useful to know.

"How about a walk up to the surface?" he said. "Maybe the sun has come out."

"And maybe Kix can speak," she said, but set off ahead of him through the square.

"Who were those children? They looked like us. Like—what do they call us? Top-siders? And what were those men doing?" She shook her head. "I didn't like those men."

"They weren't like us," Rab told her. "They'd been lost and the men were returning them home. That's all."

"I don't think so," she said. "You called them captives. I heard you. And the old man said that sometimes Top-siders steal their children. I heard that, too. Were those children stolen?"

Rab shrugged, hoping to put off further discussion. "I suppose so."

"And the men were bringing them back?"

It seemed the strategy wasn't going to work.

"Seems so."

"How?" she asked. "I mean how did they find them?"

Rab shrugged again and kept moving. "I wouldn't know."

"They didn't look happy," she said. "If I'd been born here and then stolen, I'd be happy if someone brought me back."

"Do you want to stay here?" Rab asked, surprised.

"No."

The answer sounded definite enough.

"But if I'd been born here, I would. We don't fit in. But those children, they didn't fit in, either."

"Oh," Rab said, instantly relieved. "Well, they were just confused. That's all."

"No," Gift said again. "They weren't. I mean—they were, but—I don't know. They didn't look right."

Rab nudged her good-naturedly in the ribs. "What does around here?"

She wasn't falling for it.

"Is Sunny going to sell me, too?"

Rab wasn't prepared for such a sense of resignation in her voice.

He stopped and dropped down to her level.

"No, she isn't," he told her, grasping her small shoulders with both hands. "If she was going to do that, she'd have done it already. And she certainly wouldn't have let her grandfather parade us around the way he has. Would she?"

"I suppose not," Gift agreed hesitantly. "But you asked her that yourself, Rab. I heard you."

He let go of her shoulders to run a hand through his hair. "Yes, I did. But I wasn't thinking when I said that. She has no intention of selling you, Gift." He tried on a smile, but it didn't fit very well. "And even if she had, you don't think I'd let that happen, do you?"

Gift shrugged. "Maybe you wouldn't have a choice."

Rab shook his head. "She's not as tough as she likes to think she is," he said, and hoped that was true. "We could be wrong, you know. No one has said we can't leave, so maybe we can walk right out that gate any time we like. Maybe Sunny was just trying to scare us when she said the gate was guarded."

"And even if there are guards, maybe they'll just open the gate for us," Gift suggested, brightening.

"That's right." This time, the smile he offered fitted a little better.

"But what about Fin and Stitch? We can't leave without them. Or our food and clothes."

He straightened and took her hand. "We're not going to leave this very moment. We're just going to see if we can."

Before they started up the tunnel, Rab tightened his hold on her hand. With the welcome glow of the phosphorescent walls lighting their way, there was no chance they would trip or become lost; but he felt the need to reassure her, or perhaps more honestly, himself.

They emerged at the mouth of the tunnel into the large open space, that at first glance, looked much the same. . .there sat the oversized chair . . .there the container overflowing with the wadded up scraps Sunny had pulled from inside her clothing, scraps that Rab now realised were paper . . .even the fire was still burning brightly against the back wall. The only thing missing was the old man lying curled up asleep in the chair. . .and the guards.

Gift broke free of his hand and stepped into the room.

"The fire's going, but there's no one here." She swung around to face Rab. "Does that mean they'll be coming back soon?"

Rab shook his head. "Maybe those bounty hunters were using it. And if it was them, I don't see why they'd come back so soon."

Gift glanced briefly back at the fire. "What a waste," she said, but looked relieved just the same.

Rab might have shared her response, but for what he'd just noticed. When Sunny had led them down from the surface, through the twisting, upper tunnel, they'd emerged directly into this space. There hadn't been a door or a gate or a barrier of any kind. That wasn't the case any longer.

Gift spotted the obstruction for herself then and struck off across the room to tentatively touch the door.

"This wasn't here before."

"It must have been open and pushed back against the wall when we arrived," Rab replied, joining her at the now barricaded entrance to the upper tunnel. "Otherwise we'd have seen it."

"But what is it?" Gift asked.

After testing the obstruction himself, Rab was lost for an answer. Clearly it was a door—but of what kind? Its surface felt strangely smooth and cool against the skin of his hand. A kick from the toe of his boot had no effect at all, other than to send a bolt of pain all the way up his shin. Had he kicked a little harder, he'd likely have broken his foot. Jiggling the bulky handle proved futile; the door stayed firmly in place, barring their exit. There was some kind of script, two large lines of it, running across the middle of the door. Rab traced the blocky writing with a finger. Something about the style of it reminded him of the marks he'd seen stamped on the bricks back at the factory. But even if he could read, Rab doubted the writing would have helped.

His attention returned to the door itself. Running his hand around the edges of the door, he felt a draught of colder air seeping in from the upper tunnel. And over the top of the door, another narrow gap channelled more of the icy current over their heads. The door might be a poor fit, salvaged from somewhere else perhaps, but right now, it was doing an admirable job of keeping anyone on the outside from getting in and anyone on the inside from getting out.

Gift leaned against the stubborn door. "We weren't wrong," she said. "Now what do we do?"

"Maybe that other tunnel leads to the surface a different way," Rab said, pointing to the smaller opening on the left side of the hearth.

Gift pushed off from the door. "I hope so," she said, leading the way.

After only a few steps, Rab began to suspect that the passage would only lead them deeper into the complex. Its poor condition also suggested that it was rarely used and barely improved. Time and again he was obliged to scramble over chunks of rock that had fallen from the roof, or squeeze through tight spaces where the cavity naturally narrowed.

"The shimmerers are here, too," Gift said, reinforcing Rab's own fears.

There were no shimmerers lining the walls of the upper tunnel that opened onto the surface but it seemed to him that the concentration of shimmerers in this tunnel was actually increasing.

"Oh, Rab! Come and look!"

Perhaps he was mistaken and the tunnel had taken them to the surface after all.

He rounded the corner, disappointed but startled just the same when he saw what Gift had found. She hadn't stumbled on an exit but what appeared to be the source of the tunnel city's food supply. To Rab, the cave below them resembled an enormous bowl that had been overturned, spilling its vast contents of 'shrooms. He had never seen so many living 'shrooms in his entire life. And the vast space was brilliantly lit from above by the glow from a myriad of brightworms.

Wagons, two to three times the size of those he'd seen in Market Square, were stacked up one behind the other in a line that stretched all the way into the 'shroom field from the mouth of an opening, larger than the one they were standing in, on the other side of the cave. The wheels of each wagon were perched on two parallel, elevated tracks of some kind.

Gift, black eyes agape, flicked Rab a hopeful look.

"Can we go down there, Rab? Just to see?"

He hated to forbid it.

"Look," he said, pointing to a small gathering of tunnel-dwellers at work on the far side of the cave. "We're not alone."

The tunnel-dwellers didn't appear to have seen them and Rab wanted to keep it that way.

"I think we'd better not. We might not be welcome," he said, although he was certain they wouldn't be. "Besides, there's no way out from here."

"But that opening—"

"—leads deeper into the city," Rab said, cutting her off. "See the wagons? It must be how they get the harvest in. They're not going to cart the harvest to the surface, Gift. I'm afraid we're out of luck here. This isn't what we're looking for."

Slowly the expression on the little girl's face began to alter, reminding Rab of the resignation he'd seen in the eyes of the old man's horse.

"No," she said at last in a voice that sounded small and broken. "I guess it isn't."

She hadn't paid any individual 'shroom too much attention, but Rab had and he'd picked over the ruin of too many crops not to notice the incipient signs of disease in this one. Already these 'shrooms were displaying that distinctive wrinkling of their caps and ominous narrowing at their bases. Soon the brown specks of an insidious something would appear and eat through the tender flesh. The disease wasn't widespread yet but it would be. Nothing could stop it.

"Come on, Gift," Rab said, gently taking hold of her shoulder to turn her away. "Let's go."

***

"Can't someone make them stop?"

Rab pushed Gift behind him in an effort to shield her from the noise and confusion.

He should have thought ahead about what he'd be leading them into, but by the time they reached Main Street, his mind was back on plans for their escape, so when Gift insisted they return to Stitch, he had mechanically started off for the hospital, forgetting all about the returned captives and where Sunny had sent them. And then when they opened the hospital door, it was onto complete chaos.

There had to be at least twenty women packed into the space, all screaming and pulling at once. Rab pitied the three girls whose presence had sparked the riot. The oldest of the children, the one Sunny called 'the Benson girl', was on the right of the room, straining to free herself from the nurse and a little, dark-haired woman. The two smaller children were caught up in a scuffle of their own in the middle of the room. Rab recognised the dark-haired woman who was trying to pull the Benson girl away from the nurse as the merchant they had startled on their arrival in the city; perhaps she was Lilly Benson. Whoever she was, if she didn't let up soon she'd dislocate the child's shoulder. They seemed to be the only two people in the room who weren't screaming, although in all the commotion it was difficult to be sure.

All Rab could figure was that the twenty or more screaming, pushing and pulling women were impatient to lay claim to the children, robbing Ruby, the nurse, of the chance to clean them up. He'd have thought that a city as supposedly sophisticated as this one would have had some sort of system in place to deal with these matters. After all, this couldn't be the first set of captives to be returned. Rab hated to think this appalling display went on every time some poor hapless child found themselves ushered back into the tunnels. Blaze would never have allowed such bedlam to continue unchecked. Besides, Rab couldn't imagine a scene like this ever erupting in his village in the first place. These tunnel-dwellers simply weren't as civilised as they liked to think they were.

Gift had her head buried in the small of his back and, when he glanced around to check on her, discovered that she had clamped her hands over her ears and had her eyes screwed tightly shut.

Time to retreat. Abandon Fin and Stitch to the skirmish and hope they'd found a safe corner somewhere to ride it out. They'd had nothing to do with this.

Gift might have read his mind, or perhaps he'd actually taken a reflexive step down the corridor. Her eyes popped open and her head shot up.

"We can't just leave them here!"

"But there's nothing. . ."

Rab stopped talking when he spotted Braham and a group of men heading towards them down the tunnel. They pushed past him without stopping and marched into the hospital.

"Break this up now," old Braham shouted. "Ruby, you let go of that girl and you there, Lilly, take her out of here. The rest of you, shut up. Do I need to remind you all this is a hospital?"

Rab couldn't see much around the four men who had stationed themselves across the doorway, but the screaming stopped almost immediately and the only noise he could hear then was a kind of mewling, which he guessed was coming from the two smallest girls.

"But John," someone said. It sounded to Rab like the nurse. "I haven't cleaned that girl up yet."

"Too bad," Braham replied sharply. "If Lilly's happy to clean up the filthy little thing, let her. The rest of you women will have your chance to look at the others as soon as Ruby says so. Now get! Every one of you! Or maybe you'd like me to send one of these guards after Sunny."

It seemed Rab wasn't alone in wanting as little contact with Sunny as possible. There was the predictable grumble but most of what Rab could make out then was the shuffle of feet.

Lilly Benson and her charge were the first to leave, two guards stepping to either side of the door to give them access to the tunnel. The girl wasn't screaming any longer but continued to punch and claw her 'mother'. Even Rab was obliged to dodge one of the girl's errant blows. He had no doubts that tonight, Lilly Benson would be counting bruises. The rest of the women slowly followed Lilly and Rab squeezed himself back against the wall of the tunnel so they could pass, nearly squashing Gift in the process. Now and again, as the women disappeared down the tunnel, he could still hear the odd complaint.

Nurse Ruby was left in the middle of the room trying to restrain the two smaller girls by their coat-tails. Braham was righting chairs. And Fin and Stitch appeared at the back of the hospital, looking stunned but uninjured.

"Is it over?" Gift asked, easing herself out from behind Rab and trying to peer around the four men who'd moved back to bar the entrance.

"Seems to be," Rab replied, eyeing the silent men at the door.

He bent down to Gift's level. "The boys are all right. There's nothing we can do here and it doesn't look as if the old man's interested in talking to us right now. I think we should just go back and find something to eat. What do you say?"

Nothing.

After what she'd just witnessed, Rab didn't expect anything else.

***

Neither Braham nor Sunny had told them they couldn't have free rein of the tunnels and, even if they had, Rab wouldn't have taken any notice. Though two Top-siders wandering unchaperoned in the tunnels wasn't exactly welcomed, no one attempted to stop them as they made their way back through Market Square and down Braham Street towards the old man's space where they'd left their packs and their food.

They found Sunny, back turned to the entrance, working at something on the low table. The fire was well alight again and her oversized shadow danced across the side wall as she moved along the length of the table. The gun was at its usual station, within easy reach.

Rab stopped short of entering and leaned a shoulder against the jagged wall.

"Perhaps you should have lied about the others as well," he said. "It might have averted the riot."

Sunny turned to face him, bowl in hand. She seemed surprised to see them.

"What are you talking about?"

"We've just come from the hospital where a pack of your so-called civilised tunnel-dwellers were fighting over those three little girls. You should have guessed something like that would happen." He pushed off from the wall.

"Well, that's the difference between us and Top-siders. We don't have to guess."

She returned to her task at the table. "Ruby knows to send for my grandfather."

"He came a little late," Rab said.

Sunny's right shoulder lifted slightly. She didn't answer.

"I see. It's irrelevant to you that a couple of Top-sider children almost had their arms ripped off."

"You're exaggerating. Besides," she said with a fleeting look over her shoulder, "they aren't Top-siders."

"So you say." Rab inched farther into the room, leaving Gift a pace behind. "You haven't shown me any proof that Top-siders have been abducting your young girls. And judging by what I saw this morning, it looks to me like it's the other way around."

"You can think whatever you want. I really don't care."

"Does the same apply to everyone else in this city? Did it ever occur to you that I could tell them that you lied this morning. . .that you have no idea who that girl really is?"

"Go ahead," Sunny told him, "if you think anyone would stop long enough to hear you out. Even then, they wouldn't believe you."

She was probably right, on both counts.

"You have it all worked out, don't you?"

"I'm a Braham," Sunny replied. "What more need I say?"

"That's something else that doesn't add up. For two people who appear to have a lot of influence around here, you and your grandfather have quite a few differences of opinion. About all those books you're so eager to burn, for example. Or that thing. . .that horse. And about—"

Sunny turned around and smiled.

"Ah, so you've met Kix," she said, cutting him off. "And no doubt he's talked about Safe Harbour, too. Agreed with you about all those launch pads scattered across this planet with all those space ships just waiting to whip us away to safety. For years, my grandfather has been fantasising about taking off with that horse to find one of those mythical launch pads. If I were you, I wouldn't feel obliged to help him."

"No, I'm sure you wouldn't and I don't, but why only him and that horse?"

"You are showing your ignorance, Top-sider. It was my understanding that even the few Top-siders who have heard those wretched rumours don't encourage them. You've obviously been to the library. If there were any truth to the stories, wouldn't you think there'd be something about it in those books? My grandfather could show you the plans for this city, but I'll bet you he couldn't show you a single book in that prized library of his that even mentions something called Safe Harbour. Now why do think that could be?" The bitter smile broadened. "So just how did you come by that crude tale anyway?"

"My father told me—and his father told him."

"And your village condoned that?"

Rab didn't answer.

"I didn't think so." Sunny nodded at Gift. "I suppose you're expecting me to feed her?"

"I don't expect it, but it would be the kind thing to do."

"Look Top-sider, we don't owe you anything and you're really starting to annoy me. If you want me to feed her, sit down. If you don't, leave."

"It's just like I thought then. You and your grandfather run this place to suit yourselves. You're not civilised at all. The riot in the hospital this morning proved that. At least in our village, we all have a say and our elders don't lie to us to meet their own ends."

"Just what do you think you are? What rights do you think you have here? You and your kind—you're nothing."

"Nothing but civilised."

"Don't talk to me about civilised. Maybe you do have some say in how your village is governed, but what is there to govern? You've seen enough of this place to know we live a hundred, a thousand times better than you do. Besides, Grandfather and I only advise here and the people listen to me—us—out of respect for Edward Braham. What's wrong with that? And why am I bothering to explain myself to you? The sooner you leave, the better. Maybe you could even take my grandfather and that ludicrous horse with you," she suggested with a cold, little laugh. "Heaven knows, we'd be well rid of them both. The stories he tells the children teach them bad habits and that horse of his eats their food. So why don't you just take him? I don't need anything but this." She made a sudden lunge sideways and swung the gun up to her shoulder.

Rab just shook his head. "It's only a useless weapon, Sunny."

Gift was looking up at him, wide-eyed, clearly shocked that he had dared to challenge their host.

And it had been a stupid thing to do, especially before availing himself of her food. The moment they were gone, Sunny would settle herself down in the middle of that soft carpet and eat that food he had smelled without a second thought for her fleeting argument with an ignorant Top-sider.

"Come on," he said, grabbing Gift's hand. "We're getting out of here."

His original intention was to return to the library, not to assure himself that Sunny had been telling the truth; he couldn't read anything in any of the books and had no idea how Braham had lit those little lamps, or even where he kept them. But the library seemed to be the one place tunnel-dwellers rarely visited and Rab desperately needed to be free of them for a while.

Instead he gravitated to the one place they all tended to gather: Market Square, where the conversation all seemed to be about the captive girls. Until they were spotted, of course, and the spirited chatter abruptly stopped. Once they passed, no doubt the talk would turn to Top-siders.

Rab found himself a quiet spot at the top end of the square, away from the stalls, and dropped onto the hard rock floor. Gift plopped down beside him, but all he had to offer her was a weak smile.

For a long while, they just sat, listening to the muted conversation and watching the comings and goings down in the square. Blaze had certainly made a grave error in judgement, Rab thought. He couldn't look after these kids; he couldn't even look after himself. The smart thing to do was leave them here and go on alone. Perhaps Sunny would allow Gift to stay—although that was unlikely. Maybe he would keep that promise to her, after all. If Stitch remained here, he'd at least be safe —Fin too, since it was a certainty that he'd never leave his brother behind. Their prospects of finding somewhere better on the surface were slim to none, if Sunny was telling the truth. And why should she lie about that? Their departure suited her; she'd made that clear more times than he could count. And the least of her concerns would be whether they made it or not.

"I'm hungry," Gift said, breaking into his thoughts.

He was hungry, too, and would have been a lot happier if she hadn't reminded him. Stupid! He'd been stupid to have argued with Sunny. What he should have done was put his pride aside and secure them something to eat. Too late now—for him anyway. He turned to the little girl.

"Do you think you can find your way back to the old man's space?"

Gift looked at him wryly.

Of course she could.

Rab eased himself to his feet, pulling Gift up with him. "See if you can persuade Sunny to give you some food."

"What about you? Aren't you coming?"

"You stand a better chance without me. Just wait there until I get back. I promise I won't be long."

Gift's expression turned wary. "Where are you going? I think I should come, too."

"Nowhere in particular," Rab said. "I'm not planning to leave without you, if that's what you're worried about."

Could he trust her? Would she panic if he told her the truth?

"Look, Gift," he said, deciding to risk it, "I can't stay here. Maybe you and the boys could but not me—"

"But Sunny said I couldn't stay," she reminded him. "Besides I don't want to."

"The old man would look after you. I'm sure he would. And you'd have Fin and Stitch here with you. It might be for the best."

"No!" She shook her head. "We all leave or we all stay."

"But I can't stay, Gift, and Stitch can't leave—not yet anyway."

"Then we wait until he gets better."

"That won't be for a while, Gift. And meanwhile, outside, the weather is getting worse. I can't just stay here doing nothing. I could push on, find the launch pad and come back for you and the boys after snow time."

"You can't do it alone," she insisted. "And Sunny doesn't want me."

"Sunny won't complain about you staying if she knows I'm coming back," Rab said, hoping that he would be proved right. "And as for me going on alone, that's what I'd been planning to do from the start, remember? It won't make any difference at all. In fact, I'll be able to move faster."

"You need me. I don't hold you up. Don't say that I do."

She'd spoken the truth—on both scores.

"No, you don't," he said, relenting. "All right then, it's us two—we go together and come back for the boys. But we have to go soon, Gift. We can't wait around much longer."

She glanced briefly behind her in the general direction of Braham Street.

"And if I go back to the old man's space now and get something to eat, you won't leave without me?"

"No, Gift, I won't," he promised. "Besides," he flung out his hands, "I don't have the packs or my coat."

To Rab's relief, she didn't press him further. If she'd known he was going to visit Kix again, she'd have insisted on coming with him and he didn't want Gift's enthusiasm for the horse to sway him one way or the other when he reassessed the stringy-looking beast. Worse—he didn't want to give her the opportunity to come up with the same idea he'd already dismissed. As soon as she caught sight of Kix again, she'd be certain to argue in favour of taking Stitch with them. But the horse simply couldn't carry Gift, the packs, and Stitch. Rab wasn't even convinced that Kix could carry just the packs, let alone Gift. Carrying Stitch as well would surely kill the thing within a day of setting out.

Chapter 8

RAB wound his way back towards the stall. When he passed the turn-off to the hospital, he had a momentary inclination to go there first to check on the welfare of the boys. The impulse passed swiftly. He really wasn't in a frame of mind to weather more of Fin's belligerence if he was admitted, or face up to his nagging feelings of guilt if he wasn't. Should his plan seem even remotely possible, then very shortly he'd be leaving the two boys behind—perhaps forever. He had no idea what they would find out there and, despite what he had told Gift, their return for the boys was not a certainty.

He had almost reached Kix's stall when he heard Braham's voice from inside and froze.

"We have to try."

Was the old man talking to the beast?

"But he's a Top-sider."

No. Unless Kix had suddenly developed the capacity for speech, there was someone else inside the stall with him.

"It doesn't matter. He knows about Safe Harbour."

"Doesn't mean a thing. Rumours travel. Who's to say it didn't travel down the valley from one of us."

"Nonsense. Who here talks about the past but you and me? Besides, how many of us deal with Top-siders? Sunny and a few others. And you know as well as I do that Sunny's a non-believer like the rest. And these Top-siders haven't come from the valley. They're from the south."

"More reason not to trust them. There's no one alive in the south."

Just what was the old man up to?

"You can't possibly manage such a journey," Braham's companion in the stall was saying.

"Are you offering to go instead?"

"Me? Don't be absurd. I have responsibilities here, and a family to take care of. I'm not about to abandon everything on the word of a Top-sider. We can't afford another mistake."

"There was no mistake." Braham's voice again.

"How can you say that with your own son dead and your granddaughter the only one to come back?"

"But Sunny was only a child then. Who knows what she really saw or didn't see out there. Besides, it's clear now that they went dreadfully unprepared. We have the Top-sider this time—and Kix."

Rab heard a hollow thump—the old man giving the beast a healthy slap.

"That horse! The poor thing is on its last legs. And as for the Top-sider, the young boy got injured under his care. That doesn't say much for his skills on the outside."

"An accident," Braham said. "Anyone can have an accident. Anyway there's no other choice and no one else who is willing to go. How much longer do you think we can survive here? How many more tunnels can we close off and how many more families do you propose we crowd together?"

Silence.

Braham's companion was lost for a ready answer. Evidently the old man was not as naive as the rest of these tunnel-dwellers appeared to be and was aware, just as Rab was, that the days of the tunnel-dwellers were numbered. But there was no way Rab was going to allow himself, and Gift, to be dragged down with it. And what was all that about Sunny?

". . .just give me some time," Braham was saying, sounding closer now.

Rab scanned the tunnel, seeking a place to hide. Behind him, he spied a darkened space that looked to be the entrance to one of those aborted, offshoot tunnels. He ducked inside.

"What if you don't come back?"

"Then you'll know it's over."

Two shadows passed, but Rab didn't bother to investigate the identity of the old man's companion. Whoever he was, he was right. Maybe the horse could make it—for some distance anyway—and some distance was better than none at all. The old man was another matter. He and Gift needed to get out now.

But for Gift, Rab would never have visited the hospital again; the little girl had become his self-appointed moral guide. He hoped he'd be lucky enough to find the men still there however, guarding the entrance, and he could avoid an uncomfortable, last encounter.

But instead of the four men, he found Gift, and Sunny.

Gift was seated on the mattress at the foot of Stitch's bed, Fin standing sentinel at his shoulder. Sunny was on the other side of the room, quarrelling with Ruby. Her arms were locked around one of the returned girls, who was viciously kicking, flailing, and periodically sinking her teeth into Sunny's forearm.

The other girl was sitting bolt upright in her bed, wide, red-rimmed eyes anxiously taking in the brawl in the middle of the floor and Rab's silent trio of companions on the other side of the room. The removal of a few layers of grime and the prospect of comfortable bedding had clearly done nothing to reassure the children the bounty hunters had returned.

No one had noticed him, so Rab stopped just beyond the open door.

There'd been another altercation with the tunnel women. It was the only explanation for what Rab heard: Ruby's pleas to have the men return and Sunny's repeated refusal. For some reason, Sunny looked less formidable as she stood there, still deftly overpowering a little girl less than a third her size. Finally Rab realised she wasn't carrying the gun.

From the sound of it, the dispute had been going on for some time, but not long enough for Gift to have missed securing food before Sunny had been summoned to the hospital. Every now and then, she brought her hand up to her mouth and began to chew.

Something must have alerted Sunny to his presence because suddenly she glanced in his direction.

"Well," she panted, literally swinging the nearly exhausted child off her feet into the arms of the silenced nurse, "I thought you'd be making your way to the surface by now."

Rab was surprised to see a raw and bleeding gash on the left side of Sunny's flushed face. He strode into the room, careful to avoid eye contact with Fin, whose head had snapped around.

"You haven't exactly left the door open."

Sunny sent him a wry smile, breathing heavily as she swiped at the streaming gash with the back of her hand, staining her cheek pink.

"That door is the only thing that stands between us and your kind," she said. "Did you think we'd just let you wander top-side any time you liked. . .tell your thieving people everything you've seen here?"

"They are not my people, Sunny. How many times do I have to tell you our village lies to the south and we were heading north? You have nothing to fear from us."

Sunny was about to say something, but the nurse—Ruby—cut her off.

"South?" she said, sounding genuinely puzzled. The young girl, finally drained of fight, looked more like a bunch of dirty rags hanging limply from her hands than a human child. The nurse glanced at Sunny and asked "But there's no one alive in the south anymore. Is there?"

Sunny didn't answer. Instead she thrust a hand inside her clothes and produced a thin metal ring, which she dangled in the air in front of Rab. Beneath the ring hung four short and slender cylinders. All four cylinders had rounded heads and a jagged looking profile. As she jiggled the ring in his face, the cylinders banged together, making a clanking sound.

"You'll need these to get the door open," she said. "And it's not likely I'll just hand you the keys, is it? Despite where you say you come from."

It was Rab's turn to smile. Top-siders didn't have keys; in fact he'd never seen one before, but he'd heard about them and if that's what it took to get out—fine.

"You could escort us to the door yourself," he suggested. "The keys never need to leave your hand."

Fin bolted from the side of the bed.

"I won't leave Stitch," he roared, advancing on Rab.

Rab turned to the boy. "I wasn't asking you to."

It wasn't how he'd intended to break the news.

"Oh, I see how it is now."

If Gift hadn't leapt off the bed and rushed across the floor to step between them, Rab had no doubt Fin would have fallen on him with both fists pumping.

"You're going to leave us here and it wouldn't surprise me if you hadn't known about this place all along." Fin spun around to confront Sunny. "You and him. You had this planned from the start, didn't you? It was no accident finding you out there. Just what's in it for you? Her?" His finger was pointing at Gift.

Rab's hand found its way to Gift's head. A gesture of loyalty? Comfort? Didn't matter. Gift stepped a little closer.

"Don't be ridiculous," Sunny said.

She made to shove past Fin, but he grabbed her shoulder.

"You're so ready to dismiss us as stupid. Do you think we're blind as well? Stitch and me—we saw what went on here today. Those women pawing at those girls, fighting to get at them. And you! Tossing people around like they're nothing."

Fin couldn't have frightened the little girl in the bed more if he'd come at her with a club. She scampered towards the head of the bed and balled herself up against the wall.

"Pretty big words coming from you," Sunny grunted.

"Are you paying him for her? Is that what's this is all about? Food? Information? Just what have you got that he wants so badly?"

"Not a thing," Sunny answered with another smile. "Girls are useless here. If you Top-siders ever communicated with each other like civilised people, you'd know that already." Shoving Fin aside, she turned to Rab. "Go get your belongings," she said, then brushed past him making for the tunnel.

Rab stared after her.

Surely it couldn't be that simple.

"Go on," Fin shouted at Rab. "You take Gift and try to find that imaginary launch pad." He turned away and headed back to Stitch. "We're better off here without you."

"That's right, Fin, you are," Rab said. "For the moment. But don't make yourself too comfortable. Gift and I will be back." He pointed at Stitch. "You just watch out for your brother while we're gone. He's your responsibility now." Rab almost choked on the words, but if he faltered, cut Fin any slack at all, Stitch would see right through the pretence. "And try to do a better job of it this time."

He more or less expected Fin to come flying back at him, but when Gift jumped between them again, Fin pulled back just in time to avoid knocking the girl to the ground.

"Stop it! Please stop it!" she said, pushing on Fin's waist with all her might. "We're going to find the launch pad and come back. We are!"

"And what do you know?" Fin snapped at her. "There's no launch pad. He's just telling you there is because he's too scared to admit there isn't."

"Well then," she said calmly, "we'll still be back, won't we?"

Rab glanced towards Stitch, knowing he should back up Gift's pledge to return, but the desolation on Stitch's face stripped the words away. Nothing he could say or do at that moment would make a shred of difference.

"Do whatever you want," Fin snarled. "But you'll never find it," he added and, turning, stormed across the room towards his brother.

"You're wrong, Fin," Gift sang after him. "Wrong," she repeated in a whisper, then tilted her head towards Rab. "I want to say goodbye to Stitch."

Rab nodded. "But be quick," he called to her as she ran across the room, "I don't think Sunny intends to give us much time."

Although he couldn't hear what Gift was saying, her repeated stroking of Stitch's hair went some way to calm the boy. For Fin however, there was nothing even Gift could do to win him back. He'd dropped down in the chair beside his brother's bed, stony-faced and mute now, even Gift invisible to him.

Rab caught Gift's eye and waved for her to come back. After one last stroke of the little boy's hair, she stepped away from the bed and, when she reached Rab, held out her hand for him to take. Neither spoke as they walked back through the tunnels. For Rab, each dark and doubtful glance that was aimed at them further reinforced the wisdom of leaving.

He thought they might encounter Braham and the man he'd been speaking with in the stall on the way, but there was no sign of either of them. Sunny, who had made it back to the old man's space well ahead of them, looked more her old self again now. The gun was in her arms and their packs were lying in a pile at her feet.

"I've added some extra food," she said. "You won't get far on what you had."

Something about her demeanour suddenly changed. She marched quickly into the tunnel and returned immediately.

"Where are the boys?"

She'd meant him to take Fin and Stitch! Rab's heart sank; it hadn't been that simple.

"They're not coming," he told her. "I never intended to take them with us. Stitch can't make it and Fin won't go without him. I thought you understood that."

"They're not welcome here any longer. I thought you understood that." She pointed towards the tunnel, blood-streaked face flushing angrily. "So you can go back there now and get them. I don't care how you do it, just do it."

"They won't come."

Sunny shook her head. "That's not my problem." She kicked once at the packs. "Take these, them, and get out."

"What's going on in here?" It was Braham.

"They're leaving," Sunny said with finality, then walked back to the hearth, propped the gun against the wall in its customary place, and began to fidget with something on the table.

The old man stopped in the doorway and looked at Rab. "What's she talking about? You can't leave yet."

"It seems that your granddaughter and I have had yet another misunderstanding."

Sunny swung around.

"Typical of Top-siders to lie. Not long ago, you wanted to leave. You asked to leave." She shrugged. "I'm just going along with your wishes."

Braham shook his head in obvious confusion. "No. No. This isn't right. We agreed—"

Rab interrupted. "It's true, I did ask to leave, but she wants me to take Fin and Stitch. We can't go on with Stitch."

"Then I'd suggest you go back the way you came," Sunny said, back turned.

"I can't carry the boy all that way and you know it."

"But what about our agreement?" Braham said, clearly troubled.

He was trying hard to catch Rab's eye, but captured Sunny's attention instead.

"What agreement?" Sunny dashed across the floor and grasped her grandfather's arm. "What agreement?"

Vainly, the old man attempted to shake her off. "Nothing that concerns you."

Sunny's wrath fell on Rab. "Well? I suggest you tell me if you ever want out of here, with or without the boy."

It didn't matter to him what Sunny did or didn't know about the old man's plans, and when all was said and done, he didn't owe these tunnel-dwellers a thing.

"Your grandfather has asked to come with us," Rab admitted. "To the launch pad."

He'd expected Sunny to erupt, but she surprised him by smiling.

"Should have known you weren't telling me everything before," she said. "I gather you haven't exactly agreed." She didn't give Rab a chance to answer. "Of course, you haven't. Just when were you going to inform me?" she demanded, turning on old Braham. "Or did you plan to just sneak away?" She shook her head. "Wouldn't Edward Braham be proud of us now? A fine legacy he's left. You, his oldest living descendant, so eager to abandon everything he fought so hard to build. And me —" her finger turned accusingly on herself, "— just too damn trusting and soft, believing that saving those four Top-siders was the right thing to do when what I should have done was leave them to die." Her angry glance fell on Rab once more. "Even Top-sider children are liars and thieves. You've barely been here a day and already you've spread your poison. It's in your blood and nothing can change that. Not hospitality. Not kindness. We gave you both and look how you've repaid us."

"We haven't lied about anything," Rab said, abandoning the old man in the doorway, "and we certainly haven't stolen anything. If you're talking about me going up in the tunnel, well why wouldn't I? Despite what you said about Gift not being welcome and us having the choice to move on anytime we liked, you locked us in and intended to keep us in. As far as your grandfather's leaving goes, that was his idea. You said so yourself. In fact, you even suggested that I take him."

"Only an ignorant Top-sider would take such a sarcastic and offhand comment seriously," Sunny replied with a violent shake of her head. "His talk of leaving was only talk until you came here."

Rab smiled. "I wouldn't be so sure about that."

Sunny shrugged off his reply. "I'm not interested in your opinion. Just pick up your things and go—all four of you."

"You're sending us out to die. Even a Top-sider's life must mean something to you. You bought back those three little girls. You can't tell me it doesn't bother you to know that, with Stitch along, we'll all die out there."

"Those girls aren't Top-siders. They're our people and no matter how your kind might have tried to infect them, with time and patience, we'll flush the corruption out of them. They were born with the blood of my people, not the blood of Top-siders. Four dead Top-siders is just four times better than one dead Top-sider to me."

"Sunny, you can't." The old man stepped forward. "Let Rab and the little girl go if that's their choice. But let the boys stay here. I'll go with them and we'll find the launch pad and when we do, we'll come back and show you the way. Every one of us can be saved, Sunny. I know we can."

"You're talking to the wrong person, old man. Besides, what do you think you're saving us from?" She pointed past Rab towards Gift. "They're the ones in trouble, not us. We're doing fine here."

"Sunny, that's simply not true. Our city is dying."

"You're dying, Grandfather, not us, and your incessant back-thinking has blinded you to the things we have."

Rab thought of the disease creeping through the 'shroom fields. How could Sunny possibly not know about that? And she accused her grandfather of being blind!

"I'm still a councillor here, Sunny. I'm going with this lad and you don't have enough authority yet to stop me."

She stood there for a long time, staring at the old man, seeming to size him up. Rab couldn't read her face, couldn't imagine what she might be thinking behind those cold and muddy eyes.

"All right, old man," she said finally and, turning, went to retrieve the gun. "I can't stop you," she said, walking back with it. "The moment my back is turned, you'll go with or without these two. Oh, I can send them out to die and no one here would think badly of me. But our people have always looked to a Braham for guidance. They expect it. If I knowingly let my own grandfather go alone and unprotected with these Top-siders, no one will ever trust a Braham again. And since you don't have much time left, old man, that means me." She pushed past Rab and headed for the tunnel. "First thing tomorrow morning, we leave—and the two boys stay behind."

Rab stared at the empty entrance for a long time. He hadn't expected Sunny to give in—never mind resolve to come with them. Apparently Braham hadn't either, but suddenly he stirred from his own stupor and looked at Rab.

"There's a lot to do," he said, coming to his senses.

He shot past Rab and into the tunnel, muttering to himself all the while.

Rab glanced at Gift, then shrugged, unable to explain Sunny's abrupt change of mind.

"That didn't work out quite how we'd planned," he said.

Gift shook her head. "Maybe Sunny is right," she said in that mature way of hers that always managed to surprise him.

"You mean about the launch pad?"

"That, too," she replied. "But I really meant what she said about us. Maybe we aren't worth saving. Maybe we are just liars and thieves like she said."

Silently Rab cursed Sunny. Bit by agonising bit, she sapped at the little girl's spirit.

"What do you mean? We haven't lied to anyone here and we haven't stolen, either."

"But we have," Gift insisted gravely. "Maybe we haven't lied about the launch pad intentionally, but if we say it's there and it isn't, doesn't that still mean it's a lie? And we did steal, Rab. At least Fin did. That's why we were in the hospital when you came back there. That's what the fight was about. While the nurse's back was turned, he stole food from those two girls so he could give it to Stitch. Sunny had to come and break up the fight between them. But Rab, the nurse had fed them. Stitch told me that she had. So why did Fin do it?" She sighed. "Maybe we really are just what Sunny says we are."

Chapter 9

THEY waited in uncomfortable silence well into the night for Sunny and Braham to return. But it seemed both had better things to do than come back to feed two thieving Top-siders.

Gift had been badly stung by Sunny's words and there wasn't a thing Rab could do about it. He didn't doubt the nurse—Fin probably had stolen the little girls' food. It was something he'd do. He didn't doubt Stitch either—the boys had been fed and, from his own observations that morning, fed well. He could say that about these tunnel-dwellers: they didn't let a stranger go hungry. At least they hadn't until now. Tonight though, it appeared that he and Gift would have to fend for themselves and he wondered how Gift would react to him stealing food from the back room, where it seemed Sunny kept their supplies. He could have rummaged among their own packs, of course, but was loath to deplete their meagre provisions or to ask Sunny to supplement them again in the morning.

Without consulting Gift, he made for the niche in the back wall. Of the four of them who'd start out tomorrow, the old man and Gift stood the least chance of survival. Although she'd be unpleasant and uninvited company, Sunny's skills on the surface would prove useful. Braham, on the other hand, was nothing but an encumbrance. But Braham wasn't his responsibility. If Sunny didn't think to feed and prepare her grandfather for the hardships ahead, it wasn't up to him to take up the slack. But Gift was his responsibility.

Stripped of his blindsight, Rab still couldn't sense a thing in front of him. Sunny appeared to see in the darkness just fine and all Rab could figure was that the tunnel-dwellers' eyes had permanently adapted to the lower levels of light underground. But as he rummaged around in the dark, among the shelves and benches he bumped against, Rab wondered if that kind of adaption might just pose another obstacle on the surface. Sunny had seemed to fare well enough outside. But just how long had it been since the old man had seen daylight?

When he touched something that was cold and hard, Rab instinctively pulled his hand away. Tentatively feeling around again, he realised that what he'd touched were canisters of some sort—stacked four, sometimes five, high against the back wall of the inner room. The stack teetered but he managed to grab the topmost canister from the nearest tower without bringing the whole lot down. The canister had some sort of lid that popped free with a little sucking sound. Rab instantly smelled 'shrooms.

His search for water proved less successful. Although he could hear water running behind the rock wall, he could find no way to get at it. He'd have to rely on the flasks that Sunny had filled for them. When she returned for them in the morning, if she returned, he'd have her fill the flasks again; surely she wouldn't deny them water.

Gift didn't question what he'd done or baulk at taking the food from his hands, but ate her share in silence. She accepted the flask he retrieved from his pack just as meekly.

Watching her sitting there, progressively fading more and more before his eyes, Rab realised that finding the launch pad had taken on an entirely new meaning and urgency. Gift had lost faith. Not in him—somehow he knew she'd never lose faith in him—but her own worth. She was coming to see her reflection in Sunny's eyes and she didn't like what she saw. It was no use to tell her that she wasn't like Fin, no use trying to persuade her that Sunny was wrong to generalise Top-siders. They weren't all the same.

When Gift was done with her meal, Rab saw her to the makeshift bed she'd slept on the night before, then moved to stoke the fire. Much of the tinder he found by the hearth was richly decorated, confirming Rab's earlier suspicion, and the old man's warning to Sunny. Like their counterparts on the surface, the tunnel-dwellers were running out of fuel, food and time, circumstances that might better explain Sunny's change of mind. She'd claimed that duty to the Braham reputation had forced her to go with them, but Rab wondered if, at the back of her mind, Sunny was harbouring a niggling suspicion that her grandfather might be right.

Rab slept little that night and, whether Gift in fact slept, she didn't make a sound. Braham was the first to return in the morning, followed hard on by Sunny. The old man spared Rab a quick glance before he darted into his sleeping quarters; Sunny, none at all. So he was surprised when she emerged from the back room, where he'd scavenged last night's meal, carrying four bowls brimming with more of the 'shroom concoction. If she'd noticed his pilfering of the night before, she didn't say anything about it. The old man reappeared a moment later, his arms laden with paper.

"What's all that?" Sunny asked, spotting him over Rab's shoulder.

"Edward's documents," he replied, sounding surprised. "We can't leave them here."

Sunny's face flushed scarlet. "Don't be so stupid, old man. We can't take all that rubbish."

"I'm not going to take them with us, Sunny," Braham answered sharply. "What's the point when we're coming back? I'm taking all this to the library for safekeeping."

"You'd be better off sitting down to breakfast, but suit yourself." She waved him away with a grunt. "Just don't expect us to slow down for you today. I don't intend to risk my life just to save yours."

As the old man headed back into the tunnel, he called back to his granddaughter. "You look to yourself and that little one. Rab and me, we'll do just fine."

At the mention of Gift, Sunny turned to Rab. "That one," she said, pointing towards Gift with the bowl she was still holding, "is your problem. She falls behind, she stays behind. You understand?"

"I understand," Rab said, "but there's no need to concern yourself about Gift. We're bred to life on the surface. She'll fall behind long after you will."

He hoped he was right.

Sunny snorted, then settled herself down on the floor and began to eat. When she was finished, Rab asked her to replenish their water. She hesitated for only a moment, then held out her hand for their flasks. If Sunny weren't Sunny, he'd have followed her to the back room just to satisfy his curiosity. Somehow the tunnel-dwellers had perfected a way to channel water into their city and he had to admit that, in many respects, these people had certainly bettered his on the surface.

The old man burst back through the doorway, rushed past Rab and, for the second time, disappeared into his own quarters. If he intended to burden them unnecessarily, Sunny would have her say on the matter. Still, Rab was relieved to see him return empty-handed. He was anxious to get under way and lacked the patience to be stalled by a protracted argument on what constituted appropriate baggage. But the old man seemed content to delegate that particular concern to his granddaughter, which left Rab wondering what his night-long absence had been all about.

"You," Sunny said, drawing Rab's attention.

He glanced around and found her standing by the hearth, pointing again at Gift.

"You carry only what you can manage. You do exactly what I tell you and you don't ask questions. Understand?"

Out of the corner of his eye, Rab caught Gift's sober nod.

"And you." Sunny turned to Rab. "You carry your own stuff and most of hers."

Rab leapt to his feet, enraged.

"Let's get something straight right now. Don't forget that I got us this far and it wasn't by offloading my burden onto children. I'm more capable out there than you are."

"Really? Then exactly how did that boy manage to break his leg?"

Before he could answer, Sunny turned away and set about extinguishing the hearth fire.

Rab felt a touch on his hand.

"If she hates us so much, why is she coming?" Gift whispered.

He'd like an answer to that question himself. At the back of his mind, he knew—just knew—there had to more behind Sunny's decision than a sense of familial responsibility for the old man.

***

At the junction of Braham and Main streets, the old man broke off from their party and when Sunny's effort to call him back failed, Rab flung his packs to the ground.

Their journey was destined to fail. The old man was already off on some secondary mission that he'd neglected to share with the rest of them, only revealing that there was one more thing he needed to take and that he'd meet them shortly at 'the house'.

Rab glanced at Sunny, but she said nothing. It seemed to him that there was more than one thing the old man had neglected to take with him. Neither he nor Sunny looked the least prepared for their journey. While he and Gift had donned their coats and reclaimed their packs, including the large one Blaze had prepared for the children, the old man and Sunny still wore the same clothes they'd been in the day before and, apart from Sunny's ever-present gun, their arms were conspicuously empty. This lengthy performance couldn't just be some ploy to get the two of them out of the city; there were easier ways to get rid of a couple of nuisance Top-siders.

When Sunny struck off for Market Square, Rab grabbed his packs from the ground and, with Gift on his heels, took off after her. Their transit through the marketplace drew only mild interest now; Sunny coming and going through the tunnels was too common an occurrence to warrant curiosity and the departure of two unwanted Top-siders was probably a welcome sight. Leaving the market behind, Rab trailed Sunny into the lower tunnel. He never had asked her anything about the shimmerers. Like the people in this city, he'd automatically come to accept them as an expected and unremarkable feature of life in the tunnels. With the acquired indifference, he had also developed an instinctive consideration for their fragility and, as he walked, was careful not to scrape the edges of his cumbersome burden against the walls.

As he emerged behind Sunny in the upper room, he was surprised to find the hearth well ablaze, then noticed the heap of packs and coats by the heavy metal door. Well, at least he knew what Sunny and the old man had been up to all night.

"Why does your grandfather call this 'the house'?" Rab asked. "It isn't so much bigger than his space down in the tunnels."

Sunny lay her weapon on top of the pile of heavy coats and, when the pile began to teeter, used the toe of her boot to stabilise it before she bothered to look his way.

"I seem to recall my grandfather showing you the drawings."

Rab shook his head as he lowered his own packs to the floor. "He showed me a drawing, but it certainly didn't look anything like this."

"You're talking about the windows and other rooms," Sunny said, suddenly gracing him with a rare smile. It didn't last long; the smile died away and she shrugged. "We abandoned the house when we moved deeper into the tunnels. Heating all the rooms then would have been wasteful, so we shut them off."

She pointed, drawing Rab's attention to the wall behind him. With a little imagination, he conceded that there might indeed be a blocked doorway just to the right of the hearth.

"There's another over there," Sunny said, pointing left.

Rab could make out the second relic doorway with its plug of jagged, randomly-sized boulders more easily.

"Earthquakes took care of the windows," Sunny told him as she crossed to the largest wall in the room. Back to Rab, she extended her arms across the rock face. "They were about twice this wide and made of glass four times thicker than your upper arm. In a few places, you can still see where the opening used to be." She shrugged again as she swung around.

Rab walked to the wall. "And what could you see?" he asked. "Through the windows?"

"Me? Nothing. The windows were long gone before I was born. Doors, too. I couldn't tell you what's behind them." She glanced towards the still empty tunnel entrance. "What's taking him so long?"

Rab was barely listening. His fingers had found one of those smooth edges where an opening had once been hacked out of the stone. Transparent glass was just another of those things he'd heard about but the tunnel-dwellers, or some of them anyway, had been privileged enough to see. He began to wonder what his father would have thought of this place and, how his fellow villagers would have reacted if they could have had the opportunity to see and actually touch evidence that at least some of the things his father had spoken about amounted to more than misguided rambling. But though the evidence was right in front of him, even Rab found it difficult to imagine that by standing at this window and looking up into the night sky, it was possible to see the stars.

Behind him, he could hear Sunny making repeated circuits around the room. Rest was going to be a rare commodity on the surface and by pacing, Sunny was just wasting her energy. Reluctantly, he turned away from the walled-up windows to see that Gift had found a place of comfort on Sunny's waiting packs. Their talk of smashed windows and plugged-up doorways hadn't interested her.

Beneath the echo of Sunny's marching, Rab detected an unfamiliar clacking kind of noise coming from inside the tunnel. He glanced expectantly at Sunny, but evidently she hadn't heard it. Instead she ceased pacing and pointed at Rab's packs.

"Do you have extra clothes in those?" she asked.

"Some," Rab replied, curious why she'd care. "Why?"

She didn't answer, but her head snapped around.

"Not that horse," she barked, swinging on Rab. "Don't tell me he's bringing that horse."

Rab shrugged. "Why ask me?"

"You knew about this. Don't try to tell me that you didn't. Well," she said, turning her anger on Gift. "Is that horse intended for you? Is that what my grandfather is thinking?"

"Gift had nothing to do with it," Rab said, leaping to Gift's defence. "Your grandfather intends to use the horse to carry our packs—that's all—and maybe it isn't such a bad idea."

"You think so, do you?" Sunny said. "Well, let me ask you this then, did either of you give any thought at all as to how you're going to get that horse up onto the plateau?"

It shocked Rab to realise that he hadn't. But then the old man had been plotting this venture for a very long time and the horse had been a fundamental part of his scheme from the start.

"But didn't it come off the plateau?" he asked hopefully. "I mean it got in here somehow."

"Twenty years ago and through a different tunnel."

"Then why can't—"

"That tunnel's gone! You must have experienced earthquakes top-side. You know what they can do. That," she said, pointing towards the metal door, "is the only way in or out now and the only way onto the plateau is up the steps." Her hands found her hips. "So maybe you and the old man can carry it up."

"Kix can walk up by himself!"

Horse and owner appeared at the mouth of the tunnel. The old man looked weary already and, beneath its roughly fashioned bags and interlaced network of straps, the horse just looked plain scared.

"You're a bigger fool than this Top-sider, old man."

Gift stirred on her perch atop of the pile of coats. "How will we get Kix up the steps?" she asked. "If he slips, he could fall all the way down into the valley and die."

Clearly her concerns were more for the horse's welfare than the potential loss of a pack carrier.

When the old man began to lead the horse forward, Rab was troubled to see that familiar nervous rippling down its flank again. Braham was going to have a difficult task just to control the beast, let alone coax it up the narrow steps—and that was only the start of their journey. Who knew what further obstacles lay ahead?

Rab stepped up to the old man.

"Perhaps taking the horse isn't such a good idea," he said, then glanced over his shoulder at Sunny. "If the City isn't too far, we might manage better without it."

"If you're asking for my opinion, then we're not going to manage at all." She turned away and headed for Gift and the pile of coats and packs. "With or without that relic. You do what you want." Nudging Gift aside, she grabbed the topmost coat, shrugged into it, then dived into the pile and retrieved two of the packs. "Just don't expect any help from me." With one pack flung up to her shoulder, she dumped the second on the floor and turned to Gift. "You, Gift, whatever your name is," she said and began dragging the little girl to a metal container standing in the far corner of the room, "You see this paper?"

Rab watched as Sunny began to pull out wad after crumpled wad and ram each in turn under her coat, reversing the procedure he'd seen her perform when they'd first come down the tunnel.

"You stuff that inside your clothing like this. Understand?" she said. "It helps to keep you warm. And if your Top-sider friend over there has any brains, he'll do the same."

Gift needed no further prompting. Over and over again her little hands plunged in and out of the container as she set about padding herself up in a skilful imitation of Sunny.

"Me next," the old man said.

Before he realised it, the rough strap that had been dangling from the horse's neck was thrust into Rab's hand.

"You hold Kix still. Then it's your turn."

The horse made a lunge for the lower tunnel and almost pulled Rab off his feet. His gloves were still in his pocket, so the strap tore a shallow rent in the palm of his unprotected hand. Rab struggled to keep the beast in check but the clattering of the horse's hooves on the stone floor continued to make an alarming racket that the old man dispassionately ignored and Sunny predictably found irritating.

"Shut that thing up."

Gift walked over to save him; all it took was a simple touch of her hand on its muzzle for the horse to begin to settle.

"There, there, Kix," she crooned. "Good horse. Quiet now."

Her attention fell on Rab's hand and then drifted to the telltale trace of blood that had soaked into Kix's strap. She was about to say something but Rab stopped her with a shake of his head. Sunny didn't need to know about the injury to his hand. It had been stupid to allow himself to be compromised even before their journey began and Sunny had little enough faith in Top-siders. Fortunately his gloves would conceal the evidence.

When the old man came back and relieved him of the horse, Rab took his turn at the container.

He swung around to find the old man examining the pink stain his blood had left on the horse's strap. Sunny was back by the remaining packs, retrieving her gun, so she didn't see the old man lead Kix to the container where he gathered more of the wadded up paper, which he then shoved beneath each of his own gloves.

Sunny turned and gestured for Gift. "You come here," she said, "and take this pack. It's light enough for you to carry up the steps."

Rab was about to protest, but Sunny had evidently been expecting an objection. She was looking directly at him when she passed the pack to Gift.

"We share the load, Top-sider, each according to their ability. Unless you think that horse can get itself and all the packs up those steps. If it makes it to the plateau, then we transfer the packs."

Rab nodded. She was right, of course. Even the old man had had sense enough to realise that. He had joined Sunny by the door and was loading up himself, instead of the horse, with two of the weightier looking packs.

"And if it doesn't," Sunny said, gathering the last of the packs for herself, "we each continue with the loads that we have. No one discards a pack even if it's empty and no one asks someone else to carry theirs."

"Gift is my responsibility, not yours," Rab said, stepping forward. "I decide if and when I take on her load."

"Not when I'm leader." She straightened and flipped out her empty hand. "Of course if you know the way to this city of yours and think you're better equipped to get us there without running out of food and water or stumbling into a mob of unfriendly Top-siders, then please—feel free to take charge."

She had him cornered—again. He knew nothing. The conversation he'd overheard outside Kix's stall implied that Sunny had covered at least some of the terrain north of the tunnel city. If they stood any chance at all of making it, pride had to take second place.

"All right," Rab agreed and gathered his own packs from the floor. "You win."

"In this venture. . ." he heard Sunny say as she set about unlocking the heavy metal door, "no one wins."

As soon as Kix was led into the dark and tight confines of the upper tunnel, it again attempted to escape. It seemed only Gift had the ability to calm it and so they progressed up through the twists and turns of the dark and narrow passageway—Sunny striding out ahead in total disregard of the struggle, Braham tugging and pulling the reluctant and agitated beast, while Gift wedged herself in beside it, sometimes being squeezed between the horse's belly and the ragged walls. Rab, bringing up the rear, was fearful that at any moment Gift's patient and soothing entreaties might fail and he'd be trampled in the horse's blind attempt to turn back in the impossibly narrow space.

Luckily Sunny had thought to have the gates already opened because, the instant the horse saw daylight, it bolted. Curiously it was Sunny who prevented it from careening over the edge of the cliff by making a grab for its straps. When the old man reached her, she casually passed him the straps, walked back to secure the gate once more, then struck off along the rock ledge in the direction of the steps. She didn't say a word.

As soon as he stepped outside, Rab's eyes began to sting and water. After only a few days living underground in the subtle glow of the shimmerers, he'd become sensitised to the marginally brighter light of his own world. And it even felt a little strange to see his own breath again. Perhaps her constant forays outside of the tunnels had conditioned Sunny to expect such abrupt changes, but Kix and the old man must have been practically blinded the moment they stepped out onto the ledge.

True to her word, on reaching the base of the steps, Sunny started up at once, heedless of Rab, her grandfather, and the distressed horse. She hadn't offered to relieve either one of them of their packs and, if they were ever going to get Kix onto the plateau, it was clear that they'd have to do it with the horse and themselves unencumbered. The packs would have to be left behind and returned for once the horse was on top of the plateau. As Rab dropped his packs beside the old man's, he noticed Sunny shepherding Gift up the steps ahead of her. But Kix was at the forefront of his mind right then and he couldn't spare a moment to question Sunny's uncharacteristic concern for his little companion.

Once the horse realised that the old man intended to lead it up the steeply rising steps, it attempted to bolt again. If the old man hadn't padded up his gloves, its thrashing and bucking would have ripped the skin of his hands to shreds.

Braham pulled. Rab pushed, wincing each time the horse strained. Age must have mellowed poor Kix because he had the terrible suspicion that a younger animal would have sent all three of them tumbling down the jagged steps. Whenever the old man managed to coax the horse to take another step, its hooves sent a shower of splintered rock onto the step where Rab was standing. The old man grunted. The horse brayed. And another cascade of stones came pinging down the steps. Alone, Rab could never have got the horse anywhere near the plateau.

At every chance he got, Rab searched for but failed to find any sign of Sunny and Gift above them. The only thing he knew for certain was that they'd made it safely onto the plateau.

Half way up the steps, Kix lost his footing, knocking Rab backward. As he teetered, about to fall, his left hand grazed and then managed to grab a projection in the rock face. But his right arm was left swinging freely and his boots repeatedly slipped off the edge of the step below. Finally he found a foothold, almost turning an ankle in the process. But his right foot was pinned to the spot. By some miracle, the horse had righted itself and not catapulted the old man over its flanks, but one of its hind hooves was planted squarely on Rab's right foot. Still at the head of the horse, the old man lay in a crumpled heap a few steps above Rab, while Kix stood in a fixed and silent stance midway between them. The hood of the old man's coat had been wrenched backward, revealing an ashen face.

Gingerly, Rab began to work his right foot free; it didn't appear to be broken at least. Of the three of them, the horse seemed to have fared the worst. Its shins were scraped and bleeding and a long gash had opened up in the flesh of one of its hind legs. Rab couldn't afford to spook the animal or cause it any more damage; the old man still had a hold of its straps and any sudden movement would send him down the steps.

Once Rab was secure on the step again, he looked up hopefully towards the plateau, but he saw no one—nothing—not even a head peeking down over the edge to confirm that they were all still alive. They were on their own.

Above him, Braham slowly came to his feet. Wordlessly, he glanced down, perhaps to make sure that Rab had regained his footing, because immediately he began to tug at the traumatised horse. At first the horse refused to budge, then abruptly began to move. The hoof that had been planted so painfully on Rab's foot rose to the step above. Next came a front hoof and then slowly, one tentative step after the next, Kix resumed its struggle to reach the top of the steps. In a perverse stroke of luck, the higher steps were slightly wider than those below and the horse seemed to find it easier going.

Rab scrambled onto the plateau and fell to his knees, heart pounding, gasping for breath. When he finally found the strength and will to look up, he spotted Sunny seated on a distant outcrop with a hand securely tangled in the collar of Gift's coat. The old man was lying on the ground close to Rab. His whole body was heaving and he still had one hand looped through Kix's straps. Despite the bitter cold, the horse's flanks were glistening with sweat. But mercifully the animal was silent.

"Made it, I see," Sunny said, rising. She looked at Rab for a moment longer, then released her hold on Gift and turned away. "And that's the last of our luck from now on."

Gift darted across the plateau and crashed onto the ground in front of Rab. Beneath her hood, she was grinning.

"We're going to make it now. I know we are. Sunny's just mad because you proved her wrong." She jumped up then and, grabbing Rab's arm, made a valiant effort to drag him onto his feet as well.

Rab didn't share Gift's faith. No doubt the miracle of getting the horse and themselves up the steps and onto the plateau had used up every last shred of their luck and the going wouldn't be much better from now on.

Rab found he couldn't straighten. Every time he tried, it prompted a wracking cough, but after standing some moments, bent at the waist, hands pressed to his thighs for support and with Gift periodically pumping his back, the burning in his chest began to subside. The old man should have been near dead, but when Rab looked over, he discovered him trying to stagger onto his feet. Gift rushed over to help. The horse seemed to be regaining some of its senses as well, but it was wildly flicking its head now and each new frenzied lurch threatened to wrench the straps free of Braham's hands. When Gift took the straps however, Kix immediately began to quieten.

So, Gift had found herself a friend. And just as well. Without her, the horse would be more of an encumbrance than an aid. Horses were obviously skittish beasts, something John Braham had conveniently neglected to tell them.

Gift smiled back at Rab, but almost immediately began to frown. "Where are all the packs?"

He'd been trying not to think about that.

"They're still at the bottom of the steps," he told her. "Kix couldn't carry them and neither could we. I'll have to go back and get them."

"I can help," Gift said and, flinging the straps at Braham, started after Rab towards the steps.

"No, Gift," Rab replied, bending to take her by the shoulders. "I need you to stay here and look after that horse."

She shot him a disappointed look but turned back just the same.

He could have done with Fin right then. The boy had two good hands, a sturdy and young pair of legs and an attitude of self-confidence and boldness that suited their current circumstances. Rab didn't relish the prospect of another trip down the steps and back up again, laden with all those packs. But there was no alternative. He was ten or so steps from the top when Gift called down to him.

"Sunny's gone off and left us. What should I do?"

"Follow her," Rab shouted back. "And don't let her out of your sight. I'll catch up to you. Hurry," he said, relieved when, a moment later, he heard the sound of hooves clattering on the plateau.

Five packs were too many to carry up all at once. In the end, Rab was obliged to make two trips and, by the time he returned to the plateau a second time, Kix, the old man, and Gift were almost lost inside the smoke haze that rose from the tunnel-dwellers' fires. At last he spotted a large and fuzzy silhouette and, beside it, a smaller one that seemed to be jumping up and down in the air. Kix and Gift!

Despite the added burden he was forced to carry on his back and drag behind him across the rugged ground, it took Rab less time than he'd expected to cross the smoke field and catch up with Gift and the horse. The old man was still some distance ahead and, marching on in front of him, Sunny. She wasn't doing her best time, perhaps making a concession for his delay in retrieving the packs.

With Sunny travelling so slowly, he could spare the time to rid himself of the packs. Together, Gift and he loaded four of the packs, two apiece, in the bags the old man had attached either side of the horse's flanks. Kix resisted a little, and without Gift, Rab suspected he'd have had a tougher time of it.

Once the packs were in place, Gift gave Kix an encouraging slap on the rump. The horse responded immediately. If Gift had been a bit bigger, Rab could have had her lead the poor beast up to the plateau; it seemed to bear a lingering resentment for him.

"Didn't I tell you we'd make it now?" Gift said, smiling at him around the horse's rump. "There won't be any more steps ahead and Kix is doing just fine on flat ground."

"No," Rab agreed and attempted to return an encouraging smile. "There won't be any more steps."

Or so he hoped. Sunny hadn't been exactly free with her information, revealing nothing about what lay ahead of them or how close her party had even come to reaching the City—or when. Things changed quickly on the surface and that journey couldn't have been event-free. If what he had overheard outside Kix's stall was true, and he had no reason to suspect that it wasn't, then Sunny had been the only one to come back alive. Why? And perhaps more importantly—how?

Rab was accustomed to the way night subtly claimed the sky, but the old man seemed confused by the gradual deterioration of the wan daylight and Kix travelled little better, stumbling more frequently over the now hidden hazards peppering the plateau. Sunny looked at ease, the time she spent top-side obviously schooling her to expect such tricks from the sky. She pressed on farther into the night than Rab thought wise, so he was relieved when she finally stopped.

Settling herself cross-legged on the cold hard ground, she began to dole out their evening rations from her own packs, leaving Rab's and Gift's packs untouched. The slab of that familiar 'shroom concoction she gave him was overly generous, but Rab didn't comment. For the moment, she was in control. When Sunny placed Gift's share in her outstretched hand, the little girl looked towards Rab, clearly puzzled.

Rab hadn't expected Sunny to eat with them, so wasn't surprised when, after another dive into the still bulging pack, she left. He watched her as she moved away set, he'd thought, on taking her own meal in private. Instead she kept on walking, stopping finally at the small boulder where Kix was tethered. In the darkness he could just make out her raised hand nudge again and again at the horse's mouth as she patiently coaxed the animal to take more. When she turned, seeming to sense him watching her, Rab looked away.

Her grandfather had seen it, too.

"Kix has value tonight," he said with a shrug. "This morning, he didn't. Tomorrow he might not again."

"I'll never work her out," Rab replied. "She seems to have no understanding of loyalty."

"Sunny believes in survival," Braham explained as he systematically picked at a few crumbs that had fallen onto his lap, savouring each in turn. "Her loyalty is to that and that alone."

"Then we've got ourselves a fine leader, haven't we?"

"Depends on how you look at it." The old man rose slowly to his feet. "Stay valuable—like Kix there—and she'll do everything she can to keep you alive."

Rab looked over at Braham, suddenly comprehending. "You knew all along she'd accept that horse."

The old man shook his head. "Not all along, no. But once we got it onto the plateau. . ." He smiled, ". . .I figured she'd recognise its worth."

"Then you'd better tend to your own, old man."

Rab jumped at the sound of Sunny's voice.

"And see about arranging those packs." She turned to Rab. "You, too. Set them up for bedding. The ground will freeze tonight."

Rab eased himself onto his feet. "Thanks for the warning." He stretched a hand down towards Gift. "I'd never have worked that out for myself."

Sunny didn't answer but reached for the pack Gift was about to pick up from the ground. She drove a hand inside to retrieve a slab of 'shroom loaf.

"The other was for the horse," she said.

If she was expecting him to protest, she was in for a disappointment. Rab just shrugged, retrieved the pack from her hands and, with Gift in tow, carried it to Braham.

The old man was doing a reasonable job of laying out the rest of the packs. He'd set them out in rows, three large, one small, the last obviously intended for Gift.

"Be good to have had a fire," he said, bending to place the pack Rab brought. "Do you think a wind might come up?" He glanced into the building darkness towards the spot where the horse was tethered. "Kix is used to protection."

Rab thought for a moment, then began to pull out the balled up wads of paper from under Blaze's coat.

"What are you. . ." Gift started to say, but fell silent when, one by one, Rab stuffed the wads under the thick under-layer of his clothing.

He stripped off Blaze's bulky coat.

"You'll freeze," the old man said, clearly anticipating what Rab had in mind.

"Better me than it," Rab replied with a jerk of his head, indicating Sunny. "As I'm sure she'd agree. That paper stuff of hers is more than enough, better than I'm used to." He bent to redistribute two of the packs. "I'll just sleep between these. It'll be fine," then passed the coat to the old man. "Lay it over the horse's back and tie it on with some of those straps."

Braham stood motionless for a long time, the coat dangling loosely from his hands.

"Maybe Sunny's wrong," he said at last. "Maybe Top-siders are people, too." With a shake of his head, he walked away, heading for Kix.

Rab sensed Gift's big black eyes looking up at him.

"What?" he prompted, glancing down.

"I think that might have been a mistake."

Rab smiled. "Wouldn't be my first." He bent to plump up the packs that were to be his outer protection for the night. "But Sunny was right about that paper, wasn't she? You've been warmer, right?"

Gift shrugged. "But all night, Rab? When you're not moving around? I don't know. . ."

"Just you worry about yourself," Rab said, motioning her towards the pack the old man had laid out for her.

She shook her head in a fair imitation of the old man, then snuggled down, almost disappearing into the lumpy mound.

"Go to sleep," Rab said. "I promise I'll still be here in the morning."

"You'd better be," she replied, a weariness she could no longer fight beginning to slur her words, "because Sunny wouldn't think twice about leaving me here if you weren't."

As much as he hated to admit it, she was probably right, so he was grateful to hear a subtle change in her breathing, which spared him the obligation to respond. She'd fallen fast asleep. He left her there and walked back to Sunny.

"I want you to promise me something," he said, lowering himself to the ground beside her. He spoke softly, just in case Gift wasn't asleep after all.

"I want you to promise that if anything happens to me, you won't go on, that you'll take Gift back with you to the tunnels."

"Why should I promise you anything?" Sunny flipped her hand in the air. "I can go where I choose when I choose and do whatever I want with that girl."

"Yes, you can," Rab agreed. "But she's strong. She's smart. You can see that."

"So?"

"She'd grow to be useful among your people." He glanced briefly over his shoulder towards the spot where Gift lay. "She's useful now," he added, turning back to Sunny.

"Told you before," Sunny replied evenly. "We've got enough girls."

"And not one of them could have been stolen from you," Rab observed. "You and the old man are lying. I don't know why, but you are. So there's no good reason—"

"Just can't let it go, can you, Top-sider?" Sunny said, cutting him off. "Fine, I'll explain then. . .if it'll only shut you up. We never had what you might call good relations with the Top-siders, but we got on in a manner of speaking. And we didn't always live in the tunnels every minute of every day. There used to be animals to tend up top. . .like that damn horse. We even had stands of crops growing. Not that I ever saw them. And that gate in the cliff was the only thing that kept us and the Top-siders apart. Most times it wasn't even locked. Wasn't any need until first the crops died, then the animals, then the Top-siders' young girls. When ours started to go missing, they locked the gates. But the gates were easy to break through." Another of those disquieting smiles swept across her face. "Not telling you anything there, am I? I saw you looking. . .wondering. Well, next came guards at the gates. Some were just a little too eager to be bribed. It was my grandfather's idea to erect that big door, not long before I saved your sorry skin actually. Never had the same sort of trouble after that. Happy now?" she prompted, fixing him with a challenging stare.

"All right, Sunny. Maybe that's true and maybe it isn't, but, either way, it doesn't make Gift any less valuable to you."

"Here," she said, extending her hand.

"Whatever that is, I don't want it." What he wanted was to have her promise to take care of Gift and, failing that, to have the guts to knock her head off.

"Oh, I think you do." She nodded towards his lap, where his hands were resting. "That rip should have attention."

Could he get nothing past this woman? He took the small pouch she offered, drew the string to open it, and cautiously sniffed at the contents. Whatever it was smelled kind of musty.

"What is it?"

"Sulfur," she said. "But be sparing with it. It's more precious than that little girl you're so determined to protect. And it's rarer."

Redrawing the string, Rab set the pouch aside. He always healed quickly and his hand no longer pained him at all.

"It doesn't need anything," he said.

"Do it anyway," Sunny replied. "At the moment, you are valuable." She nodded towards the sleeping Gift. "So is she. She's got a way with that ill-tempered horse."

Retrieving the pouch, Rab removed his gloves, and took a pinch of the fine powder between thumb and forefinger.

"Just sprinkle it on the wound."

After doing as Sunny instructed, he replaced his gloves and offered up the restrung pouch.

"You could use some of this yourself."

Sunny's hand flew up to her face.

"That captive girl had dirty fingernails," she said, accepting the pouch from his outstretched hand. "The scratches were deep. They bled a lot."

"Doesn't look good," Rab said casually and eased back onto his feet.

Let Sunny worry about something for a while.

Chapter 10

RAB had expected it to happen earlier, but the demanding journey was finally beginning to exact its toll on the old man. Each morning Sunny's little party started out as one, but within a short time, one that seemed to shrink more every day, she and Gift would be striding well out in front again, leaving the old man and Kix at the rear. Fearful that Braham would lose sight of them completely, Rab had taken to walking in-between where he could hold Sunny and Gift in view and still keep track of Kix and the old man. They couldn't afford to lose the horse; it was still toting most of their packs. But old Kix probably couldn't manage much longer; it was already favouring its damaged hind legs.

Sunny had relinquished only one of her packs but, even with the one she stubbornly continued to carry, she could still have outpaced Gift. As he walked, Rab mulled over what possible motive Sunny had to show such consideration, convinced there was more to it than Gift's 'way with the ill-tempered horse'. It gave him something to think about other than the cold and the gruelling journey. This morning their quest northward had taken them onto a slick downward slope, but the weather, so far, had held. When it broke, the frozen ground beneath their feet would become buried in drifts of snow. Rab held grave fears for the old horse then; if it stumbled into a snow-covered hole, its thin legs would surely snap.

Over the last few days, Rab had caught the occasional whiff of bad water, but since they had ventured onto the slope, its stench constantly fouled the air. All along he had intentionally avoided the river, but that didn't appear to be part of Sunny's strategy and so Rab wasn't surprised, only angered, when Sunny led them right up to its bank. The woman was mad; neither the horse nor old man could possible manage the boggy ground and none of them could tolerate the bad air for any length of time.

He rushed up, prepared for a clash of wills.

"We can't stay here," he gasped. "Are you trying to kill us?"

"Do you want me to take you north or not?" Sunny answered with a shrug. "It's all the same to me. But this is the only way I know. We have to cross the river."

"How?" Rab protested, then fell into a brief fit of coughing. "Just look at it," he said, recovering. "It's flowing too fast. Even if we can get through it, the horse can't."

"That's not my problem," she told him, then stamped her boot into the soggy ground. She pulled and, with a kind of sucking sound, her boot came free. "See. We can make it. This is the shallowest part of the river. I've crossed it here before."

"Just how long ago was that? How many snow times, Sunny? You can't know what the bed of the river is like now. Or how bad the water has become."

Sunny waved his protest aside. "Top-sider folklore," she said. "I wouldn't recommend drinking it, but otherwise the water's fine. It won't rot your skin off if that's what you're worried about." She took the few steps to the water's edge, stripped off her glove and dipped her hand into the filthy stream. "See any rotting flesh?" she asked, displaying her outstretched hand.

He didn't, but her hand was covered in a thick, dirty slime all the same.

"Anyway," she said, wiping the slime down her thigh. "We're not going in naked. As for the horse, well, you'll recall I was against bringing it from the start."

"If you don't get swept away in there, you'll freeze."

She just ignored him.

Gift stayed by Rab's side, observing with intense silence as Sunny shrugged off her coat and laid it flat on the ground. Delving inside her clothing, she removed wad after wad of the crumpled paper and stacked it all in a pile in the centre of the coat. Sitting on the edge of the coat, she proceeded to remove her footwear. Once everything was bundled together inside the coat, Sunny strapped the package to the side of her pack beside the gun.

"What's she doing?" Gift asked in a sharp, shocked voice. "She's going in barefoot!"

Rab shrugged. "If her boots get wet, they're likely to stay wet and then her feet will freeze. It's the only way to get across."

Gift looked up at him, clearly sceptical. "If you say so," she said, "but I'm not taking off my boots."

Rab wasn't happy about it either, but Sunny was right.

Without a word Sunny hoisted the pack above her head and began to ford the river. She made an easy start and, for a while, Rab was beginning to think he'd misjudged the river's strength. But by the time she was midstream, he changed his mind. Obliged to fight both the sucking mud of the riverbed and the quickly flowing stream, she struggled to keep the pack above her head. Still the river was much shallower than Rab had expected and, at its deepest, only reached as high as Sunny's chest. When she forded the worst part of the river without incident, Gift breathed a sigh of relief. Slipping and sliding in the muck, Sunny reached the opposite bank and turned around to face them, a mud-covered, sodden mess.

"So," he said, turning to Gift, "what do you say?"

She shook her head. "That water will be over my head," she reminded him soberly, then suddenly brightened. "Maybe I could ride on Kix. That way I wouldn't have to take my boots off."

When he'd seen the waters only rise to Sunny's chest, the same thought had briefly crossed Rab's mind, too. But what if the horse panicked? Then both of them would be carried downstream.

"How about you ride on my shoulders instead? Kix will have enough to worry about with the packs. But you'll still have to take off your boots; I don't think I can keep your feet from dangling in the water."

He didn't dare share his fears that the horse might not make it at all or tell Gift that he would have to cross the river more than once; Braham wouldn't be able to guide the horse by himself and they simply couldn't lose those packs.

"All right," Gift said at last and sloughed off her small pack.

Rab dumped his own onto the ground. "We'll have to leave these for Kix," he said. "I can't keep you and the packs out of the water."

He looked for and spotted Braham and his horse still some distance away, leaving him enough time to take Gift over and return before the old man reached the bank and took it in his head to attempt to ford the river alone.

Copying Sunny, Rab removed his coat, boots and the wadded up balls of paper. Gift dropped down beside him and began to remove her own boots as he'd instructed. He hadn't asked her to do it, but she stripped off her coat as well. Without the coat, she'd be easier for him to carry. Instantly she began to shiver; he could hear her teeth rattling. Or perhaps they were his own.

Gift had kept her gloves on, but he'd have to remove his; they were the only ones he had. With stiff fingers he worked to secure the wads of paper and their coats, boots, and his gloves to their packs. He couldn't remember ever feeling so cold and he hadn't even started across the river yet. How could he possibly cross it twice?

"Ready?" he asked.

Gift climbed clumsily onto his shoulders, throwing him momentarily off balance.

He weighed a lot more than Sunny and now had Gift's added weight as well. Time and time again, his bare feet became stuck in the greasy mud of the bank and he stumbled so often, Gift could easily have toppled from his back. Once he made it into the water, the going wasn't quite so hard; the flow of the river seemed to have scoured the bed somewhat, providing a better foothold. By the time he was waist high though, the current had started to work against him. The filthy eddies of slime that raced at him, then washed around his sides, threatened to suck him downstream. Gift had managed to hold on so far, but no matter how well he thought he'd compensated, the water's unpredictable surge kept upsetting his balance. The next surge broadsided him into the water and sent Gift catapulting from his shoulders. Head submerged, he reached out blindly to grab her, but his hands only closed on rushing water.

Gift was gone.

Panic stricken, Rab struggled to his feet in the muck, frantically searching. He heard splashing but realised quickly that the noise had come from across the bank, so ignored it. His thoughts were only on Gift. He couldn't lose her—not now—not like this. Suddenly he saw something bobbing in the water downstream. It was too big to be Gift, but he began to thrash once more, intent on reaching that something anyway. If the something was a rock, maybe Gift had managed to grab hold. Fighting his way closer, he saw at last that the thing bobbing up and down in the stream was Sunny. Again and again, she disappeared beneath the water and resurfaced. The current was dragging her downstream and no matter how hard he fought, Rab couldn't seem to reach her. Neither he nor Gift could swim; it didn't look as though Sunny could either because she was being swept into deeper and deeper water. She surfaced again, only this time, Rab could see not one head, but two. She'd come up from the bottom with Gift. He couldn't help her, couldn't get to her. Both she and Gift were flailing, heads bobbing in and out of sight in the murky water.

He stopped struggling and planted his feet as firmly as he could in the slime of the riverbed. The water was washing over his shoulders now and he had to stroke with his arms just to stay upright. Downstream, Sunny and Gift still bumped up and down, but with each bump they seemed to be gaining on the bank. He could see Sunny's shoulders now—her waist.

It was going to be all right.

Rab took off directly for the bank. He slipped and slid and fell, then fell again. Staggering out of the water, he looked downstream to discover that he'd made it out ahead of Sunny and Gift. Barefooted, he battled his way through clinging, caking mud, reaching Sunny just as she was grappling for a handhold in the sodden bank. With a rough jerk on her arm, he pulled her the last of the way out; Gift came along behind, her clothing bunched fast in Sunny's free hand. No one had the breath to speak.

As Sunny dragged herself up the bank, Rab grabbed a hold of Gift. It hadn't even occurred to him until then that Sunny might have only succeeded in returning with a dead child. But Gift began to splutter and heave and a stream of dirty water gushed from her mouth onto the ground.

Perhaps it wasn't going to be so all right after all; both she and Sunny had swallowed the filth of the river. Behind him, he could hear Sunny spitting out water as well. He hadn't managed to swallow any of it but that was little compensation if Gift became sick and died.

Rab struggled to his feet, bringing Gift up with him. He glanced back to find Sunny, lying flat on her back, her whole body heaving as she laboured to gulp air. Gift seemed to be recovering faster, but then Sunny had been out of coat and boots the longest of any of them. Her lips were blue and her cheek was bleeding again profusely. Rab scanned the bank for her pack, but they'd been dragged so far downstream he couldn't immediately see it. Settling Gift farther up the bank on firmer ground, he sped off to find Sunny's pack. As he ran, he searched the opposite bank, hoping for a glimpse of Braham and the horse.

He spotted the pack and his missing companions at almost the same moment.

"Stay there," he yelled, desperate to catch Braham's attention.

The old man was standing motionless on the other side of the river with his hand wrapped around Kix's straps. Rab didn't know if he'd witnessed Gift's rescue or not, but the last thing he needed was for the old man to strike out into the water before he'd had time to see to Sunny and Gift.

"I'm coming over for you and Kix," Rab called, then pointed downstream. "Your granddaughter and Gift are down there. I need to get them dry clothes. Understand?"

The old man waved back. Confident that he'd heard, Rab set about retrieving Sunny's pack. As he rushed back downstream, he loosened the fastenings on the pack and glanced every so often towards the opposite bank to check on the old man.

"You'd better see to her." Sunny was back on her feet, jumping up and down on the spot, but stopped long enough to snatch the pack from his hands. "And put this on her." Diving her hand into the pack, she flung something towards Rab.

He lobbed it back immediately. "You do it. I've got to get your grandfather."

His feet were beginning to freeze; he could barely feel his fingers anymore; and he still had to cross the river two more times. There wasn't a moment to waste. Without Gift to throw him off balance, the crossing was easier, but even before he reached the middle of the stream, his legs had gone completely numb. Determination alone lent him the strength to push on against the current and drag his feet up and out of the mud of the river bottom over and over again.

"No," he yelled, seeing the old man about to head into the river, "go back."

He heaved himself onto the bank, oblivious to most pain except the burning in his lungs whenever he tried to breathe. "The horse," he gasped and it felt like his ribs were about to crack. "You've got to get the packs higher up on its back."

That was all he had wind for; if the old man hadn't understood, Rab simply couldn't repeat it, every muscle in his face had seized. Something came down on his shoulders—the old man's coat. It wasn't much but better than nothing dry at all. He could hear the old man behind him, releasing the horse's restraints.

"How high?" Braham asked. "The water? How high?"

Rab couldn't answer for a fit of painful coughing. When the fit was over, he felt better. He might have swallowed some of the dirty water as well, but he didn't think so. At least he could now stagger onto his feet, although he had to lean against the side of the horse for support.

"Strap the packs tight," he said, then looked around to find the packs they'd abandoned before the first crossing. "They've got to stay out of the water."

The packs weren't anywhere in sight.

"Where are the—"

"I've got them. Yours and the little girl's. They're already up here on Kix," Braham said, then slipped to the ground and began removing his boots. "She could have warned us," he muttered. "We could have prepared much better."

Rab glanced down at the old man, a sudden thought surfacing. "Maybe that was the idea."

The old man faltered a moment, then returned to removing his boots.

"No," he told Rab with an adamant shake of his head. "That isn't her way. Besides she's been here before. She knows it can be done."

As the old man got to his feet, Rab shrugged off his coat and began to tuck it firmly under the packs that were now sitting high on Kix's back.

"You can't know that for certain," he said. The coat secured, he grasped the old man's shoulder. "I overheard what you said back there in Kix's stall. I know she was the only one to come back. Just when were they here? I asked her but she wouldn't answer."

"Oh, a long time ago. Sunny was ten years old when they set out," Braham replied with a scratch of his head. "Eleven maybe."

Rab's people weren't moved to tally their lifespan year by year, but they still appreciated the passing of time and how dramatically time could change everything.

"Eleven? She'd only seen eleven snow times?"

The old man nodded. "Why?"

"How?"

"What do you—"

"How did someone that young manage to survive out here all alone and find her way back home?"

"Sunny's smart."

"No kid is that smart. She had help." After one last wrench on Kix's straps to satisfy himself that everything was secure, Rab turned to look back at Braham.

The old man had paled.

"It's a pity you didn't think to ask then because I'd sure like to know who it was now." He gave Braham a shove. "Get going," he said, "before we freeze here to the spot."

Wordlessly, the old man took his place on the left side of the horse and began to lead it into the water. Rab stumbled to his station on the right, then twisted his hand firmly, painfully into the horse's straps. When his bare feet touched the water again, he felt nothing.

He had to give Braham credit; the old man took more than his share of the burden, leaning heavily against Kix's side, forcing it to plod a straight line through the river. Barely needing to shove from the other side, Rab could devote most of his attention to keeping the packs clear of the water. It couldn't have been easy for Braham; perhaps Rab had done him an unintentional favour, diverting his attention from the challenge of the river with his suspicions about Sunny's survival. Hard to believe the old man hadn't ever wondered about it himself. Maybe he just never wanted to think about it. Maybe he already knew the answer and his concern wasn't about how Sunny had done it, but how Rab thought she had done it. In truth, Rab had no idea.

They were nearing the muddy opposite bank of the river and it was there Rab feared that the horse stood the best chance of slipping or, worse, taking a tumble sideways knocking either him or the old man into the water. Rab wasn't up for a second rescue attempt and likely Sunny wasn't, either. While she might try to save her grandfather, she'd almost certainly allow the horse to be flushed downstream. Rab tightened his hold on Kix's straps; the horse bucked and protested but no worse than it had throughout the whole crossing. The beast was too compliant, its spirit already sapped. Three days ago, he couldn't see Kix going so meekly flank high into the water. Although its submissiveness was a bonus at the moment, ultimately it was an extremely bad omen. Rab tried not to think about that as they emerged onto the opposite bank; he'd grown quite fond of the horse. Old Kix took one stumble, but with the aid of Rab and the old man, righted itself and staggered out of the water.

Sunny was there to meet them; she'd changed her clothes and had Gift swathed, head to foot, in a coat Rab had never seen before. Predictably, she offered no assistance with the horse, but made a lunge for one of the packs and began to delve inside. The woman had a good eye and a good memory; she'd honed in on Gift's pack right away. Rab, on the other hand, couldn't seem to recognise his own pack among the jumble on the horse's back. In fact, he was becoming more and more light-headed.

Something was thrust into his hand—the pack. And someone was shaking him vigorously by the shoulder—Sunny. She was talking at him, too, but try as he might Rab really couldn't grasp what she was saying. Suddenly Gift's voice broke through into the haze. Something about wet clothes. Yes, that's right, he remembered. Sunny was getting dry clothes out of her pack. He felt a violent tug on his arms and then seemed to be sliding along on his back. When had he fallen over?

"Do something," he heard a voice wail close to his ear. "Please do something."

***

Rab felt warm and, strangely, something else he'd never felt before—safe. A constant nagging at the back of his mind told him that he had no right to be feeling that way. But he didn't want to give in to that nagging. It was better to stay where he was, better to stay safe and warm in the darkness. The nagging became a distant voice that, in the beginning, was easy to ignore. But the voice kept growing louder, dragging him with irritating insistence towards the light. Rab didn't want to go, it was pleasant there in the dark.

"Wake up, Rab. Wake up."

He wasn't asleep, just safe for the first time in his life. Why couldn't they leave him alone? But it did seem that there was something he was supposed to be doing—somewhere he was supposed to be going.

"Let him sleep," someone said, a man. "He'll come to in his own time."

"The child is right."

A woman's voice now. Rab struggled but failed to recognise it.

"The sooner he gets up and moving, the better off he'll be. Besides he needs to eat now."

The dark slipped further and further away. Rab tried to hold on to it, but it just wouldn't stay. A face drifted in front of his eyes—Gift's worried face. Where had she been all this time?

"He's awake." The sound of her voice almost deafened him.

He struggled onto his elbows—strange—it shouldn't be so difficult just to get up from the ground. The ground! He was lying flat out on the ground.

Behind Gift, another face hung suspended in the air but refused to remain in focus. Its lips appeared to be moving.

"Finally," it said. "Sunny says you have to eat now. We have an early start in the morning."

A rough tug on his arm brought Rab upright. He recalled something then—the river—and Gift's head bobbing along on the surface, rushing away from him. No—that was earlier. Kix! He and the old man had guided the horse safely across the river. But what had happened after that? He couldn't seem to remember.

Rab glanced around, curious about his surroundings. In front of him, Gift was perched on bent knees, staring into his face and smiling. Behind her, the old man and his horse slowly came into focus.

"You were out for a long time," Gift said to him, inching closer.

Her hand drifted past his face. Something felt warm at his back.

"You went completely blue," she said, the smile broadening. "But you're better now, aren't you?"

Better than what? Rab wondered. His attention wandered from Gift towards his clothes.

"They changed them," Gift said. "You were covered in mud. But then I guess we all were." She sidled a little closer. "Sunny was really mad," she whispered. "She said that no one was supposed to help anyone else, so you should never have gone back across to get her grandfather." She shrugged. "Didn't stop her from rescuing me though, did it? Sunny doesn't make a lot of sense sometimes. Here."

She reached out and took a hold of his hand.

"Sunny made food. Take it. It's nice and warm."

Rab's hands closed around the familiar shape of one of Sunny's bowls.

"How. . ." he began to say, then recalled the warmth he'd felt at his back. Turning, he glanced over his shoulder to discover Sunny on her knees, tending a modest fire.

Rab's thoughts flicked quickly to Gift, when something the old man had said flooded back to him. *Stay valuable and Sunny will do all she can to keep you alive.* Just days ago, the little girl had been nothing but an unwanted, unwelcome nuisance. Today Sunny had risked her own life to save her.

"I told you she'd been here before."

Rab swung back around. Horse in tow, the old man had come up to stand directly behind Gift.

"You should be grateful," he said. "It took her a long time to get that wood and come back here with it. Of course," he said with a smile and a gentle thump on Kix's flank, "it would have taken her a whole lot longer without our friend here." His hand wandered to Kix's hanging strap. "You should be grateful to them both," he said, leading the horse past Rab in the direction of Sunny's fire.

"It's true," Gift said, prompting him to eat with a prod of the bowl in his hand. "After she'd seen to our wet clothes, she stripped the packs from Kix's back and took off with him over there." She pointed past Rab's shoulder. "She didn't tell us where she was going of course or why, but just like he said, she came back with the horse and all that wood. Then she made us all food and started to dry out the wet clothes. She's been doing it ever since."

Rab glanced over his shoulder again. Sunny must have heard every word her grandfather and Gift had said, but she just leaned in towards the fire to stretch her hands out over the flames.

"She knew the wood would be there all along," Rab said absently.

"I guess so."

"No more talking." Sunny rose from her task at the fire and looked their way. "You know everything that's happened now," she said. "There's nothing else to tell. You finish eating and let that girl get some sleep. There'll be no more rivers, but there'll be no more wood, either. So you'd better make the most of it tonight. From here on, things get harder."

If he'd felt up to it, Rab would have got onto his feet, strode over to where Sunny was standing and punched her. Perhaps he had actually attempted to rise, because suddenly he felt the pressure of Gift's hand on his thigh.

"Don't," she said softly. "She saved our lives, Rab. Both of us." She leaned towards him then and her lips brushed against his ear. "I don't like her either, but she knows the way. She must."

Rab couldn't argue with that. Although she'd repeatedly denied its very existence, Sunny did indeed seem to know the way to the City—just like the old man had said. Fine, let Braham be right. Rab had no problem with that. In fact, it was a lot better that way. At least they wouldn't be wasting their time and worse, precious resources, in blind and empty searches. But if the City did exist, then why did Sunny protest so adamantly that it didn't? And if it didn't, then where exactly was she taking them? And why was she so secretive about the journey? She could have told them about the river before they'd left the tunnel city. If she'd thought that knowing they'd have to cross the river might dissuade them from setting out in the first place, it would have only suited her purpose—after all, she didn't really want to go. And then there was her knowledge about the cache of wood. She'd kept that from them, too.

"All right," Rab said, reaching out to ruffle Gift's hair. His little companion did look exhausted. "We'll do what she says for now. You go over to the fire." He held up the bowl in his hands. "I'll just finish this and then come over and join you."

Gift nodded and got to her feet. Rab watched her go. She'd only been partially right before; most of the time Sunny didn't make a lot of sense.

***

In the two days since they'd crossed the river, Sunny's pace had noticeably slowed. Never a great communicator, she was now confining herself to the odd grunt or two when they stopped to eat their one meal of the day and snatch some abbreviated rest. The side of her face had swollen and it looked like her eye might be starting to close up. Her thirst seemed abnormal as well; twice now Rab had caught her sneaking a drink from her pack outside their scheduled ration period. It wasn't as though he minded the peace her heightened moodiness provided, but that, and their slackened progress did give him cause for concern. Snow time drew nearer each day.

But at least he could now lend a hand to the old man without the constant threat of losing complete sight of his companions. And Sunny's grandfather was definitely in need of his help; Kix had developed a worrying stagger and constantly required the encouragement and support of them both. So far Rab had left care of the horse entirely up to the old man, but last evening, when he decided to thoroughly inspect the horse himself, he was shocked at what he found. Not only were both of its hind legs badly inflamed, but the wounds it had sustained mounting the steps to the plateau had turned an angry red and were weeping some sort of cloudy fluid. He didn't berate the old man; Braham had enough of his own problems and likely hadn't even noticed. Old men simply weren't equipped for hard journeys. Old horses weren't, either. Rab had a passing thought to mention Kix's condition to Sunny, but quickly decided against it. She'd warned them not to bring the horse and wouldn't care much that it was dying. And Rab was certain that it was dying. The polluted river water had got into its wounds, turned them bad. There was no coming back from that. Rab had seen more of his people sicken and die as a result of a simple scratch or shallow puncture than he cared to remember.

He didn't reveal his discovery to Gift either, although she seemed to sense something was wrong, and that night she'd spent an overly long time with Kix before settling down to sleep. In the darkness, its wounds wouldn't have been noticeable unless she was specifically looking for them. When the sullen day broke this morning, Rab took great pains to ensure that she didn't approach too close to the horse. He lingered behind with Braham, only starting out after Sunny and Gift had put some distance between them.

How were they going to manage without the horse? The old man wouldn't be able to carry one pack, let alone take on a share of the others and Sunny had made it quite clear that everyone was to be responsible for their own load. When the time came, it was doubtful she'd have a change of heart.

As they trudged across the barren ground together, every now and then Rab glanced over the back of the failing horse to check on the old man.

"How do we know that Sunny is leading us in the right direction?" Rab asked finally.

"The wind here always blows from the north, lad. As long as we keep heading into the wind, we keep heading north and north's where we'll find the City."

"Will it be much further?"

"Wouldn't know," the old man replied, his eyes fixed on the two, now some distance in front of them. "Sunny never spoke much about it."

The horse staggered, almost bringing Rab down. He righted himself and turned again to the old man.

"You must remember how long she was gone—how many days."

"Days!" Braham answered with a snort. "I think you've misunderstood, lad. Sunny was gone eight years."

Rab pulled up in his tracks. Again the horse staggered. "What? We can't go on that long! There isn't enough food, water—"

The old man laughed. "You're a great one for jumping to conclusions, aren't you? I didn't mean it took her that long to get there and back, only that she was gone that long. But then, I guess you weren't to know that Sunny had been a captive of the Top-siders. It's not something she likes to talk about."

"I've yet to find much she does like to talk about," Rab said. "And you could have told me that before. I asked you who helped her get home."

"I don't know who helped her escape, or whether she managed it by herself," Braham replied. "One day she just came back all alone. I asked what had happened to her father, of course, but she refused to answer." He shrugged. "Maybe she really didn't remember. Or maybe she just chose not to remember. All I know is that everyone else who set out to find the City died—including my son."

"What makes you think everyone died? I mean if Sunny wouldn't talk about it. . ."

"Just look around, what else could have happened?"

Rab shook his head, it seemed the old man had a tendency to jump to conclusions, too. "So your son believed in the existence of the City then?"

"Of course. And so did Sunny once—when she was little. It was only after she came back that she began insisting that it was all lies. That there never was any plan called Safe Harbour after the Pluming and that there never were any launch pads."

"The Pluming." Rab rolled the words around on his tongue. "You've used those words before but I've never heard of it."

"Son, you don't need to have heard of it," the old man said and laughed again. "You're living it. What do you think happened to this planet?"

"The people of my village said the ground went bad."

"That's what they said, is it? Well, I guess you could say that it did. But then I don't suppose the people of your village ever questioned why for fear of being branded a back-thinker. The Pluming, lad. It was because of the Pluming! Something that started long before you or I were even born."

"When?" Rab asked. Maybe the old man was just talking gibberish. Maybe. "When did it start?"

Braham hesitated a moment before answering. "It's not a matter of when exactly, but how long the Pluming has been going on. The world is millions and millions of years old."

Rab shook his head, a gesture Kix seemed to interpret as threatening. It pulled immediately to the right and Rab had a struggle to set it back on a straight path.

"That can't be right," he said, once the horse had settled again. "The world wasn't always like this. That's probably the one thing my father and the people in my village ever agreed on. So if this 'Pluming', as you call it, has been going on for millions of years, then why is the world suddenly so different now?"

On the opposite side of Kix, Braham had his own problems as Kix's stride was becoming increasingly unpredictable.

"You've just answered your own question," the old man said at last, "and I can assure you there was nothing sudden about it. But you are right about one thing though—the world wasn't always like this," he said, giving Kix an encouraging pat. "In fact, the world wasn't always like anything. It's constantly changing and it has never been completely one thing or another. When this last event started? Who really knows? Not long though, that's for sure, but Pluming itself is hardly something new. It just happens that you and I are around for the worst one. I guess you might call us unlucky."

The old man could certainly understate.

"Some of the books say that about some seventy thousand years ago, there was an eruption in Indonesia that nearly wiped us all out." He glanced towards Rab to qualify. "But that kind of pales into insignificance now and Toba, I think they called it, wasn't caused by a superplume. Still, what followed the eruption was a volcanic winter," with his free hand, he indicated the desolate landscape, "not all that dissimilar to the one we have now. But when you blow out a good chunk of Africa—well you've got to expect something a little more spectacular that'll last a whole lot longer. It'll see us out I'm afraid. And very fitting too, wouldn't you agree? I mean we came out of Africa; it was our cradle. It's kind of appropriate that it should end up being our tomb."

Rab snorted. "Old man, I think you're completely mad. Indonesia! Africa! If those places are so important, why haven't I heard of them?"

"You hadn't heard of a horse before, either, had you? Your village didn't have books, lad. You couldn't write and you couldn't read. But take my word for it. Maybe they were a long way from here, but those places did exist. And in Edward Braham's time, on the east coast of Africa, not one but a whole series of volcanoes began to erupt. And if Edward was right, and I've yet to find him wrong about anything, then they're still erupting to this day, spilling liquid rock from far below onto the surface."

Incredulous, Rab glanced at the old man over the top of Kix's heavy burden. "And that caused all this? Liquid rock?"

"Not the rock itself, but what comes with it. Ash and gases that are carried right across the world to block out the sun and poison the water. It's just what we've got right now, isn't it? Have you ever really seen the sun in the sky? And what about the stars at night? Don't tell me you don't believe in stars now, because I know you do. You talked to me about them. I might be old but my memory hasn't failed me yet. And then there's water. Can you drink water from the rivers? No, of course you can't. And what happened to all the trees? They must have been here once, otherwise Sunny wouldn't have been able to make that nice fire for you the other night. Think about that for a while and then try to tell me that I'm wrong."

"Well, maybe that part does make some kind of sense, but," Rab stopped for a moment to stamp his foot on the ground, "rock isn't liquid. It's solid."

Braham just smiled at him. "Not under heat and pressure, it isn't. Ice is solid, too, but squeeze some of it in your hand and see what happens."

The old man was as stubborn as they come. "All right, then," Rab said. "So where does this liquid rock come from?"

"Like I told you, from far beneath the surface. Oh, it's a real pity you didn't ask me these questions before. I could have shown you such books in the library. There are things you just wouldn't believe."

"You've got that right," Rab said, but the old man wasn't listening.

"You see it's like this," he continued, "way, way down the earth is a sort of liquid. At the centre is the core, and the inner part of that is solid I'll grant you, but the rest is very hot and liquid. Outside of that is the mantle and, outside of that, well there's you and me and every living thing just sitting on this thin, solid crust. And the heat from below is kind of steering us around on rafts made up of the crust and the very top of the mantle. Understand? Those volcanoes, the ones in Africa, well those eruptions came up all the way from the deep mantle, maybe even the core, and punched right through the thin layer of crust. It's what they call a plume. Understand now? Kind of a passage in the mantle that allows the heat from the core to rise. Now those volcanoes aren't just sitting on any old everyday plume—what those volcanoes are sitting on is a superplume."

"Plume! Superplume!" Rab said with exasperation. "I wouldn't know and I don't really care because frankly, I can't see that it matters much what caused it. You said that the world is always changing, that things like this have happened before. And if you're right, it seems to me that what's really important is what's so different now? If we made it through then, why aren't we making it through now?"

When the old man stopped to answer, Kix's step faltered slightly but, like Rab, he seemed grateful for the moment of rest.

"You heard what I said about Toba?" Braham said, leaning over the packs to look at Rab directly. "Toba wasn't sitting on a superplume. Anyway, lad, you're right not to fret too much about the cause of it. It doesn't matter now because we're going to get out, leave it behind us at last. So what exactly prompted us to leave doesn't really matter. And as I see it, there isn't much point concerning ourselves with what we're leaving behind, either. This planet was here a long time before we came along in some form or other and it'll be here a long time after we're gone in forms we couldn't even imagine. I mean just because this can't be our world any longer, doesn't mean it can't be a world for something else. And if it can change and go on, then what's to stop us? In fact, we must. There's a whole new world ahead of us now, so it's enough that you believe something happened and that some people were smart enough to see it coming and prepare. Sunny there doesn't believe. Oh, don't get me wrong, she believes in the Pluming all right, but she simply refuses to believe that the people before us were willing or loyal enough to have worked together even for their own salvation."

Rab wasn't about to admit it to the old man, but there were times, many times during his life when he thought the very same thing. They were alike in some ways—he and Sunny.

"I think you should go on ahead and get Sunny," Braham said unexpectedly; his hand was gently stroking Kix's head. "My old friend needs her medicines now."

Rab glanced at the horse's hind legs. Since they'd started out this morning, he'd consciously avoided looking at the nasty wounds. He saw now that they'd grown much, much worse and, when he put a hand to the horse's flank, even through his glove he could feel that the beast was burning up.

"It won't help," he told Braham with a shake of his head. "Besides, she might not be willing to share them with a horse."

The old man's smile was cheerless. "You go ask her for it now anyway and I'll wait here with Kix."

"Why me? She's more likely to give it to you."

"She isn't likely to give it to either of us but we have to try and it won't make much difference who asks. I want to stay here with Kix."

"All right."

Dropping Kix's strap, Rab sped off to intercept Sunny, knowing from the outset that it was pointless. Nothing could help the old horse any longer.

Gift must have heard him coming, because she'd left Sunny and was walking back to him very quickly.

"What's wrong?" she called.

Ahead, Sunny stopped to turn around.

For Gift's sake, Rab tried to soften the blow.

"Kix isn't feeling very well and the old man wants some of Sunny's medicine."

"I knew it."

Before Rab could stop her, Gift rushed past him, making for Kix and the old man.

"So it's happened, has it?" Sunny said, walking towards Rab. "Well, I guess we got a few days of use out of the brute."

Perhaps he and Sunny weren't quite so alike after all!

Right from the start, he'd realised that Kix stood a slim chance of making it all the way to the City. But even then he'd known that, when the time came, it wasn't in him to just casually let go of the old horse. Maybe heat and pressure could melt the ground beneath him, but nothing, it seemed, could melt the heart of the young woman standing in front of him.

"Your grandfather wants some of your medicine for the horse," Rab said, "and if it comes down to a vote, then mine's with the old man."

"It doesn't," Sunny said simply and pushed right past him, heading for the others.

The horse was on the ground by the time Rab returned. Braham and Gift were on the ground with it, soothing hands trying to coax the beast back onto its feet. It wasn't going to happen. Rab could see that and as she stood there, looming over Kix's head, it was plain that Sunny had seen it, too.

Roughly, she reached down and dragged Gift to her feet. "Stop that," she told the girl. "It's time. The horse knows it and so should you. That goes for you too, old man. Get up."

"No," Braham said, frantically shaking his head. And, with each stubborn swing, another tear rolled down his cheek to splash on the horse's head.

With a quick jerk of her arm, Sunny lifted and aimed that ugly gun of hers. From the mouth of it, there came a loud and unexpected crack that set Rab's ears ringing and his heart racing. He looked down, horrified to see a hole blown right through the top of the horse's head.

She was as good a shot as her grandfather claimed.

Rab was almost brought down when Gift suddenly flung herself at his legs. Speechless, he turned to find Sunny standing beside the dead horse. She bent, laid the gun on the ground, then set about removing the straps that circled the animal's belly.

At last Rab found his voice. "What kind of evil people are you to even think of making something like that gun?"

"We carry the load ourselves now," Sunny said, rising with one of the packs in her hand.

Rab's focus darted to the old man. He was still sitting there, folded over, pale and silent, a figure locked motionless in space and time. Gift was quietly sobbing. But for the horse at least, a pitiful struggle was over.

"We're not stopping to bury it." Sunny started to amble away, but stopped suddenly and swung around. "On second thought. . ."

Her stride as she returned seemed too purposeful, the expression on her face too callous.

"Get up on your feet, old man," she snapped. "The horse is dead and you should be thanking me for making death so easy for it. If you're lucky, I'll do the same for you. Now get up. There's use in that beast yet." Her attention shifted to Rab. With a familiarly irritating flourish, she flung the gun over her shoulder and smiled. "I'm betting you've never tasted—"

Rab didn't let her finish; he'd instantly realised what she was about to say—and do.

"Shut up!" he roared, then smacked her hard—really hard—across the mouth.

He was shaking uncontrollably when he reached down, disentangled Gift from his legs and took her hand.

Sooner or later, he was going to pay for what he'd done. Sooner or later. But Sunny wasn't one to act rashly. She planned well, so it was enough for the moment to have her walk off in silence. If Sunny were the rash type, there was little doubt he'd be wearing a hole in his own head right now.

The old man hadn't budged, his hand still frozen where it had been resting against the ropy neck of the horse. He seemed unaware of Rab's presence.

Rab reached down to touch his shoulder and Braham twitched a little in response.

"Get up, John. It's over. There's nothing you can do for it now. You must have known Kix was likely to die."

Slowly the old man's reddened eyes turned up to look at Rab. The tears had ended. Rab was thankful for that at least; Gift's tears were enough for them all.

"Didn't die," the old man said, surprising Rab with the clarity and strength of his voice.

He snubbed Rab's offer of assistance and came to his feet unaided. Standing now, Rab sensed a power and a determination he'd never seen in the old man before; something he hadn't expected to see now.

"She killed him," Braham said and made to push on past.

Rab grabbed a hold of his sleeve.

"You told me that gun of hers didn't work," he said, challenging Braham to deny it.

It wasn't tears he saw in the old man's eyes, but rage, when he deftly shook off Rab's hold and rushed off after Sunny.

Chapter 11

RAB'S impulse was to chase after the old man, but this wasn't his fight, although more than ever now it was his problem. Sunny had only taken one of the packs; despite the load having been lightened by the food they'd already eaten, neither Braham nor Gift could carry a full load and that left only Rab to take the place of the dead horse.

He turned to find Gift, not surprised when he discovered her diligently removing the remaining packs from beneath the loosened straps. He joined her on the ground by the dead horse.

"Here," he said, wrenching the last of the stubborn straps free. "That's got it." He flung the end of the strap aside and immediately Gift got to her feet and began an earnest struggle to pull the rest of the straps out from under the horse.

"What are you doing?" Rab asked. "All the packs are off." He stood, intending to draw Gift away.

"Kix is free now," she said, brushing at a stubborn tear. "He doesn't want all this tripping him up."

For a moment Rab simply stared at her then, nudging Gift aside and taking the end of the strap from her hand, gave it an almighty tug, wrenching it loose and almost toppling himself backward in the process. At first he hadn't fully understood Gift's meaning, but when he glanced at the horse's long face, the life-weary expression he'd grown so accustomed to seeing wasn't there. Maybe Gift was right. What did he know?

As she bent to pat their silent companion, Rab set about gathering the straps, thinking they might prove useful in the future. As he stuffed the balled up lengths of cloth into his own half-filled pack, Gift walked up.

"She had to do it, Rab. I know that. Her medicines couldn't have helped him. I don't blame her and you shouldn't either."

"I don't blame her for what she did, Gift," Rab said, glancing up as he blindly secured his pack, "only how she did it." He got to his feet. "She could have sent you and the old man away first, but it never even entered her mind." Secretly Rab suspected that having Gift and the old man witness the death of the horse gave Sunny perverse pleasure. "And I'm not too happy with that old man, either. He told me that gun of Sunny's didn't work anymore."

"Maybe that's what she told him."

Rab shrugged.

"What is it anyway, Rab? That thing? Do you know?"

"I've never seen anything like it," he answered, coming to his feet. "We've got to move on." He nodded ahead. "Sunny's not waiting for anyone."

Gift turned to study the collection of packs still lying about the body of the horse.

"How are we going to carry all this?" she asked, looking back at Rab. "Sunny's grandfather didn't take his. I could shove everything from mine into one of these and carry it instead. I'm sure I can, but you can't carry the other three as well as your own."

No—not day in, day out, he couldn't.

"Go through the old man's packs," he said. "Throw out everything but the food and water."

"Everything?"

"Yes, everything." Dropping to the ground, he reached for one of Braham's packs. "Everything that can't be eaten."

"Like this?"

Rab looked over at Gift. When he saw that she was holding up one of the old man's books, he thought twice. Paper was useful, but paper was also heavy.

"Throw it," he said, making a quick decision. Sunny was leaving them farther and farther behind.

In the pack he was sorting, Rab found a pair of sturdy boots. It pained him to toss them aside. The thick shirt he kept, but apart from food and water, that was all.

"Here," Gift said, coming to his side, arms laden with the foodstuff she'd gathered. "That pack's empty now. Will all this fit in the one you've got?"

"I'll make it," Rab said, stuffing in the items all at once. He didn't have time to waste balancing the load. Tonight, when they stopped, he could repack.

"If I take one, that leaves two," Gift said. "Can you carry three packs again?"

"Until we catch up with Braham. If you can carry one, so can he," he said and got to his feet, the pack slung over his shoulder. "Now go find the lightest pack."

Gift simply grabbed the closest.

"You can't—"

Gift cut him off. "I'm fine," she said. "And each day, it'll only get lighter."

It would that—and as each day passed, they'd trade a little of the weight on their back for more and more on their minds. Even when they won, they lost.

"All right. Just take it for the moment. We don't have time to argue."

Sunny was becoming a speck in the distance and the old man was still hurrying to catch up with her. He didn't stand a chance.

"What's she trying to do?" Gift asked.

Rab shook his head. "Just go," he said. "She can't keep up that pace."

When he stooped to gather the last pack, Rab almost tumbled over. Gift hadn't noticed; she'd taken off after the crazy old man and his even crazier granddaughter. Clearly, she was struggling with her load, but there was nothing he could do about that now. As he passed by the head of old Kix, Rab spared their lost friend one last glance. The blood had stopped oozing from its head and the pool on the ground had nearly disappeared completely, leaving only a dark, irregularly shaped stain. He almost envied the silent beast. Was this what it took to win freedom? Enough suffering? Enough hardship? He truly hoped Gift was right—that Kix was finally free.

He looked up to find Gift striding ahead. She was a little like Kix; the two seemed to share the tenacity of a single soul. Only age separated them. The beast had gone on until he dropped, and so would Gift.

"Are you coming, Rab?"

The pack she was carrying was so large, Gift couldn't even turn her head to call.

"I'm here," he sang back.

Either Sunny was slowing down or he and Gift were managing the packs better than he had hoped. The old man was gaining on her as well. He was stumbling though, faring worse than Gift despite the lack of a burden. Rab wasn't sure he could successfully off-load one of the packs onto Braham, but he really had no alternative. The muscles in his shoulders already burned and his knees buckled with each step.

"Sunny's slowing down," Gift said when Rab reached her.

There'd have been little point to her journey if she didn't. This was the old man's mission, not hers, and it still baffled Rab why she'd muscled herself into it in the first place. He doubted it was to safeguard the old man as she'd claimed.

They were almost on the old man. He'd be played out by the time he reached his granddaughter and that had probably been Sunny's intent all along.

"Wait up," Rab called. "You have to take this pack."

The old man stopped and turned around.

"What?" he rasped.

"Your pack. Take your pack."

The old man just stood there, vacant of expression.

Rab shrugged and one of the packs slipped down his stiff arm to the ground.

"Pick it up, old man."

He didn't wait around for a response or to see how Braham fared hefting the load.

Gift hurried up to his side. "He took it," she whispered.

Rab nodded.

He felt sorry for the old man. He felt sorry for them all—everyone but Sunny, who was still striding out ahead of them, packs slung either side of her back with that loud and worrying gun resting comfortably between.

***

The old man and his granddaughter had argued throughout their evening meal, but it really didn't amount to much. Neither appeared to have the heart or the strength for the battle. Although in Sunny's case Rab doubted it was either guilt or remorse over the horse that was at the heart of her sudden lethargy. And it wasn't just her lacklustre tussle with the old man that had Rab concerned; everything she did seemed to be taking a little extra time and demanding that little extra bit of concentration. The old man and Gift had collapsed in exhaustion long ago, affording Rab the opportunity to better organise their packs and to study Sunny unobserved as she set about arranging her bedding. The scratches that had opened up on her cheek remained open and her eye had closed up even further.

"You're sick," he said at last, garnering her attention.

"We're all sick," she said. "Everything on this planet is sick." She bent to her task again.

"That isn't what I mean." He glanced around for her packs. "Where's that medicine of yours?" When he looked up, he discovered her dangling a familiar-looking pouch from her hand.

"Are you looking for this?" She shook her head. "Won't do any good. The horse. The old man. Then me. Your problem is going to be who's next." She nodded towards Gift, a twisted, sleeping bundle some distance away. "Her or you? You'd better hope it's her."

Rab jumped to his feet and made a rough grab for Sunny's elbow. The pouch fell from her hand.

"The horse was dead the instant we started on this journey. The old man, too, most probably. But we're young. We're strong. Give up on yourself if you want to, but don't speak for Gift and me. We were managing before we met you; we'll manage after you're gone."

"Really?" Sunny said with a dry laugh. "Just how long do you think you would have continued to manage if you hadn't stumbled onto me out there? What were you going to do with that boy and his broken leg?" Her focus shifted to that dreadful weapon of hers. "If you'd had a gun, you could have shot him. But you didn't, did you? Of course, you could have smashed his head in with a brick or something, but somehow I couldn't see you doing that. One life for the price of three? Top-siders don't add that way."

"And nor do you or you'd have killed the old man by now. He's slowing us down and he's only going to slow us down further." He pushed her arm aside. "You talk tough, Sunny, but you never quite follow through, do you?"

"I can't see you shooting the horse."

"I wouldn't be so certain of that."

"Fine." She retrieved the pouch, then reached out to gather the gun. "Shoot me then," she said and thrust the gun into Rab's hands. "Right here. Right now. The scratches on my face are badly infected and there isn't a thing I can do about it. Even my medicines can only do so much. So shoot me now and get it over with."

Rab shoved the gun back into her hands. "I'm not finished with you yet. Just like you weren't finished with that horse. Or your grandfather evidently," he said over his shoulder as he strode back to his waiting packs.

Sleep came grudgingly and fitfully. He felt too cold, too angry, too worried. In the morning, he was the first to wake up. There was no telling sound of movement in their small camp.

Looking around, he located his travelling companions, little more than three separate mounds really. As always, Gift was sleeping close by his side. The old man lay a short distance away. Sunny had passed the night far from the rest of them. If she'd died in her sleep, no one would have been close enough to know. Somehow Rab didn't think that likely. Yes, she seemed sick, but he'd been a witness to sickness most of his life and she just didn't have that unmistakable pall of death about her yet.

The old man was a different matter.

He reached out to shake Gift's shoulder.

"Time to get up," he whispered and heard the young girl stir. "Be quiet now."

The old man might trust that his granddaughter was leading them in the right direction; Rab didn't. Before they had made camp last night, he had noticed an isolated ridge not too far away. If they moved fast enough, he and Gift might be able to make it to the top of that ridge and back before Sunny woke up.

Placing a finger to his lips, he waved Gift forward.

She glanced briefly at their abandoned packs, then followed. When they were out of earshot, she tugged on his sleeve.

"What are we doing?"

Rab pointed. "See that ridge? We're going to climb it. If there's anything out there, we might be able to see it from the top."

Gift stumbled but righted herself immediately. "Do you think we're close then?"

Rab shrugged. "That's what I'm hoping to find out."

The ground was rockier now and Gift slipped again. This time, it took Rab's quick action to prevent a tumble on jagged stones.

"We could have just asked Sunny, Rab. She'll be mad if she wakes up and discovers we've gone." Gift cast an anxious look back towards camp. "She might even leave without us."

"She won't leave. The old man will slow her down and we'll be back before she can get him up and going." He smiled down at the little girl. "And just this once, I'd like us to be one step ahead of her. Don't you want to know what's out there?"

It wasn't easy to read the expression on Gift's face and, when she didn't answer, Rab took it as a 'no'.

"Come on," he said, giving her a nudge of encouragement. "It's only a little way further."

In hindsight, as Rab looked up at the steep and unstable-looking slope he realised it would have been better to have taken this short excursion alone, but now Gift was there, she wouldn't be prepared to wait for him at the base while he scouted the terrain from above.

"Just stay here while I look around for an easier way up. I won't be long."

Gift didn't looked pleased, so after he'd walked a short distance around the base of the outcrop, he glanced back to assure himself that she hadn't followed. She was standing right where he'd left her, looking after him. Satisfied, Rab continued on. As he circled the outcrop, he scanned the rockface above. It didn't look hopeful. He was directly across from the place he'd left Gift now and in front of him stretched a sheer wall that offered no footholds or access to the top. There was no way up on this side. Turning, he leaned his back against the vertical sheet of rock to study what he could of their surroundings. It was very little. To see more, they had to go up.

Resigned, he pushed away from the wall and, as he did, his eyes chanced on something lying half buried in the ground a few paces away. It looked like the top-side of a pack and, on investigation, that's just what Rab found—an old and tattered pack. He knelt and began to disturb the soil around the pack, digging more earnestly when he came across something that looked disturbingly like bone. He didn't expose it all, just enough of it to confirm his suspicions. The skull had been stripped of most of its flesh long ago and only a few tuffs of spindly red hair remained. Large empty sockets stared up out of the ground as though silently appealing to Rab. He covered them over again with loose soil, then glanced once more at the pack. Empty—of no use to them at all. Rising, he made an easy decision. He'd leave the useless and the dead where they lay and he wouldn't tell Gift what he'd found.

"Well?" Gift asked the moment he returned.

"That side is no good. We'll have to go up this way, unless you're willing to wait for me down here," he suggested with little expectation that Gift would agree.

It was safe enough to take her; the pack and skull wouldn't be visible from the summit.

She shook her head.

And so they climbed, Rab with one eye turned to the ground beneath his feet and the other to the ground beneath Gift's. Just shy of the summit, Rab was obliged to stop. He could barely breathe or muster the wave towards Gift to let her know that he'd be all right. She continued on, scrambling on hands and knees to the reach the top. Once the fire in his lungs eased, Rab followed. He found Gift standing on the narrow rim of the ridge. It was a straight drop down the other side. She turned briefly at the sound of his approach, then looked back again into the obscure dawn. Rab turned a full circle to scan in all directions.

Nothing! There was nothing there. Just the two black shapes, Sunny and her grandfather, in camp off to the left, but otherwise more of the rocky same. Rab could see farther than he'd ever seen before, but land and sky still blended to create that familiar dirty, murky barrier in the distance.

Slowly Gift turned around, her face masked in an unreadable expression.

"What about that over there?" Rab raised an arm to point. "Does that look like an old road to you?" Crouching to match Gift's height, he pointed again towards a scattering of dark shapes down on the plain.

"Maybe," Gift conceded. "But I don't think so."

Rab was inclined to agree. The vague shapes he'd seen were peppered too randomly. More than likely he had simply spotted another distant field of boulders.

"She lied to us," Gift said at last.

Rab shook his head. "It doesn't make any sense. Why bring us out here into nothingness?" He scanned the muddy horizon again, yet still found nothing other than those same scattered boulders. "There must be something there. Something we're not seeing." He looked down hopefully at Gift. "It's possible," he said. "We still can't see all that far."

"Far enough," Gift replied and made to turn around.

Her foot slipped. She fell flat on her face and immediately began to slide down the steep side of the ridge.

An image of empty eyes in a cold, white, fleshless head flooded Rab's mind. Without thinking, he dropped onto his belly and flung his hand across the jagged rocks. Tiny gloved fingers latched onto his. He reached out with his free hand, grasping for something, anything. By chance, he caught hold of Gift's other wrist, then he pulled and pulled again. Every movement set off a cascade of rocks down the back side of the ridge. Bit by agonising bit, he managed to drag Gift back onto the narrow cusp.

Breathless, he rolled onto his back, still clutching Gift tightly. He couldn't seem to let her go, lacking the breath to ask if she was hurt and the strength to find out for himself. All he could do was lie there—feeling spent, dazed, and detached. It took the pressure of Gift's little hands leaning into his chest to get him moving again.

"I'm fine. I'm fine," she grumbled. "Let me up."

Slowly, Rab's arms relaxed; for a while, they had been beyond his control.

Gift slipped to the ground beside him and quickly scrambled onto her feet. It seemed to take an unreasonable amount of effort, but Rab raised his head and shoulders from the ground.

"Not even a rip," Gift said, inspecting her clothes for damage. She shrugged, then glanced at Rab, looking suddenly puzzled. "What's the matter?"

"You nearly fell off. Weren't you even scared?"

"Of course, I was," she said, tilting her head slightly askew. "But it's over now."

"Glad you think so," Rab mumbled, righting himself. "Let's just go. We've seen what we came to see."

Coming down was a harder task than Rab had anticipated and the safest place for Gift was behind him, something he realised the first time he set a shower of rubble downhill. Halfway down, he risked a glance towards camp and was disappointed to discover that Sunny was already up and about.

She'd be well and truly angry, but Rab really didn't care. He was more concerned about what had just happened up on that ridge. Gift had moved on from the experience; he couldn't. It almost seemed like her generation expected nothing but a lifelong chain of adversities and once one was averted, they simply moved on to the next. What if he was wrong? What if there was no city, no launch pad, no salvation—just another link in that long, endless chain of adversities?

"What are you going to say to her?" Gift asked, interrupting his thoughts.

"Depends." He nodded towards camp. "She knows we've been up on the ridge. She saw us."

Gift shook her head. "She won't care. She'd have been happier if we'd both fallen off. Then she could just do to the old man what she did to Kix and go home."

"I don't think so." He stopped, bringing Gift to a halt. "Think about it. She didn't have to come with us. And what she said about looking after her grandfather is a lie. There's something else. She needs us for some reason."

Gift pointed towards their camp. "Does she need him, too? Her grandfather?"

"Maybe. Why?"

"Because I think she might be in trouble, Rab. He hasn't moved."

Rab looked again towards camp.

"He's just tired," Rab said and hoped he was at least right about that. Like Sunny, he wasn't finished with John Braham just yet, especially now when it looked as though they were being led straight into nowhere.

When they reached camp, Rab was relieved to discover the old man, hand propped up in the dirt by his elbow, had only been watching Sunny slowly make preparations for a meal. On hearing them approach, Braham glanced their way.

"Find what you were looking for?" Sunny asked.

She was crouched on her haunches, back turned.

"Nothing like I'd have hoped."

She spun around to study Rab with her good eye. "We haven't come far enough yet. I could have told you that if you'd asked me." Her head jerked once at Gift. "What happened to her? She's filthy."

Rab shrugged. "So how much further is it then? We're almost halfway through our food now."

Sunny returned his shrug. "The horse could have made a difference to that."

"It wasn't in your original plan—or was it?"

"No," Sunny replied with a weary lopsided smile. "Five days," she said, coming slowly to her feet. "Six at the most."

"I don't believe you."

"Why? Because you can't see it? I've passed this way before." She pointed, "I've seen that ridge before," then glanced over her shoulder. "What do they call it, old man? Yes, that's it," she continued, turning back to Rab before Braham could possibly respond. "A mirage. Seeing something that actually isn't there. In this place, it works the other way around.

Often you don't see something that really is there." The twisted smile resurfaced. "But I guess you'll just have to trust me on that, won't you?"

"I've never trusted you, Sunny, and I'm not about to start now." Reaching out, he caught hold of Gift's hand and dragged her with him towards their packs.

As he bent to unfasten one of his packs, intending to find food for himself and Gift, Rab looked towards the old man. Braham hadn't moved, but it was obvious he'd been listening. His head had slipped from his hand and it was resting now on the pack Rab had forced him to carry.

"It's there," the old man said, his words directed towards the low and dismal sky. "Sunny knows. She was there and she came back. It's there."

"Crazy old man," Rab muttered, more to himself really, but desperate just the same to be proved wrong.

"Here!"

Rab turned to find Sunny standing over him. She held her hand out, offering him some of her food.

"You have my grandfather eat that while I'm away. By the time I get back, I expect him to be up and ready."

Rab got to his feet. "Just where are you going?"

"Up onto that ridge," she said. "What's wrong? You seemed to think it was a good idea."

She made to leave, but Rab reached out and grabbed her elbow. "Why are you going there? You said you knew where we were."

"I do." She shrugged him off. "But it doesn't hurt to confirm what I already know. We can't afford to lose time. We have just enough food to get there and back. No more. We don't have time for mistakes."

"Get where?" Rab called after her as she strode off towards the ridge he and Gift had just climbed. "Now you're wasting time. You can't see anything from up there."

"Maybe you couldn't."

Sunny's reply was almost lost to a building wind.

Rab turned back to the old man. "What's she up to?"

Braham just shook his head. "I told you. Sunny knows what she's doing."

"So you keep saying but, face it, old man, her story keeps changing."

He dropped to the ground, briefly concerned about Gift's whereabouts until he spotted her over by Sunny's packs, looking down at the gun Sunny had left lying beside them.

"Do you know what's really out there?" Rab asked, shifting attention to the old man again. "Because now she's insisting that there is something."

"That's just Sunny's way. If you say a thing is black, she'll swear it's white."

"And if I agree with her and say it's white?"

"She'll say it's black. When you said there was a city, she'd naturally say there wasn't. Now you say there isn't, so she'll say there is."

"So which is right? Is there a city or not?"

"You used to think there was. I still think there is."

The old man repositioned his shoulder but the effort seemed to pain him.

"And Sunny knows there is," he continued, "because she's been there. Where do you think that gun of hers came from?" A wet-sounding chuckle escaped his throat. "She didn't get it from the Top-siders. Top-siders don't have guns."

Rab shook his head. "Then why didn't she ever tell you about it?"

"Sunny told me nothing about those years she was away. Not about the journey. Not about the deaths of the others in the party. Not about her life with the Top-siders and not about how she found her way back home. I don't know why and I simply gave up asking."

Rab dipped his head to protect his eyes. The wind was blowing stronger now, picking up grit and dust.

"You'd better eat this," he said, offering the old man the food Sunny had given him.

Braham shook his head again. "Not hungry," he replied. "Give it to the little girl."

"We have our own. Eat," Rab insisted and pushed the food into the old man's limp hand. "How many people were there in that party?"

Out there on the other side of the ridge Rab had stumbled on one of that ill-fated party; he felt sure of it.

"Four—five including Sunny."

"It seems strange to have taken a child along."

The old man smiled thinly. "Sunny was never a child, only smaller, and as adventurous and inquisitive as my son. When she was young, she used to sit up with me at the old house every evening. Sometimes we'd stay there all night, just looking at those old blocked windows, imagining that on the other side the stars had finally come out."

Braham placed a shaking hand on Rab's thigh.

"It had been my idea to send out a party to look for the City. We couldn't live in those tunnels and caves forever. Even Edward Braham had known that. It never occurred to me they wouldn't make it."

"So that's what Sunny meant?"

One of the old man's eyebrows lifted slightly.

"I remember her saying that you owed her."

Braham didn't answer and Rab was distracted by the touch of Gift's hand on his shoulder.

"Sunny's coming back," she said when he turned around. "And he isn't up yet. She'll be mad at us again."

"When isn't Sunny mad at us?"

Rab got up on his knees and leaned in towards the old man, intending to give Braham a gentle shake, but stopped with his hand poised in mid-air.

"What's wrong?" Gift asked, bending over Rab's shoulder. "Can't he get up?"

Dropping his hand, Rab fell back on his heels, then shook his head. In the dirt by his knee lay the slab of food he'd given to the old man. He picked it up and passed it to Gift.

"Here," he said. "Put that back into Sunny's pack. Her grandfather won't be needing it."

Gift gave him a curious look but, taking the food from his hand, walked back to Sunny's packs.

Rab scrambled onto his feet, then turned around to find Sunny. She was striding towards camp with the hood of her coat thrown back, leaving the wind to whip at the errant long yellow strands of her hair and whirl it in every direction.

She glanced at Gift as she passed, a look of understandable suspicion on her face. After all, Gift was rummaging about in her packs.

Rab stepped forward to intercept her. Somehow he didn't think the news he had would come as a great surprise.

Chapter 12

"WE'RE not stopping to bury him, either," Sunny said with words punched into the buffeting wind. "We stay long enough to take his clothes, his boots, and his food. That's it."

When she began tugging at the old man's clothes, Rab turned and walked away.

"Fine. You want them, you take them," he called over his shoulder. "And you carry them. When you're finished, Gift and I will bury him."

"There's no time for that. We have to move on."

"We can't move in this weather," Rab said as he collapsed onto the ground beside Gift and the two packs that belonged to Sunny, now forced to shout over the rising wind. "If we wait here until it weakens, we'll save our strength."

Sunny stopped stripping the old man and, as she swivelled around on her heels, was caught by a gust of wind that whipped up the long strands of her hair and gagged her mouth. Rab had never felt so grateful for a blast of dirty wind. Sunny struggled to her feet, spitting out her hair and dusting off her knees. "All right," she agreed, battling to reseat the hood of her coat. "The wind is getting worse. We've got extra food now. We can spare half a day at most. But that's all."

"Whatever you say." Rab got to his feet and, bending into the wind, went to collect his and Gift's packs. "But we're not just going to sit here in the open." He made to point to the nearby ridge, but the wind prevented him from even raising his arm. "We can make it back to that ridge. Gift and I are going to wait it out there. You do what you like."

It felt good to be in control again. He didn't bother to seek Sunny's permission or even her opinion, just dragged the packs back to where Gift was standing. She'd risen from the ground but was fighting hard to stay upright. For once the burden of a pack would play in the little girl's favour by lending her some stability. It wasn't a long way to the ridge, but long enough. Rab didn't want to go chasing after a tumbling child. He intentionally left the old man's pack behind for Sunny to deal with. Loading up

Gift, he started off for the ridge, one hand locked tightly onto the pack on her back. Twice he lunged out to steady her and almost fell on top of her each time. By the time they reached the base of the ridge they were both exhausted and Gift crumpled to the ground the moment they reached its shelter.

Rab slumped down beside her, sliding on the loose gravel when his backside hit the ground. At last Sunny staggered up, lugging the remaining packs. She dumped them in the dirt at his feet and dropped to the ground, the sound of her laboured breathing just audible beneath the shrill whistle of the wind.

"It wasn't like this when I was here before," she said, every other syllable snatched by the wind. "If this keeps up, we'll have to turn back."

"So you admit you saw nothing from above. I told you there was nothing."

"I saw what I went up to see, Top-sider. We're on the right course and we'll make it there in less than six days. Five now maybe since we don't have the old man slowing us down. But not if this wind keeps up."

Rab leaned forward to be heard and Gift took advantage of the added shelter and nestled hard in against his back.

"What did you see? I'd really like to know. Because Gift and me—we only saw more of the same."

"To the north." Sunny's voice came ragged. "On the horizon, there's a mountain. We're heading for that. You have to know exactly where to look to make it out."

"And you saw it?"

Sunny nodded against the wind.

Rab leaned in close to grab her sleeve. "What's there, Sunny? The City? People?"

She shrugged him off, aided by the merciless wind. "Don't worry," she said. "You'll get what you left your village to find."

"Then why did you lie to us back in the tunnels? Tell us there was nothing there? Why did you keep lying to the old man?"

He was certain that she'd heard him, but Sunny just drew the hood of her coat tight about her swollen face, pulled up her legs, and dropped her head onto her knees: an unmoving, unmovable obstacle in the path of the insistent wind.

Rab adopted a similar posture, but it did little to cut the bite of the bitter gusts. Cold, hard grit pummelled against the inadequate shield of

Blaze's coat. He tasted ice. They'd left this journey too late. Behind him, Gift snuggled in closer. He pictured Stitch, lying warm and comfortable in his hospital bed, Fin sitting patient vigil beside him. Two out of four saved—in the long run, it was better odds than he, or Blaze for that matter, maybe had a right to expect.

He chanced a glance out into the wind, but could make out very little. Invisible to him now, but not too far off, the old man's body would be lying exposed to the brutal storm. Perhaps he'd be spared the effort of burying old Braham's remains.

Around midday the wind abruptly quit, leaving the three of them coated in fine dirt and the old man's body only partially concealed beneath a grainy blanket of sand and ice. With only Gift to aid him, Rab set about completing the job. Sunny busied herself cleaning off their packs while he and Gift first found, then carted, stone after stone from the surrounding plain to fashion a crude grave. The wind had prevented Sunny from robbing the old man of everything; he was missing only his coat and boots. Rab had no intention of taking the rest now or of reminding Sunny of her oversight. Let the old man go to his rest with a shred of dignity.

Once all the stones were in place, Rab stepped back to look at the long, low mound. It was the best he and Gift could manage, although he had no doubts that if it had come down to a choice, the old man would have preferred to be lying out in the open alongside the body of Kix. He glanced down to find Gift's black eyes offering approval.

"Have you satisfied your conscience enough yet?" Sunny called from the base of the ridge. She'd finished with the packs and must have been waiting on them for some time. Rab's hand tightened around Gift's. He led her away from the grave towards the ridge with the words Sunny had said yesterday turning over and over again in his mind: *Who's next? You'd better hope it's her.*

Sunny had their packs reorganised, but some of them appeared to be missing. Rab looked around but failed to find them.

"They're under there." She pointed towards a newly disturbed patch of earth at the base of the ridge. "Stored for now. Couldn't see the point in carrying it all there just to lug half of it back again. You'll remember this place?"

Rab nodded. Having just found one body and then buried another nearby, how likely was he to forget?

With their stores halved and redistributed, Sunny had reduced the total number of packs to three; one for each of them.

Skirting around the ridge, they set off north once more with Sunny, as usual, in the lead. As they walked, Rab scanned the horizon, seeking that mysterious mountain Sunny claimed to have seen. There was no sign of it, although the wind had cut a clearer channel through the air to the north, revealing more of the same barren terrain. With each step he took, doubt doubled. This didn't seem a likely place to have built a city. Then again, it hadn't always been this way so maybe Sunny wasn't lying. Six days, she'd said; maybe five. At the first chance, he cast a sly glance down at Gift, plodding silently on beside him. She seemed to be managing well enough with the pack; evidently Sunny had weighted it accordingly—but only for her own benefit, of course, knowing Rab would only stop and squander more of their time if he discovered Gift struggling.

"We should stop soon," he called ahead to Sunny. "Rest and eat."

Their last meal had been yesterday and yesterday seemed a long time ago. Sunny didn't answer, but kept walking on in that slow and irregular pace she'd so recently acquired.

In the late afternoon, Rab saw something that appeared to have escaped Sunny's attention. Low on the horizon, not too far ahead and off to the side, roiled a strange sort of dirty cloud. Rab had seen snow eddies whirl like this cloud whirled, but no snow had fallen today. He hurried Gift ahead of him and caught up with Sunny.

"There's something out there," he said.

"I've seen it," she replied without turning. "It's Top-siders and we're going to meet up with them very shortly."

Latching onto her pack, Rab spun Sunny around. "You knew they were out here?"

She staggered slightly. "Of course I didn't. But there's nothing we can do about it now. If we've seen them, then they've seen us. Just keep that girl quiet and everything will be fine." With a practised shrug of one shoulder, Sunny slipped the gun down into her hand. "Come on." She turned and struck off, heading for the dust cloud and potential disaster.

Rab glanced down at Gift. "Don't say anything," he said, "and stay right beside me. Maybe they'll just keep going."

"It's almost night time, Rab. They'll have to stop, just like we will."

"Even if they do, where's the harm? They're probably just people like us, Gift. Remember Sunny calls us Top-siders, too," he said, attempting to smile.

"But our people don't go wandering around like that."

Rab's smile came easier the second time. "We are." He shrugged. "Why can't they?"

Sunny had the gun, so Rab dropped well back and allowed her to take the absolute lead. He couldn't make out much about the band of Top-siders until they were almost on top of each other. A rough guess put their number at thirty to thirty-five and they looked a rag-tag bunch—dirty, tired, but robust enough overall and so perhaps not desperate to steal food. In the tunnel city, Rab had watched the merchants drag goods to and fro on small wheeled wagons; this band of Top-siders were equipped with similar vehicles, although these were larger in size, more like those he'd seen in the underground 'shroom field. Rab counted four wagons in all, each fitted out with two long, front-projecting handles that were manned on either side by three, sometimes, four Top-siders. Hauling the vehicles over such an inhospitable and unpredictable terrain had to be extraordinarily difficult, so whatever cargo the wagons held must be precious indeed.

Sunny and the band of Top-siders stopped, almost at the same moment. When a bearded man strode forward out of the settling dust, making for Sunny, Rab tightened his grip on Gift's hand.

He waited, expecting the worst, hoping for better, and so was astonished when he heard Sunny's sudden laugh.

The man had to be an elder sent ahead to investigate their odd little trio, and beneath the hood of his cloak Rab could just make out his grizzled beard and the wind-ravaged skin of his face. Rab's heart lurched when Sunny turned and motioned for him to approach.

"Quiet now," he reminded Gift faintly and stepped up to join Sunny and the old Top-sider.

"We'll share a camp tonight," Sunny told him. "They've come from the east, moving west," she said, then turned to follow the elder.

***

Rab was reluctant to reveal too much about the supplies they carried with them, so had Gift stay well away from the Top-sider encampment while she ate. He was inclined not to fully trust these Top-siders and the fact that Sunny appeared to, inclined him to trust them even less. She sat with them by the fire to eat, talking incessantly with the same elder who'd come out to intercept them.

By watching three of the Top-sider women build and then continue to tend the fire for Sunny and the elder, Rab had at least learned something about the contents of those four heavily laden wagons. He hoped Sunny thought to ask where the tinder had come from; if there was a cache somewhere nearby, they'd be fools not to exploit it.

Occasionally other Top-siders joined Sunny and the elder by the fire. A new group had just sauntered up when Sunny got to her feet, shouldered that gun of hers and fired it off into the night. Startled and assuming there must be trouble, Rab jumped immediately to his feet before he realised Sunny had only been offering a demonstration. The woman never missed an opportunity to impress. Rab could have done without the excitement.

Against his better judgement, he had allowed Gift to wander off with two of the Top-sider children. They seemed harmless, more curious than anything else really. Though he tried to keep them in sight, he was obliged to rely more on the noise they made scampering through camp. The sound of the children's laughter boosted his own spirits.

Gift came running up out of the darkness and scooted to a halt on her knees in front of him.

"Look, Rab," she said breathlessly, hand outheld. "That little boy gave it to me."

Rab lifted the gift from her palm. "Where did this come from?"

The gift was some kind of rock: hard, smooth-faced, and cool to the touch.

"He found it. The Top-siders find lots of different stones." She shuffled closer to him on her knees. "If you take it close to the fire, you can see this one's blue."

Rab handed back the stone.

"He said I can keep it. Is that all right?"

"I suppose so. It's just a rock." He reached out and patted Gift's pack. "No more playing tonight though, Gift. You can thank the boy in the morning, but you need to go to sleep now."

Though he sensed her reluctance, Gift crawled past him on hands and knees, making for her pack. The children in their village never played, so tonight had to have been a rare treat for her. It pleased him that she could carry away a memento.

"Gift?" he said, turning to her in the darkness. "You didn't happen to see what was in those wagons, did you?"

"You mean the firewood? I asked about that."

Rab heard another shuffle; Gift settling in for the night.

"That boy said they brought some of it with them and some they found along the way. But it's been days and days since they've found anything new to burn. I think they're running out."

"Go to sleep now, Gift."

Disappointed, Rab dropped his head and shoulders to the ground. So much for a lucky cache of tinder nearby!

Whether Gift slept or not, he couldn't say, but she stayed quiet all night; perhaps exhaustion overrode excitement. Rab's eyes never closed. He didn't know what had become of Sunny and only in the morning discovered that she'd passed the night closer to the fire. It would have been smart of him to have done likewise, but he had little faith in these strangers. Sunny branded all Top-siders the same, but Rab saw no similarity between the people in this camp and those in his village. His people were 'shroom farmers, bound to the pitiful scrap of land their parents had lived and died on; there was no telling how this roving band of people survived.

Though he permitted Gift to run off and thank that young boy, Rab hung back from the stirring Top-siders, relieved when he noticed Sunny in the midst of preparations for their departure. He set about readying himself, but Sunny seemed bent on a prolonged farewell and lingered for some time at the fire. By the time Gift returned, looking a little disappointed, Rab was long packed and anxious to go.

"What's the matter?"

Gift shrugged. "I couldn't find him," she said, stooping to retrieve her own pack. From her pocket, she pulled out the boy's present. "See." She held the stone into the dim morning light. "It's blue."

Rab smiled. "Better not let Sunny know you've got that. I'm sure she'll find something wrong about it."

Gift stuffed the stone back inside her coat. "Sunny finds something wrong in everything I do."

"Me, too," Rab said, nudging her with his elbow.

Gift's expression sobered. "She's coming."

Rab glanced up to find Sunny strolling towards them. Though some of the Top-siders looked after her, most just wandered away.

"Thought you didn't trust Top-siders," he said.

"Know of a better way to watch someone than up close?" she replied, leaving Rab to wonder if that same principle didn't go some way to explain why she had brought them into the tunnel city.

"Here." She tossed him a pair of small boots, "For the girl," then reached into the pack on her back and whipped out a heavy sweater. "For you."

Suspicious, Rab took the sweater just the same. "How about you?"

Sunny help up her hands to briefly display a new pair of gloves.

"Just what did all this cost us?"

She didn't reply.

***

"There!"

Rab couldn't see a thing. The low slung shroud of night sky appeared exactly the same to him.

"I saw it, Rab. It looked just like one of those brightworms."

Rab shook his head. The little girl was seeing things. Maybe a tiny piece of grit was stuck in her eye.

"What's she talking about?"

Sunny was lying on her back on the cold ground, head supported on an elbow. He'd thought she was asleep. Perhaps she had been or maybe the swollen cheek was to blame for the cloudiness of her speech.

"She said she could see a star."

Sunny snorted. "A star! She sounds like my grandfather."

"I'm curious," Rab said. He left Gift still peering up into the murk and scooted closer to Sunny. "You must have looked at those books your grandfather has in the library, the ones with the pictures of stars. You must believe they exist. Or are you going to tell me that the pictures aren't real simply because your grandfather insisted that they are?"

"Oh, the pictures are real all right and so are the stars," Sunny said, lifting her head from the ground. "But not for us. They're there behind the clouds, but we'll never see them."

Rab sensed her shrug in the darkness.

"Makes no difference to the stars though, does it?" she said.

"So you really don't believe they ever reached one?"

"Well, it would be kind of pointless to head right into a star, wouldn't it? But a planet orbiting one of those stars? That's a different matter. And of course they did."

She'd stunned him completely.

"Your grandfather was right. You'll say anything just to be contrary. You really should take a stand on something and stick to it. First you said that there were no launch pads and that no one was saved and now you're saying entirely the opposite."

"That's not exactly true. You should have listened more carefully."

The ground crunched beneath Sunny's feet when she rose.

"Stop that nonsense, now," she said, making for Gift. "In spite of the late start, we made good time today. With luck, we'll be there around midday two days from now, if you get enough rest tonight."

"I saw it." Gift countered in a small voice. "I don't care what you say."

"Fine! Fine! You saw it, but it's gone now. Just go to sleep."

Rab listened for Gift's protest, but heard nothing other than the rustling sound of her settling on top of her pack.

"That girl is strong and not half the trouble I'd expected her to be," Sunny observed as she joined Rab again. "For a Top-sider, that is."

The woman's slights were becoming dated.

Rab looked skyward again. Had Gift really seen something up there? He'd never known her to imagine things before.

"She could have seen something," he said to Sunny as she dropped to the ground beside him. "Well," he continued when she declined to comment. "At least I know you don't lie about everything. I'm certain you've been this way before."

"So you found Henri then, did you?" she said casually out of the darkness. "I looked when I was over at that ridge. . ."

Rab heard a swoosh—hands brushing at cloth.

". . .but I couldn't see him. You didn't have time to bury him, too, so where was he?"

"No, I didn't bury him," Rab replied. "And I didn't tell Gift about it either, so please say nothing. I found him on the other side of the ridge."

"Right where he fell I suppose. My father never did let me look."

"His pack was empty."

"It wasn't when we left him. He broke his back. At least that's what my father told me. His name was Henri Du Bois, in case you're interested. And he was twenty-five. He'd climbed up onto the top of that ridge, just like you did, to get a better look around. You were lucky—you and that little girl. Either one of you could have slipped on the loose rocks on the summit just like Henri did."

Rab shifted uncomfortably, but said nothing.

"When he fell, they had a meeting, all four of the men, out there in the dirt where he'd fallen. Henri. Jacob Sloane. Simon Deitweller. And Louis Braham, my father. I wasn't allowed to go, or to vote. Everyone agreed what was to be done, even Henri. The rest of us were to go on and Henri would stay behind to wait until we returned. And that's just what we did—left him there—with food and water, so my father said. I didn't get to say goodbye, so I was never really certain about the food and water. But since you found his pack. . .well, I guess my father told me the truth. I often wondered."

"And that's why you shot the horse?"

"The horse? No, I shot the horse because my grandfather would have just held us up, waiting for the thing to die."

Rab wasn't entirely sure he believed her. "I'm guessing you never made it back for Henri then."

"It doesn't seem so. I can show you Jacob's grave in a day or so. We did bury him. . .sort of. As for the rest of us. My father was wounded badly on the way back. By the band of Top-siders who took me. He must have died soon after. I can't tell you what happened to Simon Deitweller. He got away—at least I always thought he did—but it appears that he never did make it home. Your guess as to why is as good as mine."

"Where were you taken?"

Sunny thought a moment before answering. "A long way from here. Why?"

"By Top-siders?"

"I said so, didn't I?"

Rab shook his head. "I've seen no evidence of anyone actually living around here, Sunny, unless you lied about that band of Top-siders we met earlier."

"We never saw them either. One night they just appeared in our camp. They were just travellers like us—like those Top-siders—passing this way. They'd come from the east and had been walking a long time. Their valley had gone bad and they were moving on. Of course, none of us knew that at the time. That's what I discovered later, after they took me." She gave a weary sort of laugh. "If my father had just accepted their offer, he and Simon would probably still be alive today. It was a fair offer for a girl. A week's worth of food and water for the two of them. But my father refused and got both of them killed for the trouble."

Sunny's story had Rab spooked, imagining raiders advancing on them in the dark.

"Did they all move on?" he asked. "I mean some of them could still be here now, couldn't they?"

"How should I know? I didn't exactly count them. Maybe they all moved on. Maybe some didn't. What difference does it make? They're your kind, after all. Can't see what you've got to worry about. Besides, we've already run into one group and had no trouble."

Sunny made to rise, but Rab stopped her with a hand to her sleeve.

"Why didn't you tell your grandfather this story?" His hand fell away. "There's nothing in it he hadn't already suspected."

"If you think I was trying to spare my grandfather, you're wrong."

"What then? And why tell me all this now?"

"Simple." She was on her feet again and moving. "My journey is almost over while yours has just begun. But my grandfather, on the other hand—he never even had a journey to begin with."

"What's that supposed to mean?" Rab called after her. "Aren't we all on the same journey here?"

As usual, Sunny didn't answer. Not too far away, he could hear her shifting something about, setting up her bed for the night. Incensed, Rab grabbed his pack and did the same.

With only one pack now, the bed he made for himself was inadequate and unforgiving. And the persistent cold and Sunny's enigmatic declaration left him restless. He couldn't seem to find a spot that would stop the chill from seeping up from the ground to numb his bones or prevent the frozen night air from wrapping him in a blanket of ice. His left hip and right shoulder were in constant pain and no amount of tossing, turning or twisting brought any relief. Long before the sky lightened, he heard Sunny moving about again. Rising stiffly, he was surprised to discover Gift already up and waiting. Catching his eye, she smiled at him between mouthfuls of food. He tried to return the smile but his face seemed to have frozen in the night.

"The girl's got your food," Sunny said.

She seated herself cross-legged on the ground behind him and began to gnaw on a slab of 'shroom bread. Being forced to eat largely from only one side of her mouth, she was having a tough time of it.

Rab scooted across the ground to join Gift.

"See any more stars last night?" he asked, taking his breakfast from her hands.

His little companion frowned, obviously taking exception to his teasing.

"I did," she said at last. "But I didn't bother waking you since you didn't believe me the first time."

"Sorry," Rab answered.

He'd never known Gift to lie or fantasise. What if she truly had seen a star? They were farther from the rancid river now and here the air did seem marginally less muddied. It was possible. Unlikely. . .but. . .

"Make it fast," Sunny snapped, wrecking the spell. "And put on those new boots I gave you. Your own are almost worn through."

Rab glanced at Gift and shrugged. "Better do like she says." His knee first, then his ankle cracked loudly as he rose.

Gift laughed, then as if to make up for the small indiscretion, stood to help him on with his pack. Sunny was already moving by the time Gift had changed her boots. As they followed behind a slow-moving Sunny, Rab glanced back towards their camp. Nothing. There was nothing there to indicate that a single living soul had passed the night. It wasn't so surprising to have found no evidence of the party that had come this way before them. Just like the tracks the three of them had so recently made, all evidence of their passing had disappeared into time along with all trace of the roving Top-siders they'd come upon that day. Having stumbled across poor Henri's bones, Rab was at last inclined to accept there was some truth in Sunny's tale. But his people didn't bargain for children and they didn't murder. If it weren't for those bones, he'd have thought Sunny was making it all up. Somewhere up ahead could be the place where she'd been taken. What if they were still out there? Those Top-siders who didn't think twice about killing to get what they wanted.

"What's that?"

Rab jumped and glanced anxiously back at Gift, trailing a pace behind. She had an arm raised, finger pointing into the distance. "It must be the City this time," she said.

Rab held, then quickly released his breath, deciding the dark smudge Gift had seen ahead wasn't more Top-siders.

It wasn't the City, either. They weren't close enough yet. Sunny had said midday tomorrow and if they weren't going to reach it until then, it was unlikely they'd be seeing any signs of it now. He thought he knew what it was though.

"There's another." He stopped walking and, taking hold of Gift's shoulder, turned her slightly to the right. "It's those things we saw from the top of the ridge. Large boulders or something."

"Oh, yes. I can see them now. There's more that way." Gift's hand swung to the left. "What do you think they are?"

"They're roosts," Sunny sang out. "At least that's what Jacob said they were. He'd seen a picture of something similar in a book in our library, only those were built to shelter birds. Don't know what these here were supposed to shelter."

Rab glanced at Gift. She looked unconvinced. He gave her a gentle prod.

"Come on."

They soon caught up with Sunny, who turned at the sound of their approach.

"Since I don't have any better suggestion, I guess I'll have to believe you. Never having even seen a bird, other than in those pictures your grandfather showed Gift and me, it doesn't make a lot of sense."

"You'll see when we get there. We're making good time, so we'll shelter in one of them tonight." Her arm swept a wide arc. "They're scattered all over this plain. I suppose there were once hundreds—maybe thousands. I don't know. Most of them are ruined now."

"Who built them? Top-siders?"

Sunny shrugged. "Of course not. I told you. No Top-siders live here. Besides, those roosts have been here a long time."

Her brief bout of civility ended. She sounded tired, worse than tired. Rab kept a close eye on her from then on. Twice she stumbled, but Rab made no effort to help her.

"They look like upside down 'shrooms," Gift said, breaking the long silence.

Rab could sort of see it, too. Three of the dun-coloured roosts were plainly visible now and, while none of the tops were exactly alike, the bases of all three were uniformly broader than their tops. Three-quarters of the way up, the tapering columns were sheared off horizontally and each of the resulting platforms was capped with smaller structures. The closest of the roosts had five, maybe six small cones ringing the perimeter of the platform about a centrally-placed, broader and slightly taller cone. The roost to the left of it appeared to have a single solid cone perched on top of the platform, much like the stem of an upturned 'shroom. From a distance the structure looked to be intact. As they drew closer, the signs of extensive damage became obvious. The roost with the 'shroom stem cap was missing one whole side of its base, ragged edges revealing its inner core—another dun-coloured cylinder nested within the first. Unlike the smooth-faced outer cylinder, the entire surface of the inner cylinder was diagonally pierced with holes and it looked to Rab as though the inner wall of the outside cylinder might also be pierced. The passage between the inner and outer cylinders could take three, perhaps four, people walking shoulder to shoulder. On one side of the structure, halfway to the top, an undamaged bridge connected the walls of both cylinders; on the other side, there were signs that a bridge had collapsed. But the platform that had once ringed the stem was entirely gone and rubble blocked the circular passageway below. It seemed an incredibly elaborate construction all for the benefit of birds.

Rab had expected Sunny to stop; she'd said they would spend the night there. Instead she pressed on. She was walking fast but with that now familiar awkward gait and Rab easily caught up with her.

"I thought we were stopping here."

"Wrong one."

"What do you mean 'wrong one'? What's the difference between this one and the next? These don't look like houses for birds to me. What is this place?"

"Look, Top-sider," Sunny snapped, "I'm only telling you what Jacob Sloane told me. I hadn't seen anything like these things before. He said the ones he'd read about housed birds and that they used the bird droppings to fertilise their crops. He said they looked like these. There's a dry riverbed down there. My father and Simon Deitweller found it. So maybe there were crops here once. Or maybe these aren't bird houses, but something else. I don't know and I don't care. There's nothing here now. They're useless—defunct—finished—just like we'll be very soon if you keep wasting our time."

She pushed past him, making for another of the towers.

"What's she looking for?" Gift asked, coming up behind Rab.

"The right one apparently. Come on," he said, "we'd better follow."

He lost sight of Sunny the moment she reached the tower. She'd slipped through a narrow opening that Rab only discovered when he approached.

"Not here," she said, emerging through the opening with a difficult stoop.

"If you tell me what you're looking for, maybe I could help."

"The packs we left behind," she said, striking off again.

"Why? The food will be spoiled by now," he called after her.

"Not looking for food. Or water either. The Top-siders took all that—and anything else they wanted. It's the stuff they didn't take I'm after."

She worked her way out of the second tower, again empty-handed. Rab didn't bother to question her or look through the narrow opening. Sunny made for the next tower, with Rab and Gift on her heels.

"I hope she finds it soon," Gift said, sounding tired and disgruntled.

Rab reached down for her pack. "Stop here for a moment while I take your pack."

Gift shook her head. "It's my pack. Besides, it's not that heavy. But we're just walking in circles. She's the one wasting time, not us. Why can't she just pick one? If all the food and water is gone. . ." She shrugged ". . .I can't see the point in finding the packs."

"But Sunny does," Rab said, failing to find her again when he glanced around. "Now where's she gone?"

He headed for the closest tower, hoping she had ducked inside while he'd been talking to Gift. But there was no response when he called her name. Rounding the tower, he found the gap at its base and bent to call again.

Nothing.

"Maybe she's hurt," Gift suggested, tugging on the tail of his coat.

"I'm not hurt. I'm over here."

Rab spun around and spotted Sunny at the entrance to the tower directly behind him.

"This is it," she called, then disappeared inside again.

"Just what are you looking for?" Rab asked, stooping to squeeze through the tight opening.

It took a moment for his eyes to adjust to the speckled splay of light lining the circular passageway.

"Over here," Sunny called.

When he couldn't find her, Rab realised she was on the opposite side of the ring. The upper half of the outer wall at the back side of the complex had collapsed, littering the circular passage with rubble. Rab stepped carefully and listened for Gift, who was threading a slow but steady trail behind him. Those same curious niches cross-hatched the surface of the walls on either side of the passageway and soared diagonally up to what remained of the ceiling, the underside of the truncated platforms Rab had seen from the outside. The overall effect was disorienting.

"Did you hear me? I asked you what you're. . ."

He found Sunny, seated on the ground with her back against the outer wall. She looked up at the sound of his voice.

"He didn't even make it out of the tower."

A crumpled pile of bones lay half buried in the dirt beside her.

"Someone tried to bury him," Rab said, bending onto one knee.

"Simon, I suppose," she replied with a nod of her head.

"This is what you came to find?" Rab asked.

"No." Using the wall of the tower for support, Sunny scrambled to her feet. "I came to find the packs. I didn't think. . ." She broke off and headed deeper into the tower.

Rab hurried after her, leaving Gift alone with the bones of Sunny's father. She'd come this far; it was no use protecting the little girl now.

"If your friend Simon buried your father, then he probably took what was left in the packs with him."

Sunny was inching her way down the passageway, painstakingly scanning the ground in front of her. Every so often, she stopped to kick at something.

"He was all alone and heading home. He wouldn't have bothered to take what I'm looking for. He wouldn't have needed it."

Rab tripped and his brief curse prompted Sunny to spin around.

"What was that?"

Rab shrugged and dropped to the ground. "Probably a rock."

He began to dig and Sunny immediately joined him. The sooner he helped her find what she was looking for, the sooner they could get into another tower and rest. This tower wouldn't do; there'd be no rest in here, not with the bones of Sunny's father lying half buried around the corner. The instant he felt something hard, his thoughts flashed back to what he had discovered in the dirt beneath the ridge.

Simon Deitweller hadn't made it home. Simon Deitweller's body was still missing. Rab stopped digging and glanced over at Sunny.

"Simon Deitweller?" he asked.

She shook her head. "He wasn't injured. He got away. I'm certain of it."

"That other one then?"

"Jacob? No. Not here." A moment later, she stopped digging. "Just a piece broken off the tower," she said.

"Is this what you're looking for?"

Rab turned around to find Gift standing behind him. In her hand, she was holding up something that, at first, Rab took to be ragged strips of clothing.

"I found it under those bones," she said.

When Rab looked again he could see that what Gift had brought them was actually the filthy remains of a pack.

Chapter 13

"YOU should be resting."

Sunny glanced up. She was sitting in the dirt, leaning against the inner wall of another of the roosts, the old pack lying open on her lap. Once Gift had found the pack, she'd done her best to set the bones of Louis Braham right again by covering them with a fresh layer of dirt and rubble. As they'd passed the shoddy grave on their way back out of the roost, Rab had been the only one to notice the little girl's efforts. Sunny hadn't even bothered to look.

"You're tired. You should sleep now and do that in the morning."

"No time," Sunny said.

When Gift came up beside Rab, holding out some of Sunny's food, he nodded and she continued on to Sunny and offered her hand. Sunny took the food without comment.

"That cut on your face is weeping again."

Sunny ignored him. She was making two piles either side of her, distributing the scarce contents of the pack. A twist of rope was laid to the left of her; a battered, hole-ridden canteen to the right. On top of the rope she placed something Rab immediately found disturbing. The outside was scuffed and dirty but overall, it looked like two miniature versions of the gun Sunny so prized fused together by a bridge half way down the length of each tube.

As she crossed in front of him to reclaim her spot on the floor, Gift cast Rab a troubled look.

"Have you found what you're looking for?" he asked, hoping to put an end to Sunny's fussing.

"This is it," Sunny said and confirmed Rab's worst fears by showing him the look-alike weapon.

Rab hesitated. "Another gun?" he said at last.

Sunny stopped scavenging and glanced towards the object she'd returned to the top of the rope.

"I suppose it does look a bit like a gun, but it isn't. They're binoculars. They let you see things way off in the distance. I was hoping Simon had left them behind. He wouldn't have needed them to get home and carrying them would have only added unnecessary weight to his pack."

Rab leaned forward. "If there's a city out there, Sunny, why would we need something like that to see it?"

Sunny just continued emptying the pack. The pile to the right was growing, the pile to the left remained scant. It contained only three items: the coil of rope; the binoculars; and a pair of heavy gloves, four out of ten fingers ragged. Upending the pack, Sunny shook it, but nothing else fell out.

"That's it," she said and flung the pack aside.

"If that's all that's in there, why did anyone bother to hide it?"

"So the Top-siders couldn't have it."

Weary, Rab got to his feet. "Why would they want it." It wasn't a question.

He left Sunny inspecting the binoculars and went to where Gift had set up their beds for the night. Lying down beside her, he glanced up at the towering walls of the broken roost. Light from day's end was struggling through each of the diagonal niches. By squinting, Rab could almost fool himself into believing that each of the delicate dots of light was one of Gift's imagined stars.

"She's dying," Gift whispered.

"Maybe," he answered softly. "She has medicine though. Better than anything we've ever had. Just because—"

"She's not using it, Rab. I've been watching. Besides. . .look at her face."

"I'm still here," he said, desperate to offer the little girl comfort, but unable to comfort himself.

***

In the morning, Sunny gathered all their packs, shook each out in turn and set to redistributing their stores. Rab didn't ask what she was doing. She probably wouldn't have answered and didn't even object when he reached into the pile and claimed some of the food for himself and Gift. She took none for herself.

He found a spot a discrete distance from Sunny where Gift and he could eat in peace.

"She won't eat anything," Gift said. "She's saving it for us, isn't she?"

His small friend was too clever.

"Come on," he said, putting a hand to Gift's shoulder. "She's finished and if I know Sunny, she'll expect us to get moving."

Sunny came walking towards them, dragging all three of the packs. The coil of rope was looped over her left shoulder, the gun slung across her back.

"The girl stays here."

Rab jumped to his feet. "What?"

"You and I go on alone now." She dropped the packs in the dirt behind her.

"No! Absolutely not! It's only half a day's walk from here. That's what you said. Gift can do that easily."

"I meant 'til we made it to the roosts. We got here sooner, so shoot me. It isn't too much further but there's no more shelter for her between here and there. We'll be back in three days and I'm leaving her with most of the food and water."

"No, Sunny. I won't leave her behind. Gift comes with us."

Sunny shook her head. "It's too hard for her. She's too small." She tossed the rope to Rab.

Instinctively, Rab reached out to catch the rope as it came flying at him. "Gift's made it this far just fine. Why can't she come?" He held up the rope. "And what's this for?"

"There's a steep climb." Sunny bent to collect the largest of the packs.

"I can help her," Rab said, glancing over his shoulder.

Gift was on her feet. She seemed more confused than anxious until Sunny stepped forward and placed the large pack right in front of her.

"Here. It's your job to look after this. You're going to need everything that's in it to get back to the tunnels."

Gift snatched Rab's hand. "But I want to go with you," she begged. "What if the people in the City want to take you right away and you're not able to come back for me? I don't want to be left here all alone."

"And I don't intend to go without you." Rab knelt down in front of her. "Remember the plan? We find the launch pad first. And if the ships are still leaving, then we go back for the others." He rose and turned to Sunny. "Gift is strong. You said so yourself."

Sunny smiled at him in that hideous crooked way she'd developed and walked back to retrieve one of the remaining packs.

"She almost fell off that ridge back there, didn't she? I saw how she looked when you came back. Her stride just isn't long enough. We have to use hand- and footholds and they're too widely spaced for someone her size."

"You did it."

"I was older. . .bigger."

"I could pull her up then—on the rope."

"She'd be cut to pieces," Sunny answered with a snort. "And what if you drop her? I can't deal with a broken leg out here."

There was no question; Sunny knew just where and how savagely to wound.

Rab dropped the rope in the dirt. "I don't understand any of this. We're heading for a city. Why do we have to climb a mountain to get there? Can't we just go around it?"

"No. You want to see one of the ships, don't you? Isn't that why you came?"

Sunny struck off for the entrance, leaving Rab in a quandary. If he tried to take Gift with them, Sunny wouldn't go on. He'd never get to the City and he'd never find the launch pad.

Gift's hand found his again.

"Go," she said, settling the matter. "If the climb is too hard, then it's too hard. Sunny wouldn't have left all this behind if she thought something could happen to me. You go and find another way for Stitch and me to get to the launch pad. When you get back, you can tell me about everything you saw. I'll wait for you. It's all right."

Gift turned around and dropped down in the dirt beside the over-stuffed pack. "This is a good shelter and I have everything I need right here."

Her small hand patted the top of the pack. It wasn't even trembling, which was more than Rab could say for his own. The last thing he wanted to do was leave her, but if Sunny were telling the truth, the worst thing he could do was take her.

Leaving the rope where it lay, he went to collect the remaining small pack. He could feel Gift watching him the whole time. On his way back, he snatched up the rope again and, on reaching Gift, bent to gently touch her head.

"I'm coming back," he whispered.

She smiled up at him.

As he rounded the circular wall about to lose sight of her, he glanced back. The smile was still on her face.

Sunny was struggling to draw up the hood of her coat when Rab finally caught up with her.

"The girl will be fine. It's much better for her to stay behind and protected than to freeze to death waiting for us out there."

"You're sure we'll be back here in three days."

Sunny shrugged. "That's as long as it takes. To get there and back."

He reached out and grabbed Sunny's sleeve. "Then Gift will be alone longer than three days."

"How do you figure that?"

"We need time inside the City as well, don't we?"

"I know where to go," she said and shrugging off his hold, set out once again towards the north.

Suddenly Sunny seemed in too big a hurry to get there. She was sick, very sick. If she didn't slow down, she wouldn't make it.

Perhaps it was better for Gift to stay behind, because nothing about Sunny's latest claim or her behaviour back there in the roost made any sense. If there was a mountain out there a day's or so walk away, then why couldn't he see it?

***

"Stop."

Sunny halted and turned around.

The day was almost ended. They'd rested only briefly around midday for Rab to take a little food, but Sunny had been anxious to press on.

He'd had enough.

It would be a treacherous walk in the cold and dark, but if they turned back now, perhaps they could reach the roost and Gift just after daybreak tomorrow.

"Where is it?" Rab demanded, advancing on Sunny.

"Where's what?"

"This mountain we're to climb. The one that's too steep for Gift."

"I lied."

He could have strangled Sunny then and there or, better yet, shot her with her own damn gun. Flinging the rope aside, he lunged, but there was more fight left in Sunny than he realised. She deflected him and, as he staggered backward, his boot caught on a rock and he went down hard on the ground.

"I knew you wouldn't leave the girl behind if I asked you to," Sunny said. Even that brief struggle with Rab had left her breathless. "I had to lie. The girl can't see what I have to show you."

"Why?" Rab demanded as he struggled out of his pack. "What's so terrible she can't see it? Dead bodies?" he shouted, coming to his feet. "Well, she's seen those before, hasn't she, Sunny? She even buried your own father, not that you cared or noticed. So what is it?"

"Telling you is no good. You need to see it for yourself, Rab."

Rab faltered; she'd never called him anything but Top-sider before.

"You've got to give me a reason to go on, Sunny," he said eventually. "Or it's over right now. We turn around and go back."

"The lengths you've already gone to get here. The risks you've already taken. Aren't those reasons enough for you?"

"Not if there's nothing out there. Not if it's just more of the same."

Sunny brought the gun down from her shoulder, then let her own pack fall to the ground.

"Here," she said, offering him the gun. "You take this and we make a deal. You give me until midday tomorrow and if by then I haven't shown you a good enough reason, then you use this on me."

As tempted as he'd been only moments earlier, Rab shoved the gun aside. "I don't know how that thing works."

"Simple," Sunny said. "It's loaded with bullets. You pull the trigger and a bullet goes into my brain and kills me. Just like I did with the horse." She held out the gun once more.

"I don't want it," he said, but grabbed the gun from her hand just the same.

He couldn't trust her; she was just as likely to put one of those bullets into his brain. Then where would Gift be?

"Is it a deal?" she asked, lowering her hand.

Rab turned around to look back the way they had come. Madness. It had been madness to even contemplate walking back to Gift in the freezing, black night.

"I wouldn't have brought you all this way for nothing."

He swung around to face her.

"You didn't want to come at all," he reminded her.

"That's not quite true. I didn't want anyone to come. Stopping my grandfather was easy. Even he knew he couldn't make this trip alone. But you and that older boy were another matter. I couldn't have stopped you indefinitely. Sooner or later you'd have got yourselves out of my city." Her lips twisted into another of those warped smiles. "Guess I should have worried more about the girl. You knew to head north. You'd have found the way eventually. Maybe not so soon, but that didn't matter. So you see—I had to go with you."

"So you could lead us nowhere?"

"No. Tomorrow, you'll understand though." She finished with a shrug.

"Why tomorrow?"

Behind the exhaustion, Rab caught a trace of puzzlement on Sunny's face.

"Didn't I just tell you? Tomorrow you get what you came for."

It wasn't exactly an answer, but it appeared that was the only answer Sunny was prepared to give. She stooped to collect her pack.

"What's it to be?" she asked, righting herself with effort. "North or south? Forward or back?"

Rab looked at the gun in his hand, then back into Sunny's face. "You have until midday tomorrow."

Sunny nodded. "Then we'd better keep going. There's still a little daylight left. We should make the most of it."

She turned and started off, leaving Rab to shoulder the gun and gather his pack. The hard metal barrel cracked against his back, momentarily aborting his reach for the pack. As he passed by the discarded rope, he gave it a boot, sending up a spray of icy dirt.

"I guess we won't be needing this rope then. Nice of you to have me carry it all day for nothing."

"Bring it," Sunny called without bothering to turn around. "We still might need it."

Rab retraced his steps, collected the rope, and angrily flung it back onto his shoulder.

"If you want this rope so badly, how 'bout you carry it for a while?"

Predictably, she ignored him.

He followed Sunny until he felt he couldn't possibly follow her any longer, until it became a challenge to see the ground beneath his feet or feel his face. At last she pulled up.

"Rest if you can," she said. "Eat if you want."

Rab sloughed off pack, gun and rope and crumpled onto the ground. A moment later, he heard Sunny slip down beside him. Reaching out for his pack, he scavenged inside it. His hand found Sunny in the dark, tapped her shoulder with a canteen of water. She took it along with the scraps of food he offered. When a sudden flicker of light to the south caught his eye, he was briefly tempted to ask Sunny if she'd seen it, too. But it was only there for a moment and then gone. Besides, it was only imagination. The flash lay too low on the horizon to be one of Gift's stars—just a trick of the eyes that were almost frozen shut and a mind too worried and exhausted to care.

Rab didn't sleep. Instead he passed the night listening to Sunny toss and turn on the ground beside him. Were the cold and sickness responsible for her restlessness or was it something else? The deal she'd made with him perhaps? Fear that he might just take her up on that offer to put a bullet through her brain if she didn't make good on her promise?

She was up and moving before daylight. Rab, too, was anxious to go on. By midday, he'd be on his way back to Gift, either with an answer or empty-handed. He almost didn't care which anymore. As he walked, he tried to keep his mind on Gift and struggled against the cold and exhaustion to keep an image of her inside his head—warm and safe—deep inside the shelter of the roost. If he could keep that image of her alive, perhaps it would go some way to keep himself alive. There was nothing he could do for Sunny; will power alone kept her moving now. Time and time again she stumbled, coming down on both knees, and after each stumble, dragged herself up again, refusing his aid. Her determination had him almost convinced. This trial she'd put them through couldn't be for nothing at all.

For a while now they'd been climbing a gentle rise. The gradual ascent slowed Sunny more than it should have. Rab's pace dropped to a crawl and he kept anticipating the moment when Sunny would give out completely. When she suddenly stopped, his first thought was that the moment had come. But she'd only paused to shrug off her pack.

They'd reached the top of the rise, where the strong wind blowing from the north snapped at them more chillingly. Ahead of them, the ground sloped gradually downward and, some distance away, just as steadily up again. They'd come to a shallow valley.

Sunny began to rummage inside her pack and produced the strange twin-tubed device that Rab had initially taken to be another gun, binoculars she'd called them. Bringing the thing to her face, she positioned the tapering end of the tubes hard up against the sockets of her eyes. Despite the pain that must have caused, she didn't even flinch.

"We break off here," she said. "Stop going north."

From the moment they'd left the river, they'd constantly headed into the south-blowing wind. Tracking off course now could only increase their odds of becoming lost.

"Don't worry," she said, reading his concern. "It's not far now. I just have to—there!" Dropping one hand from the binoculars, she pointed in an easterly direction.

Rab scanned the shallow depression below them, but found nothing unusual.

Sunny thrust the binoculars into his hands.

"Take a look. That way."

She pointed again.

Rab copied what Sunny had done and brought the tubes up to his eyes, cold metal threatening to fuse with his exposed skin. He struggled against wind and exhaustion to see through the tubes, achieving little but a shaking, restricted view into the distance.

"Forget it," Sunny said, taking the binoculars from his hands. "You're shaking too much. You have to hold them steady." Stooping, she re-stowed the binoculars in her pack. "It takes practice."

Rab didn't press her. When she struggled back into her pack and started off down the incline, he simply followed. She veered east—towards whatever it was she claimed to have seen in the valley. Every step they took sent a shower of pebbles tumbling downslope. If one of them fell now, it would be the final irony.

Gradually, the ground levelled off and the biting wind dropped back. At last Rab spotted something ahead. At first it appeared to be only another dark smudge but, drawing closer, he could see that the smudge was actually some kind of elongated hill resting low on the flat and dun-coloured floor of the dried up valley. That long ridge-like bump was where Sunny was heading and she seemed in a hurry to get there.

***

"I promised you we'd get here before midday."

Rab flung his pack to the ground. He'd forgotten about the gun though and it slipped from his shoulder, landing heavily beside the pack. He was furious—broken to the point of collapse and too discouraged to even make good on their deal and shoot Sunny right on the spot.

Ruins! All she'd brought him to was another ruin, different to the factory he'd come across by the river, different to the roosts they'd encountered on the plain, but it was another ruin all right. Lying half buried in the sand, with a thin elevated rim of windblown dust marking its outline, Sunny had needed those binoculars of hers to even pick it out on the valley floor. The building was huge, gigantic if more of it lay below ground. Long, yet narrow in comparison, its roof was rounded and fashioned from an odd kind of black metal that, here and there, looked to have been scorched by fire.

"Get where?" Rab spun a full circle. "There's nothing here but this ruin!"

Sunny slipped to the ground at his feet, the signs of exhaustion evident on her face and in the laboured intake of her breath.

"Look again. This isn't a ruin. It's a wreck." She jerked her head, indicating the long bump in the sand behind her. "The winds have covered more of it since I was here. There's a door somewhere. You'll just have to clear it out again."

"A door!"

"Yes! A door!" She shook off her pack and flung it far out in front of her. "I guess the joke's on me! I needn't have come back after all. You'd never have found this place alone. Not you or anyone else coming after you." She slapped the ground beside her. "In a few months' time, the dirt and the wind could have hidden this place completely."

Suddenly she began to laugh, a crazy kind of desperate, feral outburst that prompted Rab to step clear. . .until he remembered the gun. He inched back, intending to retrieve it, but Sunny lunged sideways and beat him.

An instant later she had the gun up to her shoulder and Rab was looking directly down its barrel.

"Dig," she said.

Would she really shoot him? Probably. . .this was Sunny, after all. . .and where would that leave Gift?

Rab stepped up to the long and partially exposed wreckage, stripping off his gloves as he walked. Better to suffer the numbing cold for a while than permanently destroy the only protection he had for his hands. Coming down on his knees, he started to dig.

Sunny came up and stood behind him. He could sense the gun pointed at the back of his head as he continued to scoop away at the loose dirt, uncovering only the same strange, scorched material.

"It's not here," Sunny said at last. "Maybe it was closer to the front."

"Front of what?"

Rab stood and watched Sunny slog down the length of the wreckage. Every so often, she stopped to brush dirt away from its base.

Clearly she'd lost her mind.

"Here. I can feel something here," she said, raising a shoulder to swipe grit from her good eye.

When Rab came up behind her, she grabbed his hand and pulled him to the ground.

"Feel that?" she said, slamming his hand flat against the wreckage.

Rab could feel something—a horizontal indentation in the smooth surface of that strange metal. It could be the top of a door—just like she said.

"It's here," she said and, slinging the gun across her back, began to dig.

Rab cleaned off the thin layer of earth she'd left clinging to the surface. After all, he could be as mad as Sunny now, imagining that something was there when it wasn't, simply to rationalise digging hole after hole in the middle of a dried-up river valley. But it was there all right—a tiny but real gap. If this was the top of the door, then they still had a lot of digging to do. The windblown soil was loose, finer than sand and easy enough though time-consuming to remove. Beside him, Sunny was making a cloud of the stuff, sending it everywhere at once.

"Stop. Stop. You're going to choke us both doing it that way," Rab told her.

She wasn't listening, so he reached out and stopped her.

"You have to shift it slowly," he said. "Or it'll all just fall back in the hole. Let me work at it by myself for a while. You're exhausted. Rest, then you can take over."

Sunny fell back on her haunches, appearing to understand and shifting only when it became obvious that she was blocking his progress. Whenever the trench he'd made threatened to collapse, he simply shallowed the sides of the hole. Sunny must have been watching him carefully because soon she set the gun aside and took on the task of shallowing the sides herself, leaving him to execute the heaviest part of the trench work. She hadn't bothered to strip off her gloves and, like her face, they were soon filthy and covered in powdered earth.

The work warmed him up and he managed to clear at least three-quarters of the entrance fairly quickly, but the door was much wider than he'd expected and the trench he was obliged to dig quite broad. The door itself was equipped with a handle and locking system far more complicated than anything Rab had seen even inside the tunnel city. Two flat sheets of metal, bearing drawings and text of some kind, were bolted to the door, one above and a smaller one below the handle. He hoped Sunny could read the words, or interpret the diagram, because Rab couldn't immediately see how they were going to get the door open.

"Switch," Sunny said.

"I'm fine."

"Switch!"

"All right, you dig." Rab scrambled onto his feet and changed positions with Sunny. "This was your idea, after all. Assuming we can work out how to open this door, what do we do if it's stuck?" he asked, scooping a collapsed mound of earth out of the trench.

"The latches are all broken. It was hanging half open when we came. My father and Simon sealed it up again when we left. But if it is stuck. . ."

"It would have been a lot less work to leave it open," Rab said, frustrated by the inefficiency of Sunny's digging. He didn't bother to ask the obvious question: why had Sunny's father taken the time to reseal the door at all? If they managed to get inside, he'd find out. If they didn't, then it didn't really matter.

Finally Sunny had the door completely cleared, leaving only one last barrier—the door, itself.

Rab's heart skipped a beat when he saw Sunny stand and begin to pull on the handle. If the door had only been shoved back into place as she'd said, then it could easily come down into the trench, pinning her beneath it.

"Sunny, don't. . ." he called.

"It is stuck." She stopped tugging at the handle and turned to Rab. "Get the rope."

He knew what she had in mind, and now why she'd insisted on bringing the seemingly useless coil from the roost.

Rab dragged the rope through the trench, threaded one end of it through the gap between handle and door, then shoved Sunny aside.

"Stand clear."

Once Sunny had scrambled up the side wall, he grabbed both ends of the rope and made his way back up the trench. One almighty pull brought the door straight down with a dull thud and a splattering of fine dust all around. When the air cleared, he found Sunny standing on top of the toppled door, beckoning to him.

"Come on."

Rab dropped the rope and walked up the trench to the open doorway. He leaned around Sunny and looked into the semi-darkness, smelling dust and something else—something stale—something old—something dead.

"We can't go in," he said, wrenching Sunny back by her shoulder.

One corner of her mouth twitched slightly.

"That's just Jacob. No one was ever afraid of Jacob before and there's even less reason to be afraid of him now. Come in." With a hand placed on the doorframe to steady herself, she stepped over the threshold, then turned back to look at Rab. "I promised to show you where we buried him and he was dead when we put him in here if that's what's bothering you. It's a good tomb and it wasn't like he didn't have a lot of company." She waved Rab on again. "It's dark in here, so you'll have to be careful not to step on someone's bones."

Rab baulked at the open doorway, now more reluctant than ever to enter. "What is this place?"

Sunny had stopped a pace or two inside. She was looking back at him and, even though her face was only dimly lit, he couldn't miss, or ignore, that familiar unnerving way she had of smiling at an ignorant Top-sider.

"Why, it's what you came all this way to find, of course. Weren't you looking for a ship?" Her arms flared out from her sides. "Well, you've found it."

Rab shook his head. Why did Sunny persist in playing these cruel tricks?

"Stay there, then." She disappeared but continued calling to him from inside the wreckage. "Pity to have come all this way just to stand out there in the cold though."

On the outside, Rab could hear the hollow clanging that signalled Sunny's progress down the wreckage.

"So few people come to these graves. The least you could do is say hello."

Bang!

She'd stopped walking and was tossing things around now.

Rab dropped onto his backside in the dirt.

He didn't know what Sunny had brought him to, or why, but it was no ship; he was certain of that. If this was one of the ships, then where was the launch pad? The City? There wasn't a trace of anything else but these ruins on the lonely valley floor.

The clanging began again—Sunny—making her way back.

"Here."

Something flew over Rab's head and landed in the dust at his feet. Glancing around, he found her standing by the open door.

"The Captain's log," she said, then jumped clumsily into the trench. "Part of it anyway."

Rab leaned forward to collect what she'd thrown through the door. It was a book, not unlike the ones he'd seen in the library. He flipped it over in his hand. Dirty and smelly, with pages that were badly warped, it meant nothing to him.

Sunny settled herself on the ground beside him. "There are a few more hand-written logbooks inside. The rest's stored some other way. Don't know where that is or what it looks like. Probably couldn't read it anyway," she said with a shrug.

"Other way?" Rab asked.

"Never mind." She tapped the book in his hand. "If you could read, you'd see that the answer you've come looking for is in there anyway. Well, that one and the others."

Lies. Nothing but lies. It had been that way all along. There must be a terrible evil inside this woman; a foul and sinister something feeding her pleasure from other people's pain.

She scooted forward awkwardly, drawing closer to Rab. "Would you like to know how many people are dead in there? Hundreds," she said, before Rab had the chance to decline. "There are windows all along both sides of the ship and they weren't all covered up with silt when we were here before, so we could actually see well enough inside to search—oh what—maybe half of what's accessible, I guess."

Rab shook his head. "So?"

"Come inside," she said and tapped the book again. "Even if you can't read what's written there, you can still listen to the bones."

Chapter 14

SUNNY was accustomed to threading her way through those occasional black spaces that persisted down in the tunnels, but Rab's blindsight was only good for sensing, not seeing, so together they found and began to clear away dirt and grime from more of the buried windows. Sunny struggled through the task and even allowed Rab to work on the fourth window alone. Sitting slumped, head bent to her knees, she didn't notice when he had finished clearing the window. Seizing the opportunity, Rab glanced around for her pack.

She looked up just as he had opened it.

"What are you doing?" she yelled, rising awkwardly to her feet.

"Looking for your medicine."

When he couldn't find the pouch, Rab upended the pack, but only food and water containers tumbled out.

"There isn't any in there." Snatching the pack from his hand, she stooped to re-stow her supplies. "I left it all with the girl."

"But—"

"But nothing. Medicine can't help me anymore." She flung the filled pack back where Rab had found it. "I haven't got much time left and you're wasting it. So will you please just go inside? There should be enough light now."

"All right, Sunny. All right." Rab began to make his way back to the trench. "But I wouldn't have thought you were the type to just give up like that. I thought you were a fighter."

Sunny grabbed the collar of his coat, almost pulling him off his feet. He couldn't imagine where she'd found the strength.

"Here," she said, wrenching up her sleeve to reveal the bare skin of her forearm. "It's called septicaemia in case you're interested. I'm sure you've seen it before. My blood has been poisoned. Those cuts I got from the captive girl opened up and got infected in the river water. Same thing happened to the horse." She jerked her sleeve back down, concealing the angry purple streaks and splotches. "It's moving all through my body—

has been since we left the river. I tried my medicines. They didn't work. So don't you dare tell me I'm no fighter. I'm a good fighter and a good fighter knows when the battle is over." She gathered the discarded logbook and pushed past him. "The question is: are you a good enough fighter to know that your battle isn't over?"

Rab was left standing in the trench outside the door, struggling with opposing feelings of defeat and defiance. As disagreeable as Sunny could be, he still didn't want her to die. Maybe she was right. Maybe her fight was over, but like she'd said, it didn't mean he should give up the struggle for himself—or for Gift.

He followed her through the door.

"This is Jacob," Sunny said. "Simon thought he'd like to rest here, where he could guard the entrance."

Rab didn't want to look, but couldn't seem to stop himself.

There was Jacob Sloane, what remained of him anyway, sitting bolt upright on the floor, propped against the splintered remnant of the wall behind him. The flesh of his face had collapsed; the skin had dried. Rab was reminded of the old papers Braham had shown him on his first night in the tunnel city. Although Sloane had been left the dignity of his clothing, Rab wished someone had thought to close his eyes. Whatever colour they had once been, they were an inhuman-looking yellow now, sort of powdery and drained in appearance.

"Just me, Jacob," Sunny whispered, in the mistaken belief Rab couldn't hear her, and lightly touched the dead man's bony shoulder as she passed. "You'll have more company soon."

The dire prophecy grabbed Rab's attention.

"Come on," she said, louder now. "There are so many more to meet." Catching hold of his sleeve, she dragged him towards the left. "Have to go this way," she told him. "The other end is impassable. All busted up. Pretty well flattened really. My father tried to crawl through it but he didn't get very far."

The farther he ventured inside, following Sunny, and the better his eyes adjusted to the comparative darkness, the more Rab came to appreciate that the wreckage she'd led him to might just be that of a ship. Most of what he saw had been gutted—intentionally and meticulously gutted. Though some of the walls exhibited the signs of a wanton or perhaps hasty destruction, it was obvious that great care had been taken to remove large sections of many walls intact, leaving only the supporting framework. Curious, Rab removed his glove and touched the strange grey-coloured metal skeleton the wreckers had left behind—cold—just as he had thought—chillingly cold.

Slipping his glove back on, he took off again after Sunny, who had just disappeared behind one of the rare undamaged walls ahead of him.

Rounding the corner, Rab came on a passageway littered with debris. Frail light leached through the cleared external windows, making it possible for them to pick their way safely over the jagged pieces of wreckage. The wall to Rab's right had been stripped right down to its cold metal framework, like those near the entrance of the ship, but the wall to his left was completely intact and it continued that way for some distance. He was beginning to suspect that Sunny intended to have him walk the entire length of the ship semi-blind, when he noticed a narrow but markedly stronger shaft of light just ahead of her.

"Now how's that for luck?" Sunny said, stopping at the leading edge of the light to point. "One of the windows we cleared is in this room, so you'll be able to see exactly what we did."

When he drew up behind her, Rab finally saw what Sunny was pointing at: a door hanging partly on, but mostly off its hinges. With a shove from her boot, she sent the door crashing to the floor, broadening the shaft of light.

"It's the first cache we found," she said, motioning him forward.

Hesitantly, Rab peered through the opening and immediately wished he hadn't.

Bones, as far as his eyes could see, lay knee-deep in places upon the floor.

"We figured they must have collected the dead in here," Sunny said by way of explanation. "We found that a lot of the leg bones had been broken. During the crash probably. But most had their skulls or ribcages caved in. Would you like to see one of those? They're easy to find."

Rab shook his head.

"We didn't expect to find any other caches like this, but we found two more—or was it only one?" She ran a shaking hand through her hair, obviously frustrated that the exact number eluded her. "I suppose it doesn't matter," she said at last. "They were all dead, of course, and had been for a very long time."

"Why didn't someone bury them?" It seemed so terribly callous to have just dumped their dead companions that way. "I mean, if there were people left alive to scavenge the wreck. . ."

"Noticed that, did you?" Sunny shrugged. "The living come first, Rab."

"How many people did die here?" Rab asked, more of himself than Sunny.

"Who really knows? The ship is enormous. If it weren't half buried, you'd be able to judge that better for yourself. We figured that there are levels underneath this one but we never found a way to get to them."

"But what is it doing here?"

"Its job," Sunny said, backing away from him. "What it was built to do."

"That's no. . ."

He turned around and finding Sunny, logbook hugged to her chest and clutching a section of framework on the opposite side of the corridor, reached out to offer his support. As soon as he touched her, he could feel she was burning up.

She shrugged him off and pushed away from the exposed frame.

"Come on. We go that way," she said, waving him forward with an unsteady hand. "But you have to be really careful from now on. The mess gets worse."

Rab took the lead, soon coming to an area where the walls had been entirely stripped again, allowing more light to seep through to the interior of the ship. The floor was in total chaos. He scrambled, bumped, and tripped his way forward.

"Why didn't they take all this stuff as well?" he asked, glancing over his shoulder towards Sunny, who was threading her own cautious passage.

"Maybe they had no use for it. Maybe it was too damaged. Or maybe they just couldn't carry it."

"Carry it where?" Rab asked, turning his attention ahead again.

"To the City, of course."

Behind him, Sunny slipped and staggered. She had herself righted before Rab could help her, but her stumble convinced him to stop their exploration. What was the point in going on? The ship was in ruins; everyone here was long dead. If the people had taken every useful thing from inside the ship to the City, then the City was where they should be taking themselves as well.

"Is it far off—the City? Can we reach it before nightfall? Remember we still have to get back to Gift."

Sunny smiled. "You've already been to the City, Rab."

"What. . ."

"This was one of the ships built for Safe Harbour."

"Thanks but I've worked that out already, Sunny—and it crashed leaving Earth."

"Leaving? No. It crashed arriving." Raising a hand, she slapped a section of damaged framework. "This ship is where everything inside my city came from. Of course, my people don't know that. They think Edward Braham brought it all there from the towns and cities on Earth. And I suppose in some respect that's true. But he had to get it here first—and here isn't Earth."

The woman's fever had her raving. If only she hadn't left all her medicine with Gift, he might have been able to. . .

"Down there," she said, tapping his shoulder with the book she'd been carrying, cradled in her arms all the way through the wrecked ship. "That's the Captain's cabin. It's where we found these books anyway. The floor is clear there. My father and Simon hunted through it, looking for anything important, but the gun and these books were all they found. Go on," she said, nudging him with the spine of the book.

Sunny was failing; if her wild claim wasn't proof enough, even in the poor light, Rab could clearly read the signs of her decline in her pale and swollen face. This time she didn't resist when he lent her his arm. He hoped she wasn't as delusional about the condition of the Captain's cabin—once down, Rab had the horrible suspicion that Sunny intended to stay down and he couldn't just abandon her—not even her—in a gloomy corridor full of wreckage.

The room had been gutted and cleared just as Sunny promised. Otherwise there was nothing remarkable about it, beyond the welcome openness it offered.

Once inside, Sunny broke free of his arm and made immediately for the darkest corner. Rab couldn't see what she was doing, but when she returned to him, her hands were empty. She'd put the logbook back where she'd found it.

"If my grandfather had made it here," she said, lowering herself to the floor just inside the open doorway, "he could have read it all for himself in those logbooks. That's why I never wanted him to come here and he never would have tried to if you hadn't turned up. He wasn't silly enough to think he could set out from the tunnels alone and would never have come out here with one of our own. But you're a Top-sider—if a Top-sider died trying to find the City, who would care?"

"He came out with you, Sunny," Rab reminded her.

"I'd been out here before. I could make it—he knew that. I think he also knew that the chance had come too late for him and he'd probably die on the way. I knew. And it's better that way—for everyone. No Topsider could accidently stumble on this place; they'd never waste their time in a dry river valley. There's nothing here for them. That only left you and that little girl," Sunny said, clumsily shifting position. "When we left the tunnels, I never had any intention of bringing you here. You must have suspected that. But when it became clear that my medicines weren't going to work, well. . ." She shrugged. "You can't read the logbooks, Rab, so you're just going to have to listen and make up your own mind. If you believe me, then it'll be your choice what you do with the knowledge."

A part of him didn't want to listen, but another part, the rational part, knew he had to. Sunny was right; she was dying. Would the last words she spoke be more lies? It seemed so needless now.

"All right," he said and slipped down beside her. "Tell your story."

Sunny nodded faintly. "Then I must start at the beginning. What my grandfather told you is partly true. Edward Braham was the man behind Safe Harbour and it did happen, just as my grandfather always believed. But he was wrong about when Edward Braham lived. Safe Harbour is older, much older than he thought."

"But your people and mine—they don't believe it ever happened."

"My grandfather did. Your father did. And they weren't the only ones. Legends just won't die despite the best attempts to quash them. There's always someone who'll keep them alive. But the legend isn't quite right. They never are, I suppose. Ships did leave Earth. I don't know how many. The logbooks didn't say. Maybe there are other colonies from other ships here. Maybe we're the only ones. Don't you get it yet? They built the ships, they launched them and this is it—the salvation planet."

A strange sound escaped her lips. To Rab, it sounded like a laugh.

"Only problem is they took themselves off one rotten planet and landed smack on another."

She stopped talking then, whether to rest or give Rab the opportunity to absorb all she'd said, he didn't know. But as far as he was concerned, there was nothing to absorb.

"This ship crashed leaving, Sunny," he said with surprising restraint. "This is Earth."

"Only because you want it to be."

Of course he wanted it to be, but. . .

"What about the factory where Stitch broke his leg?" he asked. "Those roosts? And what about your own city? It's a long way from here. If the people who were on this ship scavenged everything from it to build a city, then the city would be here."

Sunny couldn't seem to find a comfortable place on the floor and shifted position again.

"Maybe you should have looked around better when we were outside, Rab. There's nothing here. No shelter. No water. Nothing to keep them alive."

"So they just wandered around until they found those tunnels of yours and then carted everything from here to there? Over and over again."

"I doubt it was as simple as that. But yes, that's what it says in the logs."

"And the factory down by the river?" Rab pressed her. "They built that, too, I suppose?"

"Hauled what they needed from here to do it. All the metal and such. Not the bricks, of course. No bricks in these babies," she said and patted the floor with the palm of her hand. "The brick making doesn't seem to have worked very well though. The river's bad. Maybe they got sick and moved on. Maybe they just died. I don't know. There's nothing recorded in the logs, but it doesn't—"

"The roosts then?" Rab said, interrupting her. "They're old. Much older than that factory. Ancient."

"Yes, the roosts are ancient," Sunny agreed with a weary kind of half-nod. "But the roosts aren't ours. Someone else built them—something else anyway. Maybe there are still some of them left alive, too, a long way from here. I wouldn't know. They obviously farmed the land, when it was farmable. But other than that, we know nothing about them. The logs only mention those roosts. But those roosts mean there must have been other animal life here, too. Things that flew, but they appear to be gone just like their keepers."

"No, Sunny," Rab said with a shake of his head. "There's too much that doesn't make sense. If the people on that ship crashed on another planet, they'd know it. And we'd still know it."

Sunny's glance shifted briefly from Rab to the dark corner of the room. "All I can tell you is what was written in those logs. There was a schism, a three-way division among the survivors. A small party that included the

Captain stayed with the ship and it was their job to distribute the resources. The largest group went south, while the third dispersed, most going east and west, some north. The group who'd travelled south returned to the ship again and again, but no one from the other groups ever came back. It was the returning southerners, my people, who reported the discovery of the roosts."

Rab shook his head again. "Then where did my people come from?"

Sunny just shrugged. "From one of the roving groups, maybe, who found nothing but bad land elsewhere. Or another ship. What does it matter? It's what's in those logbooks that matters."

Rab pointed towards the corner and the Captain's logs. "If those books matter so much, Sunny, then why were they just left here?"

"Can't you see how big a mistake it would have been to take them? This is Earth now. The clever bastards even started calling it Earth. Does it make sense now? Where the rules against back-thinking came from? You. Me. We both have them. And that's because they'd settled on those rules long before they even reached this place. My father and Simon. . . they figured that out from things that were written in those logs. But people don't forget so easily and the legend lived on until it became a dream. And in time, the dream became something more—a hope. And for us, what's there better to hope for than a way off this stinking planet?"

"But your grandfather had books," Rab said. "He could read and the truth would be in them."

"Yes. The library. My grandfather's precious library. I wondered about that, thought about it a lot when I was living top-side."

Sunny shifted again and, when she softly moaned, Rab made to help her, but she pushed him aside, wasting some of the little energy she had left.

"Doesn't it seem strange to you," she continued after a moment, "that they even brought books with them in the first place? They're heavy. . . take up a lot of room. I mean if they could travel from one planet to another, seems they should have had a better way of carrying information with them. Then there were those logbooks. . .they only began when the ships arrived here. I thought about that a lot."

"So?" Rab prompted.

"Like I said before. . .everything else is stored some other way, but we can't read it anymore. So those books they brought with them had to be special."

"Special how, Sunny? You're not making a lot of sense."

"I'm making perfect sense. You must have seen the books in the hospital. . .Ruby's books. There are books in the council room, too. Books the croppers use. Books on how to weave cloth, build things, fix things that are broken. They're not in the library. Used to be books about animals, but my grandfather. . .when he was a little boy, he helped his father take them down into the library. He told me so. There are other books in the library, too. Early books I'm thinking. Ones written before they came up with their better way. And ones with pictures they wanted to save." She waved a feeble hand. "Others kept for a lot of reasons we can't even imagine anymore."

"Then where are my people's books, Sunny?"

"If your people are from a different ship, then maybe they burned them," she said after a pause. "We had the tunnels. Yours didn't. Or maybe this was the ship that carried the books. Just because I can't explain everything, Rab, doesn't mean it isn't so. I thought you'd be the last person to argue that."

When she spoke again, her tone was hushed, kind of reverent really, and that alone made Rab take notice.

"There's a story the children always tell," she began, "though it's discouraged of course. That a long time ago, the library used to be locked because a monster lived inside it and, when the monster died, they opened it up again. I guess a monster really did live there once, but now the library is just a home for books no one wants to read, about things no one is supposed to talk about anymore."

The strain of so much talking had begun to show. The skin of Sunny's face looked more drawn and seemed thinner somehow. And if it weren't for the muddy brown of her eyes, she'd have had no colour at all.

When she began to cough, Rab glanced around for one of the packs, then remembered they'd been left outside.

"Stay here," he said needlessly. "I'll be back with some water."

He left Sunny propped against the wall in the doorway and threaded his way back down the maze of passageways. Twice he tripped in the debris, grimacing when he turned his right ankle. The packs and the gun were right where they'd left them. Unless another of Sunny's roving bands of Top-siders appeared, no one was around to steal them. He grabbed her pack and hurried back.

"Here."

Her hands trembled when she took the flask from him and raised it to her misshapen lips.

"We have to get you back to your city," he said, dropping onto one knee in front of her. "To the hospital."

"Too late." She straightened and leaned back against the wall. "You still don't really believe me, do you?" she said after a while.

"No, Sunny, I don't. You've lied about everything so far. You lied about the gun. You lied back there in the tunnels when you said Safe Harbour never happened. You lied to get me to leave Gift behind. You even lied to your own grandfather. You've done nothing but lie. Why should I believe you now?"

"If you walk just a little further into the ship, you'll find the reason."

"What?"

"No," she said with another shake of her head. "You have to see it for yourself."

Rab got to his feet. "I'll go," he said, "but when I get back, we're leaving. Both of us."

"Keep going that way," she said, pointing past the entrance to the cabin, "until you come to some wooden doors. You'll recognise them. They're just like the ones in the tunnels back home."

Rab stepped into the littered corridor and set off into the belly of the ship. With each stumble, he silently cursed the woman he'd left behind. He'd almost convinced himself that Sunny was playing another of her perverse tricks when he noticed something unusual ahead of him—the splintered remains of what could just be a wooden door.

Rab hurried on, tripping and stumbling. If the broken wreckage was part of a door—just like Sunny said. . .

This time Rab cursed aloud.

She should have warned him!

He kicked the ruined door aside, barely noticing the ghost of its incised panels, and stepped inside. Slowly he began to count the row after row of pens. Each had been stripped down but from the vestiges of their footprints on the floor and the bones lying scattered all about, it was plain to see what they had been and easy to guess what they had been built to hold. There were hundreds of bones, but unlike their human companions, the dead here seemed to have been left where they had fallen. . .or been killed. . .and, for reasons Rab could not understand and chose not to question, that disturbed him more.

Poor Kix. So this was where his predecessors lay. Though fleshless now, the elongated skulls were unmistakeably horse.

Rab picked his way among the remains. There were other less identifiable bones too: short but massive leg bones suggestive of some sturdy but smaller beast; triangular shaped skulls with broken, protruding horns; frail skulls that narrowed and curved downward to a sharp and lethal looking point at the front.

When a fragile fragment of bone, too small for him to notice, crunched beneath his feet, Rab faltered and, with a hollow, lonely sound, sent another bone skimming across the floor. How many of these beasts had ultimately been saved, Rab wondered. And for what?

Returning to the entrance, he scanned the corridor ahead. There was no end to the wreckage of the ship and seemingly no end to the corridor—it simply disappeared in the darkness.

He turned away and headed back to Sunny. She looked up when he walked through the doorway.

"Well?"

"I found them," Rab answered glumly, lowering his head.

Sunny appeared to relax. "Seems strange, doesn't it? To have used wooden doors to pen in livestock. Simon thought he knew why." She shifted slightly, but the effort clearly distressed her. "It would take time for the seedlings they'd brought with them to grow. So they used wood inside the ship wherever they could. That way, the seedlings could be left to mature and they wouldn't have to fell the trees too early." Her left shoulder twitched. "The nurseries must be somewhere deeper inside the ship, or maybe lower down, because we never did find them, but they're here—they must be. Nurseries for the plants. . .and the babies."

"Babies?" Rab's head snapped up. "Are you—"

"How long do you think it took to get here, Rab?"

She was right. He hadn't stopped to think about that. And what about the fallen forest Fin had found? How long did it take a tree to grow? He didn't know. How long did it take to fail? He didn't know that either. But it didn't really matter what he did or didn't know because surely she was right about that, too.

"It's time to go, Sunny. You've proved your point." He offered her his hand. "Get up! I won't leave you here to slowly die."

"That's why I want you to shoot me. There's only one bullet left. We only found a few, so please aim carefully."

"No, Sunny, no." He pointed a shaking finger. "If you want to die so badly, I'll bring you that gun and you can shoot yourself."

"Fine," she said, after a long and unpleasant pause. "It won't be easy. But you bring it and leave the job to me, although I'd have thought you owed me that much."

"Owed you? For what?" Rab shouted.

"Giving you a reason to go on."

"You didn't."

The shadow of a smile crossed her face. "You still don't understand, do you? Why I let my grandfather believe a lie when I could have told him the truth. Why I denied the truth when I knew it. Do you think I did it just for spite?"

"It wouldn't surprise me."

"How would you rather live and die, Rab? With purpose—or without? The hope of finding a launch pad gave my grandfather purpose, but if he ever learned the truth. . .the same goes for everyone else on this lousy planet. Let the believers go on believing. Let the rest go on making the best of this place."

"Until the end?" Rab asked unhappily.

"Until the end," Sunny whispered back. "You said before I was a liar. The bastards on this ship made me one. Now it's your turn."

"I'm not going to lie about what happened, Sunny, just because a group of people a long time ago decided that we should."

"Yes you will, Rab, because long before you get back to the tunnels, you'll understand. . .just like I came to. They were bastards all right. . .but the decision they made was the right one."

Rab reached out and grabbed her arm. "I don't have time to argue with you any longer. There's a young girl back there depending on me. We have to go."

"Go then. You'll get there if you keep the wind at your back. Just leave me a little water."

He pulled, probably too roughly.

"Get up. You're not just going to lie there and die."

There was a little fight left in her still.

"If you won't shoot me, then the least you can do is leave me in peace."

He dropped her arm and slipped to the floor beside her.

"What purpose is there in that, Sunny? What hope?" he said at last.

"The hope that you'll do what I ask."

"I'm not going to burn books for you, Sunny."

"Burn them. Don't burn them. You find your own way." She raised her hand with effort and placed it on his forearm. "But sooner or later, someone will want to come looking again. I've done my part. Now it's your responsibility, however you do it, to make certain this place is never found."

"You're mad, Sunny. I wish you'd never brought me here."

"My name's not Sunny. That's the name the Top-siders gave me. My father called me Faith."

Rab felt like laughing. Of all the names …

Slowly he rose to his feet and walked off to get the gun.

Chapter 15

JACOB Sloane had been left guarding the entrance to the ship; Sunny insisted on being left to guard the logs. Rab made her as comfortable as he could and, beside her, placed her gun and water.

It was dark there in that corner, hard for him to make out her face very well and that was a good thing.

"Won't you change your mind?"

He had to try one more time. "There's a chance you might make it back to the tunnels."

"No, there's not," Sunny said.

Her voice had grown so feeble now, Rab could barely hear her.

Reluctantly he rose and, without another word, started back towards the entrance of the ship. At the door to the Captain's cabin, he wrestled with the temptation to look back. As he walked, he kept listening for the sound of a gunshot, but never heard it.

She couldn't do it.

He hurried back to the cabin. Maybe she was aware of his return. Rab didn't know. He lacked the courage to look at her face, so just stooped quickly and picked up the gun. It had to be now—this instant—or never. She'd told him to aim carefully; he hoped he had.

A blast hit him in the shoulder; he hadn't expected that. The gun clattered to the floor and Rab crumpled to his knees beside it.

After a long and terrible silence, he looked up. It was too dark for him to see the damage he'd done, so he reached out to find Sunny's face. Still. Drawing back, he found her hand. Limp. He'd done what she'd asked and aimed well, but there was no satisfaction in it for him. There was little of anything. He felt nothing at all.

Finally, he reached out to collect the gun. It had no bullets left, but something told him to take it just the same.

***

Rab walked until he physically couldn't walk any longer. He passed the night in silence, alone now, but not lost. All day the wind had been at his back, keeping him moving in the right direction.

Gift.

She was all that mattered now. Not Sunny's death. Not what he had done back there. He told himself that, but didn't really believe it and knew he would never tell Gift what had happened.

The cold bit harder now; the darkness ran deeper. Before, he'd always cursed Sunny's presence; now he found himself longing for it. He'd never felt so alone. In the early morning, he set off, anxious to reach Gift before nightfall. He didn't want the little girl to suffer another night by herself. He'd never really understood before how empty the world could be.

As he walked, he fretted over what to tell Gift. He owed her honesty, but perhaps Sunny was right, and he wrong. Where should the line be drawn? Even in death, Sunny could still confound him. Had she even told him the complete truth? Perhaps he'd never really know—not with absolute certainty—but, as the day wore on, Rab gradually came to accept that the truths she'd told greatly outweighed the lies. This wasn't Earth and for generations now the survivors from that ship and maybe others like it had bred foreign stock in a foreign land that hadn't invited and couldn't sustain them. They didn't belong here. They didn't belong anywhere now.

Rab didn't stop to rest or eat again; he just walked and at the first suggestion of a bulge on the otherwise featureless horizon, he started walking faster. Suddenly the packs he carried didn't weigh him down any more; the thumping of Sunny's gun against his back didn't hurt any more. Suddenly his lungs didn't burn. And though it was well into the afternoon, even the light seemed to be a little brighter.

By the time he reached the first of the roosts he was already running and calling out loudly to Gift. Stupid. She couldn't possibly hear him yet. This wasn't the roost they had left her in. He remembered that particular roost well; he'd made sure he would. As he ran, he kept his eye on the distinctive single turret. When he was almost on it, he called again. Gift didn't answer, but he wasn't concerned. All she'd had to pass the time with was sleep and she was probably asleep now, unable to hear him through the thick, sound-shielding walls of the ruin.

Rab dropped the gun and his packs just inside the entrance and rushed inside to wake Gift. Rounding the corner, he was surprised to find the spot where he'd last seen her empty. To fill in the time, had she taken to wandering around outside? Had he mistaken the roost after all? He called Gift's name again. Only the low whistle of the wind through the passageway replied. He had chosen the wrong roost. Making his way outside, he called once more.

Silence.

He could run to every other roost, frantically searching, but he knew now that he would never find her in one of them. This was the right roost. And Gift wasn't wandering around nearby killing time; she'd have heard him. Rab sank to his knees on the ground. Nothing mattered at all anymore. Nothing had substance. Time didn't seem to exist.

Slowly he came to his senses. He couldn't just give up. The little girl couldn't have simply disappeared. Something had to have happened to her and that meant he had to find out what.

Perhaps she was lying hurt out there somewhere. And if she were, how could he find her? Start at the beginning—it was the only way—go back to where he'd last seen her. Rab headed back into the roost, wound his way down the passageway again. He looked with sharper eyes this time. The earth all around was disturbed with footprints and scuff marks. This was exactly where he and Sunny had left her. There was no doubt. But there were too many footprints and scuff marks to credit to Gift alone. The light he'd noticed on the horizon that night made sickening sense now. Not one of Gift's stars at all. Top-siders!

As he painstakingly searched the ground for any more signs of Gift, a tiny light reflecting off the tip of a little blue stone caught his eye. Gift's little blue stone! If the dying sun hadn't angled its stunted ray on that very spot at that very instant, Rab could easily have missed it. He fell to his knees and began to dig. Just below the surface, he found the over-stuffed pack Sunny had left with Gift. Clever girl. She'd heard them coming and hidden the pack, leaving the stone as a maker for him to find. He'd have food. He'd have water and Sunny's medicine. And when he made it back to the ridge, he'd have the cache they'd left behind as well.

Gift was missing but she was alive and that mattered the most of all. It meant she could be found. He'd track his way back to the spot where they came upon the Top-siders on the slim chance they'd still be there. He couldn't be certain it was even that same band of Top-siders who'd taken Gift, but it was a place to begin. The fact she'd left the blue stone for him to find hinted that it was that same band, but perhaps that's all she'd had time enough to leave. And if he failed to find the Top-siders, he'd press on to the tunnel city, find those bounty hunters Sunny had paid off before.

Sunny! Was she responsible for this? Was this the price they had paid for a sweater, a set of gloves and a second-hand pair of boots?

Rab slept poorly that night. He was anxious to start searching. As long as Gift was alive, there was hope and he had purpose. The damnable woman was right. . .just like the bastards on the ship were right. Without hope. . .without purpose. . .they had nothing. The past was finished. . . done. . .and like the truth, better forgotten. So he would do just as Sunny intended and never stop looking for Gift and he'd lie and mislead and evade. . .just like she did. . .if that's what it took to keep the past forgotten until even the future was denied them.

In the morning, he sacrificed some precious time equalising the weight of the two packs he'd take with him. Alone now, he'd have to shoulder the whole load. The gun was out of bullets; it made better sense to leave it behind. But recalling how the Top-siders had reacted to Sunny's deliberate show of power, he changed his mind. If Gift had been taken by the same band of Top-siders, they'd remember. The gun might still serve him well.

The wind was blowing hard from the north when he stepped outside the roost. It set his course straight. Turning his back to the driving wind, he began to walk.

THE END

Thank you for reading COLD FAITH.

We hope you enjoyed it.

If you would like to be kept informed of further
releases in The Safe Harbour Chronicle, or other new books from
Hague Publishing, why not subscribe to our newsletter at:

www.HaguePublishing.com/subscribe.php

And if you loved the book and have a moment to spare we would
really appreciate a short review. Your help in spreading the word is
gratefully received.

About The Author

SHAUNE Lafferty Webb was born in Brisbane, Australia. Her father was an amateur astronomer and her eldest brother, an avid science fiction reader, so perhaps it was inevitable that she developed an early enthusiasm for writing speculative fiction.

After obtaining a degree in geology from the University of Queensland, Shaune subsequently worked in geochemical laboratories, exploration companies, and, while living in the United States, at a multinational scientific institute involved in exploration beneath the ocean floors.

Her short stories have appeared in AntipodeanSF, The Nautilus Engine, Blue Crow Magazine, and The Vandal and her novels, 'Bus Stop on a Strange Loop' and 'Balanced in An Angel's Eye', were released in 2011 and 2012, respectively. These days, Shaune keeps herself busy completing The Safe Harbour Chronicle trilogy and pandering to a pair of wayward canine companions.

Shaune lives in Brisbane with her husband, a research scientist.

Hague

Publishing

www.HaguePublishing.com

PO Box 451 Bassendean
Western Australia 6934